## "I'm not sure I know what safety is anymore," Serena admitted.

"Yes, you do," Rafe chided. "Otherwise you wouldn't stay."

"Perhaps you're right." She lifted her eyes to his, feeling the full impact of their warmth. Their whiskey color worked into her bloodstream as surely as if she'd just drunk half a bottle of hundred-proof liquor. Along with safety, she'd abandoned her good sense. A nagging part of her desperately wanted to retrieve both—before it was too late.

She just wanted to stand there drinking him in—from his eyes to his long, corded legs. She cleared her throat. "I imagine I'd feel a good deal safer if you were dressed." It wasn't true, though, she thought. Clothes were not the issue anymore. Rafe Sugarman could be wearing seventeen layers of cotton and wool, and she'd still be aware only of that powerful, purely male body....

Dear Reader,

This month brings you *The Sorceress,* by popular author Claire Delacroix, an intriguing medieval tale of dreams and magic. It's the prequel to the author's *Romance of the Rose,* the first of the Rose series.

And from Merline Lovelace comes the next book in her Destiny's Women trilogy, *Siren's Call,* the story of an Athenian sea captain and the Spartan widow he claims as his captive. And when Rafe Sugarman returns home to Mississippi, he finds peace in the arms of Serena Quinn, in *The Sugarman,* by author Mary McBride.

And last but not least, our fourth title this month is *Brides for Sale* by Ana Seymour, a rollicking Western where a woman arrives in Seattle with high hopes for a respectable marriage and ends up falling for the town's most notorious bachelor.

As always, Harlequin strives to bring our readers the finest stories and the most memorable characters. We hope you enjoy them.

Sincerely,

Tracy Farrell

Senior Editor
Harlequin Historical

Please address questions and book requests to:
Harlequin Reader Service
U.S.: 3010 Walden Ave., P.O. Box 1325, Buffalo, NY 14269
Canadian: P.O. Box 609, Fort Erie, Ont. L2A 5X3

# MARY McBRIDE

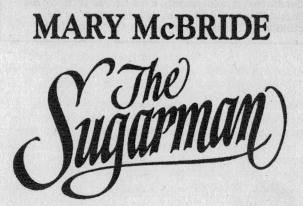

## Harlequin Books

TORONTO • NEW YORK • LONDON
AMSTERDAM • PARIS • SYDNEY • HAMBURG
STOCKHOLM • ATHENS • TOKYO • MILAN
MADRID • WARSAW • BUDAPEST • AUCKLAND

ISBN 0-373-28837-9

THE SUGARMAN

Copyright © 1994 by Mary Myers.

**Books by Mary McBride**

Harlequin Historicals

*Riverbend* #164
*Fly Away Home* #189
*The Fourth of Forever* #221
*The Sugarman* #237

---

## MARY McBRIDE

can't remember a time when she wasn't writing. Before she turned her talents to fiction, her poetry was widely published in "little magazines" and college quarterlies.

Her husband is a writer, as well. "It's wonderful," she says. "I have my own live-in editor and proofreader. The only problem is our combined libraries are threatening to crowd us and our two boys out of the house."

They live (and buy bookcases) in St. Louis, Missouri.

**For Merit Vogt Myers...**
**The Sugarboy**

# *Prologue*

*April 1865*
*Appomattox Courthouse, Virginia*

Ulysses S. Grant couldn't sleep. Or wouldn't sleep. His new aide wasn't sure which as he stood on the grassy hillock, sharing the night's quiet with his commander. Today the general had earned the laurel of victory when he accepted the surrender of Robert E. Lee, but tonight the bearded, stoop-shouldered man seemed more vanquished than victorious.

Soft Virginia moonlight glossed the gold buttons on the general's coat and glinted on the silver flask he lifted to his lips. Before he joined Grant's staff a week ago, the major had heard the gossip, but he thought if anyone deserved to celebrate with a taste of demon rum tonight, it was this man.

Below them, among the scattered campfires, the regiment had settled down in sleep. Dreaming of home, perhaps. A thousand dreams of home rising through the fragrant spring night like a thousand prayers about to be answered.

"It's over, sir," Major Parker said quietly, hoping to lighten the general's mood.

Grant didn't reply. His gaze flickered toward motion in the field below, to a man who moved like smoke through the sprawl of sleeping soldiers.

In silence they watched as the big man approached the picketed horses, where he singled out a sturdy chestnut mare. Her ears flicked once as he loosed the rope halter and let it fall. Her moonlit flank shivered and her withers twitched under the spread of his hands, and then she took the bit like sugar from his open palm. She stood still for the cinching, even seemed to welcome his weight when he swung up on her back. Then he turned her toward the open road—south—and she answered the press of his knees with a burst of speed.

"Deserter," snapped the major. "Shall I have him detained, sir? I can have a patrol mounted in ten minutes." The major was turning on his heel even as he spoke.

General Grant caught his sleeve. "Let him go." He sighed then, and when he spoke there was a catch in his voice. "By God, I believe it now. The war *is* over, Major."

"Yes, sir." The major's tone was respectful with an undertone of urgency. "But, even so, surely you don't intend to let the men desert. It's only a matter of weeks until most of them can be mustered out."

"True enough, Parker." Grant took a quick swig from his flask. "But a man can't be mustered out if he was never mustered in."

"I don't understand, sir," the major said.

"How long have you been with me, Major?"

"Just over a week, sir."

The general nodded thoughtfully. "That man hightailing it south was with me for three years. I suppose you've heard that story about what the president said when he was advised of my, er, imbibing?"

Major Parker mumbled noncommittally.

"Mr. Lincoln laughed and said he wished to send my personal brand of whiskey to all his generals." General Grant laughed now as he lifted his flask in salute. "It wasn't the whiskey, Major. That's my secret weapon riding away right now. That's my Mississippi Yank."

Major Parker squinted toward the fast-disappearing horse and rider. His breath whistled through his teeth.

He'd heard those stories, too—rumors of a giant of a man who had materialized out of the gunsmoke near Corinth, who had picked up a rifle, then hunkered down with the beleaguered Fifty-second Illinois and bullied those young farm boys into victory.

Grant's Mississippi Yank. The Sugarman. A Hercules who was said to be able to stride through hellfire and brimstone and a hail of bullets without so much as a scratch. A Southerner who wore whatever uniform they gave him and who turned up, like Lucifer himself, wherever there was trouble. They said he could smell a rebel regiment five miles away and put a minié ball between a man's eyes at a distance of half a mile. They said he could break a man's neck with a single snap of his wrist.

The general whispered an oath.

"Sir?"

"Damn fool," Grant muttered as if to himself. "I offered him a permanent place on my staff. Your place, in fact, Major. I told him I'd take him to Washington with me and make damn sure he got his proper reward. Medals, if I couldn't get him money. But he wouldn't have any of it. All he wanted was to go home."

Major Parker frowned. "I don't imagine he'll be receiving a hero's welcome there."

"A hero's welcome?" Scowling, General Grant swigged from his flask again, then twisted the cap tight. "Hell will have him sooner than Mississippi."

# Chapter One

*April 1870*
*Quinn County, Mississippi*

Rain. It was God's gift to growing things. And this one in particular. Soft and steady, it would soak through the soil and bathe every tender root. He could almost hear those young shoots sighing underground, could almost see the green above get greener still.

The air was heavy, dripping with dogwood and hyacinth. Spring in Mississippi. Green-up. Dear Lord, there was nothing like it, Rafe Sugarman thought. He was thirty years old and he still believed in magic and miracles.

Well, he believed in spring, anyway.

His fist clenched on the handle of his wet leather valise as he studied the town before him where false-fronted frame buildings gathered around the square like frail chicks around a mama hen. In the center was the stately, white-columned courthouse. The Quinn County Courthouse. Flanking that were Quinn Mercantile and Quinn Feed and Grain. Across the street, the Quinn Bank.

His mouth quirked sideways. No doubt about who *The Man* was around here. No doubt about that at all.

Valise in hand then, soaked to the skin with rain dripping from the brim of his straw hat, Rafe Sugarman sauntered toward the group of men idling around the courthouse columns. The half dozen old-timers sat slack jawed. Their eyes were cool and cautious as they watched him coming.

He dropped his valise as he planted one foot firmly on the courthouse step, then he raked his wet hat from his head and wiped his forehead with his sleeve. Then he grinned—wide, warm and winning. "Hell of a morning, gents."

"Now that's a fact," drawled an old-timer in denim overalls. His eyes tightened in a squint as he perused the big stranger standing before him. "You from around here, boy?"

"Near enough," Rafe said. He poked his chin over his shoulder toward the bank. "Looks like Quinn's the man handing out the jobs around here."

The man in the overalls nodded. "Yep." The other men merely stared.

Rafe sighed quietly. Hell, it was always a struggle. Made him wonder again why he even tried. Still, he managed another grin. "Y'all don't happen to know where I might find him, do you?"

"Con's been ailing," the old geezer with the bald pate offered. "He ain't doing much business these days."

Another nodded. "That's right. Keeps to his bed mostly."

And now they all nodded. Almost in unison they crossed their arms over their chests as if to say, "Conversation closed, boy. We don't want you here."

Only Rafe wasn't finished. And he for sure wasn't leaving. There was no place left to go.

"His bed's in his house, I expect," he drawled.

The old men blinked their watery eyes.

"Yep," one of them said.

"And just where might that be?" Rafe asked.

The man in the denim overalls cleared his throat. "Here now. If you want to do business with a Quinn, try over to the mercantile. Miss Serena's there. She'll set you straight."

"Or set you on your way," somebody snickered.

Rafe planted his hat back on his head. "Much obliged, gents."

Then the bald man cupped his hands and shouted out. "Hey, you. Little Joab. Come on over here and take this man to Miss Serena."

Turning, Rafe watched as a boy as skinny and dark as a licorice whip came racing across the street.

"You call me, Mr. Wells?" the boy asked.

"I did. You take this here fella over to the mercantile. He's wanting to see Miss Serena."

The boy's eyes flicked up to the big stranger, then down to the valise. "Carry your bag, sir?"

Rafe put a hand on the child's wiry head, winked, then bent to pick up the bag. "I got it, son. You just show me the way." He yanked the brim of his hat in the direction of the men. "Morning, gentlemen," he drawled, and turned to follow the little boy.

The rain had stopped, but the air was still heavy and wet. A few frail shafts of sunlight cut through the clouds as Rafe walked with the boy along the muddy street.

Little Joab craned his neck up at the tall man. "You got business with The Shawl Lady, mister?"

"The Shawl Lady?"

"Yessir. Miz Serena. That's what most folks call her 'cause she always wears one. Don't matter how hot. Miz Serena's always got that shawl on her."

Rafe slowed his strides so the boy could keep up with him. "Well, then, I've got business with The Shawl Lady."

Again Little Joab peered up. "You the biggest man I ever did see. Must be tall as that beanstalk giant."

"Nah. I'm just a hair over six foot three. Giants are a lot taller."

"How much you weigh?"

Rafe cocked an eyebrow. "Before or after I've eaten a little boy for breakfast?"

Little Joab swallowed hard. "You got a name, mister?"

Rafe stopped now. "Sugarman," he said, his eyes homing in on the boy's face, anticipating surprise, shock, perhaps even disgust.

But the sole emotion that registered on the child's face was mirth. His big brown eyes glittered and he began to giggle. "That's some sweet name you got."

Realizing he had been holding his breath, Rafe let it out slowly. He realized, too, that it wasn't the rain alone that accounted for the wetness of his shirt. He was sweating. Like a hog in the hot July sun, he thought disgustedly. And his hands were shaking—bad.

He gripped the valise more tightly. "Anyplace a man can get a shot of whiskey around here, kid?"

"The hotel." Little Joab lifted a thin arm and pointed to a nearby door. "I ain't welcome in there, though."

Rafe reached into his pocket, then squatted so his eyes were level with the boy's. "Tell you what. You go on ahead. I think I can find my way to the mercantile now." He pressed a coin into the boy's hand. "Pick out some sweets with this."

The small black boy stared at the money. He shook his head slightly. "Miz Serena's gonna think I stole this."

Rafe closed Little Joab's hand over the coin, engulfing the boy's small fist in his. "You tell The Shawl Lady you got it from The Sugarman. I'll be along in a while." He took the boy by the shoulders and turned him toward the mercantile. "Go on, now."

"Yessir. Thank you, sir." On the run, Little Joab called back over his shoulder. "I guess you really is The Sugarman."

"I guess," Rafe muttered as he stood. And he guessed if he didn't have a shot of whiskey soon his hands were going to shake right off his wrists. There'd been a time when he hadn't had to drink for his courage. But that was a long time ago.

Serena Quinn was not a dainty woman. She was as tall as most men in town, and her flesh was sturdy if not ample. So when Little Joab came barreling through the door of the mercantile and ran right into The Shawl Lady, it was like hitting a brick wall. The coin dropped from his hand and clattered to the floor.

Clutching her shawl, she watched the boy scramble after the nickel. Try as she might, Serena couldn't manage a stern expression even though her tone was severe. "You're two hours late, young man."

"Yes'm. I know. Our shoat got through the fence this morning and I had to shoo him all the way back from the creek." The little boy clutched the coin and got to his feet. "Then my daddy…"

Serena let go of one edge of her shawl to cradle his chin in her hand. "Your daddy's back?" Big Joab Inch had been in jail for the past two weeks over in the next county, not so much for anything he'd done but because the former slave just seemed to rile people. The wrong people.

And just as the boy was about to reply, one of those "wrong people" walked through the door. Constable Arlen Sears was a wiry man with a mean mouth and a quick temper—in Serena's opinion anyway. In a town as small and quiet as Quinn, where a badge would have sufficed, Sears insisted on wearing a side arm. He walked with a swagger that reminded Serena of a banty rooster.

That ungenerous mouth of his twitched a greeting in her direction now, then he gave his hat a brief tug before glaring down at Little Joab.

"I hear your old man's back, boy. That true?"

Little Joab's fine-boned chin trembled in Serena's hand as he nodded up at the lawman.

"You tell Big Joab I'll be watching him, boy. Every minute. You tell him if one little pig or mule disappears, I'll be out to your shack faster than lightning down a rod."

"Leave the child alone, Arlen," Serena said sharply. "He's done nothing. I seriously doubt that his daddy did anything either."

The constable held up his hand to silence her as he continued to pin the little boy with his glare. "What's that you got in your hand, boy?"

Little Joab edged sideways into the protective folds of Serena's skirt. "Nothin'," he murmured.

"I'll just bet." The constable grabbed his wrist and squeezed, forcing Little Joab's fist open and disclosing the coin. "Don't look like nothin' to me. Where'd you get that money, boy?"

With a firm hand on the child's shoulder, Serena nudged him behind her. "You go on in the back room now, Little Joab. There's sweeping to be done and crates that need opening."

The boy didn't need to be told twice. He bolted for the back room.

Serena's eyes were level with the lawman's then, and they were hot, fierce as blue flames. "I gave him that nickel." She lifted her chin. "Any more questions?"

For a moment Serena thought the man was going to hit her. His thin lips tightened. A muscle jerked in his cheek. His words ripped through his teeth.

"You damn Quinns. You think just because—"

The constable's harsh invective was interrupted when the door opened and a bright voice lilted, "Good morning, everyone. My heavens! I thought that rain was going to just keep falling forever, didn't you?"

Esme Quinn closed the yellow parasol that matched her dress, then stood there smiling. Beaming. Serena thought her sister-in-law looked like a freshly bloomed jonquil. Arlen Sears reacted immediately to her presence, Serena noticed. His angry features softened, and the lawman even smiled as he scraped his hat from his head and quickly finger-combed his hair.

"Mornin', Miz Esme. You put me in mind of a sunbeam, ma'am."

Serena rolled her eyes. Poetry from a man who had just been breathing fire and nearly spitting in her face. But then, her late brother's widow seemed to have that sort of effect on the opposite sex.

The little blonde was blushing. "Aren't you sweet, Arlen. That's the nicest thing anybody's said to me all day."

"It's only ten-thirty, Esme," Serena said sourly. Sometimes Esme's natural flirtatiousness purely grated on her ears. She slanted a scathing glance at the constable. "Surely somebody will do better than 'sunbeam' before the day's out."

Esme fidgeted with the organza frills on her bodice. "I always appreciate a compliment, Serena, even though I didn't come in here searching for one. The fact is I'm on my way to the sewing circle at Mary Ann Stanton's and I stopped in to deliver a message to you." Her gaze swept over Arlen Sears before returning to Serena. "A private message."

Taking the hint, the constable made a little bow in Esme's direction. "I'll wait outside, Miss Esme, and walk you on over to the Stantons'."

"How gallant of you, Arlen. Thank you."

Serena bit her tongue. The trouble was that Esme meant every word she said. She truly did believe that nasty man was the soul of chivalry. Well, why not? He always *was*—around Esme.

Once Sears closed the door behind him, Serena spoke a bit more testily than she'd intended. "What's this private message, Esme? What does Daddy want now?"

The blonde's pert little face nearly glowed as she wagged a gloved finger at Serena. "Not Daddy Quinn. I'm bringing you a message from an admirer, Sister."

Serena scowled and drew her shawl more closely around her shoulders. "I don't have any admirers. There's only..."

Esme flew toward her in a rush of yellow organza. "There's only John William Pettigrew, and he's up at the house right now looking like a cat who just swallowed a canary, cage and all. Oh, Serena. I just know he's going to propose to you."

"John William's in Savannah," Serena insisted.

Her blond curls almost jingled as Esme shook her head. "Not anymore he's not. He's sitting on our veranda, looking delirious and dignified all at once, waiting for you."

Esme fluttered about her, clucking her tongue softly as she tried to subdue Serena's stray auburn curls, then sighing when it was obvious those efforts were in vain. She tugged off a glove then. "Crook your knees, Sister, so I can reach you."

She licked her fingertip and ran it across one of Serena's eyebrows, frowning all the while.

"Oh, it's too bad you can't sneak home and slip into a prettier frock. Something a little gayer than this blue serge. Maybe something soft."

Serena sniffed. She didn't "slip" into clothes. She battled her way in and out of them. Clothes were necessary, serviceable, not a means of expression as Esme seemed to think. She swatted at her sister-in-law's hand.

"Stop fussing, Esme. You're tying my nerves in knots."

The little blonde's hands swooped to the fringe of Serena's shawl, untangling and arranging. "You don't have any nerves, Serena. You're just like your daddy. All cool and collected and in possession of yourself."

Esme stepped back then, crossing her arms as she inspected the woman before her. "Stop frowning. I swear, your brow looks more like a corrugated road than a female forehead."

It was a struggle, but Serena managed to lift the corners of her mouth. "How's that?"

"Better. You're almost smiling." Then Esme glanced at the clock on the wall and gulped. "Oh, my gracious. I'm ten minutes late for sewing circle."

Bending slightly, Serena kissed her sister-in-law's soft cheek. "Run along, then. And you keep this to yourself, Esme Quinn. Don't you go telling everybody I'm already halfway down the aisle, you hear?"

Worry clouded the petite woman's expression. "You are going to tell John William yes, aren't you?" When she didn't receive an immediate answer, Esme asked again, her voice lower now, more cautious. "Serena? You are going to say yes, aren't you?"

Serena blinked. Her chin snapped up. "Well, of course. That's what I'm supposed to say, isn't it?"

With a sigh of relief, Esme floated toward the door. "I'm so happy for you," she called back over her ruffled shoulder.

Through the window Serena watched her sister-in-law thread a delicate hand around Arlen Sears's proffered arm, then lean toward him slightly—like a yellow jonquil in a breeze—as they started down the sidewalk.

That kind of flowery, feminine grace came so easily to her brother's widow. Conn Quinn, Jr., had been killed at Shiloh in '62, and Esme had worn black for seven long years, but even in mourning there was always something colorful about her—her golden laughter or the bright green glint in her eyes. She was twenty-five, a year older than Serena, and yet Esme seemed so much younger. She was like a girl, glowing with life and promise. The way Serena herself had been, once.

She drew her shawl more closely about her shoulders now as her lips tightened. Then her lashes fluttered and her eyes opened wide.

John William! He was back from Savannah and he was waiting for her, right this minute, back at the house. Serena had completely forgotten about the man who had been courting her for the past five years and who now, apparently, intended to bring that lukewarm courtship to a boil.

"Good Lord," she breathed. She never thought the day would come. Five years of summer strolls and picnics, of exchanging cautious Christmas gifts and birthday mementos, of hand-holding and an occasional kiss. And now...

Now her stomach was clenching like a fist and when she looked down, her knuckles were pearly white on the edge of her shawl. The notion that she and John William Pettigrew would one day marry was one thing. The fact that he was currently cooling his heels on her veranda, waiting to propose, was quite another.

Serena's hand flitted upward toward her hair, a riot of curls now after getting caught in the rain on her way to the store. Esme was right about her apparel, too. The blue serge skirt and jacket were just plain dull. For an instant Serena wished for a frilly yellow dress. A wispy, petal-soft frock with delicate lace and tiny bows and little covered buttons that...that would take her big, clumsy fingers half a day to do or undo. "What are you thinking, Serena?" she admonished herself, running her damp palms down a length of skirt.

She had come to terms with her own substantial body years ago; she was even grateful for her hardiness and health. And as far as John William was concerned, the fact that she didn't have kitten bones or twiglike wrists had never seemed to make an impression on him one way or another.

She was being silly, behaving like a tremulous girl. She had known John William all her life. They had attended Sunday school together. They had shared numerous books and even a few secrets. When he had joined the Sixth Mississippi, they had exchanged locks of hair—a thick, flame-tipped auburn curl for a fine, tawny sheaf. John William was courteous and kind. He'd make any woman a fine, considerate husband. No, she corrected herself. Not any woman. Her. Serena Olivia Quinn.

"Miz Serena, I got the back room all swept out. Got them crates open, too." Little Joab peeked out into the main room. "That constable gone?"

"What?"

The child sidled up to her. "I asked you if that nasty lawman was gone, but I can see that for myself now."

She smiled down as she touched her fingertips to his cheek. "I'm sorry Mr. Sears was mean to you, Little Joab. He had no right to do that."

He shrugged, then held up his nickel as his glance strayed to the countertop and its array of lemon drops, licorice twists and peppermint sticks. "S'pose I could buy me some penny candy now?"

Her smile increased. "Well, I suppose if anyone's entitled to candy this morning, it's you. But before you go spending that money, you're going to have to tell me where it came from. I know your mama doesn't have whole nickels to spare."

"The Sugarman, Miz Serena. He done give it to me."

Her brows drew together and she tilted her head. There was more than a hint of suspicion in her tone. "The Sugarman?"

"That's what he told me," the boy insisted. "He said when The Shawl Lady asks you where you got that nickel, you just tell her The Sugarman gave it to you. I ain't lying, Miz Serena. I ain't."

"I know that, Little Joab." Serena looked at the clock now and had a quick vision of John William on her veranda, drumming his fingers on the arm of a wicker chair. There wasn't time to untangle all the twists and turns of a child's imagination right now, she thought.

With a sigh, she led him over to the counter where she handed him a small paper sack. "You go ahead and fill that up. And don't eat it all in one sitting, you hear? I don't want you getting sick."

A grin flashed across the boy's face. "Here's my nickel," he said, offering her the coin.

Serena took it and put it into her pocket, intending to remind herself to talk to Hester Inch about her son's sudden unexplained wealth. Then, while Little Joab made his selection, she eyed the top shelf behind the counter. If John William intended to propose to her, gentleman that he was, he probably also had a gift for her, some token of his affection. It would only be fitting to return the gesture. He enjoyed a good cigar now and then, Serena recalled, and she'd been told the ones from Havana, Cuba were exceptionally good. In fact, she had been forced to move them to the top shelf because when she kept them on the counter they had a tendency to disappear.

"I'm all done, Miz Serena."

Little Joab's paper bag looked about ready to burst at its glued seams. "Well, I'd say you made a fine selection." She winked. "Got your money's worth, too. Why don't you go on home now and have a peppermint or two. I'm going to close the store down for the afternoon."

"How come? It ain't a holiday."

No, it definitely was not a holiday, Serena thought after the child had left. She sighed, then strode around to the rear of the counter, disregarding the stepladder. The necessity of reaching to one of those high shelves was the rare instance when she was grateful for her height.

But even on tiptoe now, she couldn't reach the humidor. Serena clenched her teeth, squinted her eyes and stretched her fingers for all they were worth. She felt her shawl slide from her shoulders, but ignored it as she touched a cool corner of the metal box. Trying to slide it closer, she only ended up pushing it farther away.

"Damn!" She pulled her arm back and let her heels drop to the floor.

Warm hands pressed her shawl to her shoulders. In that instant Serena breathed in a fragrance clean as the spring rain, rich as the earth itself. It was tinged with the spice of rye whiskey, touched with a muskier scent she could only define as male. The hands lingered a moment, then the warm pressure dissipated, only to be replaced by the warmth of a body as it moved closer—touching close, shoulder to thigh—behind her.

Then a brawny arm reached up and a big hand closed around the cigar tin and brought it down.

# Chapter Two

She whirled around, ready to give the impudent stranger the tongue-lashing of his life, meaning to scald him with her hot, indignant gaze. But, instead of meeting a pair of eyes, Serena found herself staring at a damp shirtfront drawn tight over a massive chest—an acre of white cotton. Her eyes swept over it, then up to the dark chin stubble, then farther to—finally—warm, whiskey-colored eyes.

She stepped back, gripping her shawl as if it would keep her upright.

The stranger held out the humidor. "Is this what you were reaching for?"

For a moment Serena didn't know. The box looked like a tin toy in his huge grasp. She barely recognized it.

"Miz Serena, I done forgot my—" Little Joab halted at the far end of the counter, big eyed, pointing up. "That's him. I told you I wasn't lying. That's The Sugarman."

Serena snapped out of her daze. Anchoring her

shawl with one elbow, she snatched the humidor out of the man's extended hand. "Thank you," she said stiffly.

"My pleasure, ma'am." He took off his hat, and when a mass of dark, damp curls cascaded over his forehead, Serena felt her fingers twitch.

Little Joab was tugging at her skirt now. "You ask him, Miz Serena. You ask The Sugarman if he didn't gimme that nickel." The child's big brown eyes appealed to the tall man. "Tell The Shawl Lady, mister. Tell her I didn't steal it."

Rafe glanced at the boy, then settled his gaze on the woman before him. "The Shawl Lady's standing there thinking I snuck up behind her trying to steal her cigars, Little Joab. I don't know if she's of a mind to believe either one of us right now." He grinned. "Are you, ma'am?"

Serena blinked, not knowing if she was reacting to the accusation or to the gleaming, cocksure smile that cut like a swath of sunshine across his full lips while it carved deep slashes alongside his mouth. "I assure you, sir, I never..." The flush that spread over her cheeks seemed to swamp her words upon her tongue. She sputtered now, and fell silent.

"You feeling awright, Miz Serena?" Little Joab quizzed.

The little boy was regarding her as if he expected her to fall into a faint. And the other one—the huge stranger—was grinning slantways at her like a cat contemplating a mouse. In all her twenty-four years, nobody had ever looked at Serena quite like that. Gracious.

She cast a baleful glance at the clock. John William Pettigrew was waiting, and here she stood all flushed and flustered like a giddy schoolgirl. She found her voice again and directed it sharply at the child.

"I meant what I said, Little Joab, about closing the store. Now you go on home." She gave his shoulder a small shove to encourage him. "Scoot."

After the boy had skipped out the door, Serena crossed her arms and raised her face to the stranger. Her tone was businesslike and cool. "If you're intending to make a purchase, sir, you'll have to return tomorrow. We're closed for the afternoon."

Closed. Now that about described her, Rafe thought. When he'd first glimpsed this woman—on tiptoe, reaching as if she meant to grab a star—she'd been open. Beautifully open. But now, standing there hugging her shawl and chewing on her lip, she was closed up tight as a fist. Even her hair seemed to have curled tighter.

Still, she was a beautiful woman. Beautiful and sturdy and tall as a live oak, with the edges of her shawl looking like a fringe of Spanish moss. No wispy blossom, this one. And here he was grinning at her like a silly kid when he should be bowing and scraping to his potential boss lady. Lord knew he needed her good opinion a lot more than her affection. Rafe bit back on his grin and leaned a hip against the counter.

"That nickel I gave the boy was just about my last, Miss Quinn, so a purchase is temporarily out of the question." He crossed his arms now in imitation of her pose. "The fact is I'm looking for work and I was told to talk to a Quinn."

"You've got the wrong one, I'm afraid. My father does all the hiring around here." Her reply was crisp, and ordinarily she would have let it go at that, but Serena studied his face a moment, imagining what it had cost this giant's pride to admit his impoverishment. She wondered, too, about a man who would give his last nickel to a child. "My father's been doing business from his bed of late. If you'd like, you may accompany me home."

"I'd like that," he drawled.

His tone left her unsure whether it was the prospect of seeing her father or of walking with her that appealed to him. Then she decided it didn't matter.

Her own tone was businesslike. "Well, then, shall we go, Mr. . . ?"

"Sugarman. Rafe Sugarman."

He perused her face for any sign of recognition. Those cornflower blue eyes didn't blink. Her generous lips didn't thin but rather turned up at the corners in a polite if somewhat cool smile before she turned and walked toward the door. Rafe breathed a sigh of relief as he followed.

On her way out the door, Serena picked up her black silk umbrella. Unlike Esme's parasol it was plain and serviceable, utilitarian rather than decorative, ungainly rather than dainty. She gripped its wooden handle firmly as she halted outside.

Tarnation! It was raining again. She was going to have to greet John William looking like a bedraggled river rat. Glaring at the muddy, shoe-sucking street, she moved her toes inside her slippers to get a better purchase on the leather, then muttered another oath and turned back to lock up.

Her breath hitched in her throat as she watched Rafe Sugarman crook his knees slightly and bend his head as he came through the door. There was ample clearance, but he did it automatically, with a practiced grace as if the world were forever putting obstacles in his path in the form of low doorframes and chandeliers.

Her gaze swept to his good-sized boots. Heavens! That man's feet must hang over a mattress by a mile, she thought, and then felt her cheeks burn with the indecent and unbidden notion.

"The rain's back," he said, straightening to his full height and smiling out at the downpour.

Serena sniffed. "You sound like a man who's just spent six months in the desert."

He settled his hat back on his head. "I sound like a farmer after a long, dry winter, Miss Quinn. I'll bet your daddy's grateful for this rain even if you consider it a terrible inconvenience."

"I consider it a personal affront today, Mr. Sugarman," she said, and edged past him to lock the mercantile door. Then she snapped her black umbrella open and hiked up her skirt. "Shall we go?"

Rafe picked up the valise he'd left on the sidewalk and, with his free hand, gestured toward the muddy street. "After you, ma'am."

Serena gritted her teeth, stepped off the planked sidewalk and promptly sank to her ankles in muck.

The look on her face was such a sweet combination of fury and befuddlement, it was all Rafe could do not to sweep her up in his arms right that minute. The befuddled part of Miss Serena Quinn might have been grateful, but her fury would have overridden her gratitude, he was certain, and he'd only wind up getting slapped for his efforts. He didn't need that, especially now. He needed work, he reminded himself. And in this town, a Quinn—no matter how helpless or fetching—meant employment, pure and simple.

"I'm waiting, Mr. Sugarman," she called over her shoulder.

"Ma'am?"

Serena twisted to meet his quizzical gaze. She gave her umbrella a shake. "I'm willing to share my shelter, such as it is."

He stepped off the sidewalk into the mire. "That's right generous of you, Miss Quinn, but I don't mind getting a little damp."

"Nonsense." Serena readjusted the umbrella to cover his head, but because he was so tall, rather than shelter him she succeeded in poking him in the eye with one of the metal spokes. "I'm so sorry, Mr. Sugarman. Perhaps if you could just squinch down a bit." She tried to lift the black silk higher, this time knocking his straw hat askew.

"I said I didn't mind the rain," Rafe said, resettling his hat, then rubbing his eye.

"I insist."

He clamped a hand on the metal rod before she did him serious damage, then stood looking down at her, at the determined set of her mouth and the stubborn angle of her chin. It occurred to him that those lips were lush and soft in spite of all the chewing she did on them. And that chin, stubborn as it was, was pale and delicate as porcelain. His eyes swept lower, noting the ample swell of her shawl-draped bosom.

Rafe sighed. "You insist, do you?"

Serena nodded.

"Well, seeing that's the case..." He let go of the umbrella, set his valise back on the sidewalk, then whisked her up high against his chest. "I can't very well say no to a Quinn in Quinn County, can I?"

"Put me down, sir," Serena hissed.

"Well, I would, Miss Quinn," he drawled, "but seeing you're so insistent about our both keeping dry, I figure with my height and your unwieldiness with that parasol, this is the only way we can accomplish it."

His face was mere inches from hers, his breath warm and whiskey tinged. Serena could feel the heat radiating from his chest as it seeped through the wool of her shawl and the various layers of clothing she wore, as it spread across her own skin like a warm bath. She could feel the muscular arms bracing her knees and cradling her shoulders, and for a split second she felt delicate and almost breakable.

"Please," she said, her voice thready now. "I'm much too heavy."

He grinned, then hoisted her—effortlessly—higher. "Not for me. You fill my arms just right. Now which way's home, Miss Quinn?"

For a moment she wasn't even sure. For a moment her whole body felt light and translucent as a raindrop skittering down a pane of glass. And her head was light as a feather, too, she reminded herself when the word *home* finally registered there. "It's down that side street, then up the hill about a quarter mile." She narrowed her eyes on his. "It's a long hill, Mr. Sugarman."

"Yes, ma'am. Most of them are around these parts." He reached back to grab his valise, then started walking.

"I mean for transporting such a burden," she added, adjusting the umbrella over both their heads.

"Well, it might be if I were to have to carry a bale of hay or a barrel full to the brim. Something solid with no give to it. But a woman has a good deal of give to her, Miss Quinn." He moved her more closely against him as if to prove his point.

Serena shifted away, one hand tugging to close the edges of her shawl. She started to frame a curt reply to his rather indecent remark, but remained silent. She closed her eyes for a moment, allowing her senses to enjoy this surprising experience. The smooth length of his stride. The feel of his arms encompassing her. The dampness where their clothes touched and clung. And the smell of him. It was like nothing she'd ever known before. It was pungent as whiskey and sweet as springtime and—something—what? An overtone of something wild and dangerous.

Rain splattered her face. Serena's eyes flew open.

Rafe Sugarman's brandy-colored gaze was fixed on her face. His lips teased up at the edges and he seemed oblivious to the rain that was cascading from the brim of his hat and soaking his shoulders, unmindful of everything but the woman in his arms. He was going to kiss her! Serena's heart leapt into her throat as she imagined that sultry mouth moving closer to her own. This sudden stranger was going to kiss her. And—heaven help her—she was going to let him.

Then that enticing smile slid into a full-blown grin. "Sort of defeats the whole purpose, Miss Serena, don't you think?"

She could hardly speak for the tightness in her throat. "Pardon?"

Rafe angled his head sideways. "Your parasol. Correct me if I'm wrong, ma'am, but up's the way to keep the rain off."

Reality hit her now like the rain splashing on her face. The umbrella was canted like a wilted bloom. Immediately her lax grip tightened and the black canopy swung back over their heads.

In the shade of the black silk Serena felt her damp cheeks nearly boiling with mortification as she bit her lower lip. What had gotten into her, even contemplating something like a kiss? From a total stranger, to boot. It must have been the whiskey fumes from his breath making her behave like a silly girl. She was rarely silly, and she hadn't been a girl since...

Her eyes snapped up to his face. "You needn't tote me any farther, Mr. Sugarman."

He kept walking, his arms still tight around her. "I'm just hitting my stride, Miss Serena. It'd be a shame to stop now."

She pushed the flat of her hand against his chest hoping to extricate herself from his grasp, but when she felt the hard and unyielding curve beneath his damp shirt Serena drew her fingers back as if they had just been burned, while a hot little flame licked inside her. She wanted to touch him again, and she quickly squelched the desire as well as the thought.

Serena lifted her chin and cleared her throat. "What sort of work are you looking for, Mr. Sugarman?"

"I'm a farmer," he answered, keeping his eyes straight ahead as he continued up the hill. "I'm looking for a little piece of land to work. On my way into town I happened to see a fallow stretch of bottomland. You wouldn't happen to know anything about that, would you?"

"Down by Chickapee Bend?"

"About five miles west."

Serena nodded. She knew the place well. The last person who'd sharecropped there had disappeared two years before, owing her father plenty. "It's good land," she said, "though it needs a lot of work. How many hands do you plan to use to work it?"

"Just these two," he drawled as his hands moved slightly on her back and beneath her knees.

Her heart picked up a beat from his touch, then settled back into a regular rhythm. Drifter, she thought. A man who needed a place to rest, a cash crop to raise. He'd stay at Chickapee Bend till the cotton and corn were in, then he'd be on his way—in the dead of night—owing Con Quinn and smirking about how he'd caught the eye of Miss Serena.

"Well, good luck to you, Mr. Sugarman. My father takes a hefty share of the first year's crop, as well as keeping an eagle eye on his land. He doesn't take kindly to losses. As a matter of fact," she added, "neither do I."

He stopped, midstride, shifting Serena so her face was even closer to his. There was a touch of amusement in his eyes, but he wasn't grinning now and there was a harsh, almost taunting quality in his voice.

"Just what do you figure you've got to lose, lady?"

Her heart flipped over again, and now Serena didn't have a clue what it signified. Nobody had ever spoken to her so rudely. "Nothing," she snapped, then sputtered when she realized that wasn't what she meant at all. "Something. It's really none of your concern, sir."

His cool gaze latched onto her face a moment longer, dropping to her mouth, then returning lazily to her eyes. "I expect you're right about that, Miss Serena. I apologize, ma'am. Still, it's a damn shame to let all that 'concern' go to waste."

Serena stiffened in his arms as he began walking again. He seemed to be having a glorious time riling her, and it was probably her own fault, she thought,

for succumbing to his blatant virility and rather du-
bious charm in the first place. It was something she
never had done before. Something she intended never
to do again.

"There's the house," she said, pointing to the big,
redbrick, white-columned mansion at the top of the
incline. It was nestled now among glossy, wet mag-
nolias and rain-battered rhododendrons. Her father
had begun laying its bricks with his bare hands before
success and wealth allowed him to bring masons down
from Memphis and carpenters up from New Orleans.
Next to the courthouse it was the finest building in
Quinn County. "The hot-damnedest house in Mississippi," as Con Quinn called it.

A wide veranda flanked the house on three sides.
And there sat John William Pettigrew, feet tapping the
floorboards and fingers drumming on the arms of a
chair. Serena had completely forgotten about him.
Now she watched as he plucked his watch from his
pocket, opened and closed it, then stuffed it back.

Her first impression was how very small he looked
in that fan-backed wicker chair. Frail, somehow...and fit to be tied. She swung the umbrella down
like a shield.

"There you go again," Rafe muttered, casting his
eyes down to the mossy brick path and cutting his
stride by half. He'd already seen the big house and the
slick-combed dandy waiting on the porch. He'd felt
Miss Serena's limbs grow stiff, and could almost smell
the renewed starch in her clothes not to mention her
attitude. But how she thought one pitiful umbrella was

going to hide an ample woman and one overgrown man was beyond him.

When he told her so, she sniffed—indignant as a queen caught without her crown and in the arms of a peasant, to boot.

He set her down on the veranda. When she snapped the umbrella closed, the silk-shirted dandy shot out of his chair as if it had just gone up in flames.

"Serena, what's the meaning of this?"

Rafe stood back and watched her lift her chin, draw in a fortifying breath, then lean—like a full-bloomed rose—to offer her cheek for a kiss.

The dandy grazed her skin with his pursed lips, then glared at Rafe. "I don't believe I've had the pleasure, sir."

Rafe doubted it, too. He was thinking about the pleasure of meeting Miss Serena Quinn, how his arms felt empty now and how his wet shirt felt chilly without her substantial warmth against him.

Serena stood between them like a referee, well aware of John William's cool suspicions, keenly aware of what felt like waves of heat coming off Rafe Sugarman's body. The man was like a furnace at her back. And John William—the fool!—seemed eager to stoke the coals.

She quickly linked her arm through the dove gray of his sleeve, tugging him toward her. "John William Pettigrew, may I present Mr. Rafe Sugarman."

It was the big stranger who first extended his hand, and Serena stood transfixed by the surprising grace and shapeliness of such a huge hand. She remembered the way that hand had turned a humidor into a toy, and now it swallowed up John William's fingers like a whale making a snack of minnows. A shiver coursed down her spine.

Her eyes flitted to the face of the man she'd known all her life. Suddenly, rather than lukewarm and pallid, John William struck her as safe. That quality took on an entirely new appeal now.

She left the two of them to call through the front door. "Uncle Peter, could you come here, please?"

A moment later an elderly man appeared. His white grizzled hair matched his white cotton coat. His face was as black as his trousers. "Did you call me, Miz Serena?"

"Uncle Peter, would you show this gentleman upstairs to my father's room. He has some business to discuss with him."

The old man nodded, first to Serena, then to Rafe. "You can just leave that grip right here," he said as he aimed a gnarled finger at Rafe's valise. "I'll be stowing it for you whilst you're talking with Mr. Con."

"Thanks, but this goes where I go," Rafe answered firmly.

Serena hadn't even realized he was carrying that bag at the same time he was carrying her. Good Lord, now that was a load indeed. She stood aside to allow Rafe and his suitcase to pass through the door, but his arm still managed to brush against her sleeve, and his honey-colored gaze drew hers upward.

He took off his hat once more and those dark curls sprang free. "Thank you, Miss Quinn."

"You're quite welcome, Mr. Sugarman." Her hand moved almost of its own accord, as if it, too, longed to be engulfed in his huge grasp. Then it was, and the warmth of it seeped up her arm and flared across her bosom.

"Right this way," Uncle Peter said.

Serena stared at her empty hand after he let it go, then raised her eyes to watch him cross the vestibule, carrying that satchel as if it were a feather pillow with a handle on it. For such a giant, he had an amazingly trim waist. Her gaze moved down his long, powerful legs. When she saw the muddy boot prints he was leaving on her daddy's polished terrazzo floor, Serena's mouth tipped into the smallest of grins. Rafe Sugarman was making his mark as soon as he entered the house as surely as Con Quinn did whenever he came through the door.

She glanced up the wide, winding staircase. "Daddy," she thought, "you're about to encounter yourself in a six-foot mirror."

"I know that name," John William muttered behind her now. "I just can't for the life of me place it."

Serena turned. Once again she had completely forgotten John William was there. But there he was in the crisp gray suit that matched his eyes and echoed the wan brown of his finely combed hair. She tugged her shawl more tightly across her bodice. "I'm happy to see you, John William." Well, she was happy, she thought, despite the stiffness in her voice. "I hope your early return doesn't mean things didn't go well in Savannah."

"No, not at all. In fact, things went extremely well, Serena." He grasped her elbow. "Come sit with me. I believe Aunt Pete is preparing a pitcher of lemonade for us."

She settled her damp skirts in one of the big, fan-backed chairs. John William was dragging his chair closer when Aunt Pete came out the door with a heavy tray wedged into her ample stomach. Tall and trim and diffident as Uncle Peter was, his wife, Aunt Pete, was round as a billiard ball and about as hesitant to express her opinions as a crow in a cat patch. She lit into Serena immediately, depositing her tray of lemonade and ginger snaps on a table, then snatching the wet shawl from Serena's shoulders.

"You gonna catch your death in this soggy thing, child." Aunt Pete held the garment well out of range. "It sure is nice to see you back, Mr. Pettigrew. Yes, it is."

John William cleared his throat. "Thank you, Aunt Pete. It's nice to be back, although..."

The hefty black woman nudged Serena's shoulder. "You go on and pour that lemonade, Miss Serena. I got to get back to my kitchen. I'm fixing a fine roast for this prodigal man's return. And don't go spoiling your supper with too many ginger snaps, you hear?"

Serena rolled her eyes, exchanging glances with her longtime beau. Aunt Pete's flagrant familiarity was well-known to him. The woman had mothered Serena since Caroline Quinn had died giving birth to her. Servant or not, Aunt Pete was about the only one who ever talked back to Con Quinn, or to Serena, for that matter.

"I hear you," Serena said. She raised a meaningful eyebrow then. "But I've barely had time to hear a word from John William, Aunt Pete."

The big woman grinned as she turned to waddle back into the house. "I'll be in my kitchen if you two lovebirds need anything," she announced. The screen door slapped on its hinges behind her. Serena stifled a giggle as she heard her muttering about the no-'count who'd tracked up her nice clean floor.

John William's face was flushed now. A sheen of perspiration shone above his thin upper lip. He scooted his chair closer to Serena's and reached for her hand.

"We've known one another all our lives, Serena, dear," he said huskily.

Her heart jammed in her throat as she remembered Esme's nervous question—*Serena? You are going to say yes, aren't you?*—and her own sharp reply. *Well, of course. That's what I'm supposed to say, isn't it?*

"Yes, we have, John William. All our lives."

# Chapter Three

She couldn't stop looking at their joined hands. Hers and John William's. Equal in size. Alike in shade and shape. Both smooth. Familiar. Serena wondered vaguely what that meant, and whether her hands were unusually masculine or John William's were feminine, or if both of them were in some nether land between the two. His palms were damp and clammy. That she knew for certain.

His Adam's apple was bouncing above his tight collar now. "I suppose," he said, "there have been . . . well . . . expectations."

"I suppose there have been." She lowered her gaze again, thinking they weren't her expectations so much as everyone else's—the town gossips, Esme, her father. Mostly her father. He seemed to believe her unmarried state reflected poorly on him somehow. "Your mama married when she was seventeen," he kept reminding her. Serena would simply smile and say, "Yes, but she had *you* to marry, Daddy."

John William's fingers tightened as the palm of his

hand squished against hers. "I—I don't know how to say this, Serena. I'm afraid I'm going to disappoint you, my dear."

She opened her mouth to offer him a polite word of encouragement, to bolster his floundering tongue, but he cut her off, squeezing her fingers harder and speaking almost passionately now.

"I'm desperately in love, Serena."

Her lashes, still damp with rain, fluttered up. She was startled by the intense emotion on his face. She had never expected...

"Head over heels in love," he exclaimed, "with Miss Opal Hammersmith of Savannah, Georgia."

Serena blinked, and a raindrop loosened from a corner of her eye.

John William sighed. "There. Now I've wounded you. Oh, my dearest, I can't tell you how sorry I am. Had I known the fate that awaited me, I never would have gone."

"Fate." Serena echoed the word tonelessly. She felt as if she'd been on a speeding train that had suddenly and inexplicably stopped. She couldn't quite retrieve her momentum or her balance. As she floundered, the sound of raucous male laughter drifted from a window overhead. Her father's window. Her father's deep, rumbling laugh. And another—deeper still, dark somehow.

"Don't cry, dearest. Please."

Snatching her hand from his, Serena wiped at her rain-sodden lashes. "I'm not crying," she snapped. She wasn't, was she? Of all the emotions swirling through her right now, Serena was sure that none of them would have reduced her to tears.

He clucked his tongue sympathetically. "Who could blame you? I never meant for this to happen. I never meant to hurt you." John William reached for her hand again, but Serena pulled it away.

She should have hurt, she thought, but she didn't. Her heart should have felt an ache or even a twinge, but it didn't. "I'm confused, is all, John William. What, exactly, has happened?" she asked.

Without further prompting, her longtime, luke-warm beau launched into a passionate description of his sudden and inexplicable attraction to one Miss Opal Hammersmith, who appeared one evening "all tiny and adorable in rose-colored taffeta and Belgian lace." The reticent Mr. Pettigrew was suddenly nearly in song, and the words that formed his refrain were "tiny, petite, delicate, demure."

Serena stopped listening. Rather, she tilted her head and caught rough strains of laughter overhead. The pungent smell of cigars drifted around her and mingled with the sweet-smelling rain. It had been a long time since she'd heard her father do anything but groan and curse. He was laughing now. Hooting and guffawing. And his laughter was embellished by The Sugarman's, forming a harsh chorus to John William's lovestruck tune.

But John William had stopped. He was looking at her now with wide, pale eyes and a rather baffled crimp to his mouth.

"Miss Hammersmith sounds lovely," Serena offered. "I'm happy for you, John William. Truly."

"You're not just saying that, are you, Serena? I know, after all these years…you and I…well… This must be quite a disappointment for you."

"It isn't," she replied. Then, seeing his eyes widen even more, she added, "I mean, yes, of course, I'm disappointed, John William. But my happiness for you is independent of my own, um, my own…."

"Disappointment?"

Relief, Serena thought. Overwhelming and blessed relief. She could feel it coursing through her like a glittering river on its way to the open sea. She wanted to smile, to shoot straight out of her chair, twirl in the rain and shout a hallelujah chorus. Instead she let John William take her hand.

He murmured another apology, which Serena interrupted, tipping her head in the direction of the upstairs window. "Are you going to tell him, or shall I?"

John William's face froze in a kind of panic. A bead of sweat trickled down his cheek. Then he lurched up from his chair and practically tore his vest pocket to get at his watch. "Well, I would," he mumbled as he checked the time, "but I've a great deal of packing to do before my return to Savannah. Clothes. My mother's china. All those books."

Serena rose from her chair now and placed her hand on his arm. "I don't blame you," she said, arching an eyebrow toward the second-floor window. Then she laughed and leaned to kiss his smooth, clean-shaven cheek. "You go on home and get to that packing. I give you my blessings, John William. Daddy will, too—eventually.''

It wasn't true, of course, Serena thought as she watched John William nearly trot down the wet brick path toward the road. Right after she gave her daddy the news, she would undoubtedly have to find a carpenter to fix the hole where Con Quinn had gone through the roof.

The rain had slowed to a drizzle, then had stopped completely as the sun forced its way through the last scudding clouds. A fine mist was rising from the bright green lawn now as Serena stared from the veranda.

She paid scant attention when the screen door thumped on its frame, thinking it was probably Aunt Pete coming to reclaim the tray of refreshments. The porch boards creaked slightly, then boot heels came to rest right by her chair.

''Where's your gentleman caller, Miss Serena?''

''Gone,'' she answered without even thinking. ''Permanently.'' Then, as she realized just who was standing beside her chair, she gave a small gasp as she turned toward the voice. What she encountered, however, was not a voice or a face, but rather a pair of trousers—just below the belt buckle.

''Then he's more of a fool than he looked,'' Rafe drawled.

Her eyes flashed up to his face. ''It's not your concern, Mr. Sugarman.''

''Yes, ma'am. You told me that before.'' He shifted his stance. ''It doesn't strike me that you're all that concerned yourself. Do you make a habit of showing men the door, Miss Serena?" His mouth edged sideways as he cocked his head.

"No more than you make it a habit to irritate me," she responded crisply.

His expression sobered suddenly while his gaze roved over her from the top of her head to the hem of her skirt. Unnerved by the lazy appraisal, Serena smoothed the damp blue serge over her knees.

Then his eyes fastened on her bodice, not only unnerving her but making her skin prickle. Out of habit, Serena reached to gather her shawl more closely around her. Her hands fluttered in midair as she realized the shawl was gone.

And now his voice was a deep, beguiling bass. "What is it you believe a few flimsy yards of fabric can protect you from, Shawl Lady?"

Hands clasped in her lap now, Serena sat rigidly, refusing to meet his gaze. Without her shawl, she felt exposed and—yes, damn the man—unprotected. "Are you through interrogating and inspecting me now?"

Not yet, Rafe thought. He could have stood there and looked at her for hours—at the wild, rain-curled hair that had escaped its cautious knot, at the rise and fall of her breasts beneath her careful clothes. What he saw was making his blood run hot, but it was more what he didn't see that fired his mind. And he very badly wanted to see beneath the prim surface of Miss Serena Quinn. He reached out, feathering a finger along the side of her face, feeling the soft, errant curls and the smooth warmth of her cheek.

For a single, unguarded moment she leaned into his touch like a kitten. Then, like a cat, she hissed and bared her claws.

"Stop it."

From the upstairs window then, Con Quinn bellowed her name, not once but several times. Rafe's hand held still. Don't touch what you can't have, boy, he told himself. Haven't you learned that by now? Don't you know when to quit, Sugarman?

He slid his fingers to cup her chin, then winked into her face, all flushed with cat anger and kitten yearnings. "The boss is calling you." He picked up his suitcase then and gave it a playful heft before he sauntered down the veranda steps. Without even turning, he gave her a backhanded wave and called, "I'll be seeing you, Miss Serena."

Her cheek still tingled as she watched him—drifter, down to his last cent—amble down the walk like a man who hadn't a care in the world. Serena lifted her hand to touch where he had touched, half expecting to encounter a blister or a streak of blood. The mark of The Sugarman. But the heat her fingertips met there was her own.

Then her father's voice boomed once more from the window. "Serena Quinn, I'm calling you."

"Yes, Daddy," she breathed.

"Who gave you permission to shut the store down early, missy?"

"Nobody, Daddy." Serena punched her fist into the pillow to plump it, then shoved it behind her father's back. Her eyes were squinted against the cigar smoke curling toward her. "I'm in charge of the store, if you'll recall."

Con Quinn grunted as he leaned back against the headboard. The ropes under the mattress creaked as he shifted his bulk. At the age of fifty-four, his muscular frame was now equal parts muscle and fat. His hair was the color of gunmetal. His voice was loud as a cannon, especially in the confines of his bedroom. He had the disposition of a man who regularly dined on liberal doses of pepper and gunpowder.

"As I recall, Sister, I was the one who put you in charge. And I don't remember closing early being part of the deal." He pulled on his cigar, then his face nearly disappeared behind a curtain of green-gray smoke.

Serena waved it away. "Will it make you feel any better if I told you I came home to receive a call from John William?"

"Well, now," he muttered. "I was under the impression that Mr. John William *Petticoat* had taken himself to Savannah."

She plopped into the rocker next to the bed, sighing, then studying her nails. "He came back."

Silence and smoke lingered between them for a long moment before her father raised a dark eyebrow and asked, "For what?"

Moving her hands to the wooden arms of the rocker, Serena began a slow back-and-forth motion. "He came back to inform me that he has fallen in love."

Now her father's eyebrow shot even higher on his furrowed forehead. "With you, Sister?"

Calmly Serena shook her head. "No. Not with me, Daddy. He plans to marry a young lady in Savannah."

"By God, I'll kill him first," Con Quinn boomed.

It was the reaction she had expected—the reaction that the anticipation of had sent John William scurrying home earlier. Her father's face was nearly purple with rage. His dark eyes narrowed to slits.

"Where is Mr. Petticoat?" he demanded. "Downstairs cowering in some corner of my parlor?"

"He's gone, Daddy." Cowering in some corner of his own parlor, Serena added to herself.

"Damnation!" he thundered, lugging his big frame upright. "Uncle Peter! Get yourself in here right this minute." Con's hot gaze shot toward Serena. "I'll have Arlen Sears drag that pantywaist back here by the scruff of his neck. I'll sue him for breach of promise, that's what I'll do."

"There were never any promises, Daddy."

"He spent the last five years keeping company with you," he countered at the top of his lungs. "Five years, riding in my best carriage, eating at my table and drinking my best brandy.... Whiling away his time at my expense. If you don't want to call it a promise, Serena, then let's just say Mr. John William Petticoat is deeply in debt."

She shot out of the chair, which continued to rock behind her. Her hands clenched at her sides. "This is not one of your business transactions. I won't be handed over to satisfy a debt."

Con chewed on his cigar a moment, glaring at her. "I didn't mean—"

"Yes, you did, Daddy. You most certainly did." Tears welled up in Serena's eyes, though she fought to keep them from spilling. Her father had never seen her cry. She vowed he never would.

His rough features immediately softened. "Now, Serena, honey..."

It was Serena who was glaring now, her eyes like blue flames behind a screen of mist.

Con sighed. "You're twenty-four years old, Sister. By the time your mama was your age—"

"She was dead," Serena cut in.

"Leaving two fine children to carry on," he finished.

Now a tear did loosen to slide down Serena's cheek. "Daddy, please. Let's not—"

There was a soft knock on the door, after which Uncle Peter's grizzled head poked through the opening. "Did you want me, Mr. Con?"

Con Quinn looked from his servant to his daughter. His gaze lingered on her before returning to the door. "I did, Uncle Peter, but I can't for the life of me remember why. You go on back to what you were doing and I'll yell if it comes to mind."

The black man's head bobbed in the doorway before disappearing.

The room was silent then, save for the ticking of a clock and rainwater dripping off the eaves.

"All right, Sister," Con said at last, his voice low and warm. "I never did think much of that Petticoat fellow, anyway. I don't suppose there'd be much sense in dragging him back."

Serena smiled. "No sense at all, Daddy." She began to straighten the pile of papers on his bedside table.

"You're not off the hook, though, missy. Not by a long shot."

"All right," she murmured as she placed a glass paperweight on the neatened stack.

"All right," he said gruffly. Then he took her hand in his, pulling her closer to the bed. "I've had plenty of time to do some serious cogitating while I've been cooped up in this bed these past few weeks. I've been thinking about my life, Sister. I've been thinking about Quinn County and what it'll be like after I'm gone."

She touched his shoulder. "Don't, Daddy."

He lifted a hand. "No. Now hear me out. I'm not a young man. Young or not, I'm not going to live forever. Not me, anyway." Con Quinn's eyes glistened now as he raised them to his daughter's. "I want grandchildren, Serena. I long for them. I ache to know that my blood will still be flowing in Quinn County long after I'm gone."

Serena started to speak, then merely averted her eyes from his beseeching gaze.

"I love you, Serena. You're all I've got left in this world." He paused and let his breath out in a withered and mournful sigh. "But that's not enough. It's not near enough."

The Tallahatchie River bent like an elbow five miles west of town. The spring rain had it running high and fast.

"If you're in the mood to flood," Rafe muttered as he watched the tumbling, white-tipped water, "I'd just as soon you did it before I do any planting." He lobbed a hickory stick into the river and watched the current rip it away, then he picked up his valise and strode to the cabin.

He'd lived in worse places, he thought as he approached the unpainted shanty. A quick appraisal told him the front porch needed shoring up and the brick chimney was sorely in need of some tuck-pointing. He mounted the front steps with caution and pushed open the front door with his boot.

Judging from the litter and the smell, a raccoon had probably been the last one to call the place home. "You're moving up in this world, Sugarman," Rafe said under his breath. "Leastways you're one rung up from a coon."

With a sigh, he set his valise on a dusty oak table, opened it and stared at the neatly folded blue uniform.

*Come to Washington with me, Rafe.*

*Thank you, General. It's a flattering offer, but I'm set on going home.*

*Stubborn, cussed fool! What do you think's waiting for you other than the business end of a rope?*

Rafe closed his eyes now, picturing himself leading that other life, the one he'd ridden away from in Virginia five years ago. Grant was in the White House now. The White House!

His eyes took in the littered floor, the spiderwebs that hung like so much bunting, the broken window glass.

*Pride, Sugarman. You've got an unhealthy dose of it,* Grant had told him. *Do you read your Bible, son?*
*Some.*
*Pride goeth before a fall.*

The words echoed in Rafe's head as his mouth curved into a lopsided grin. "Hell, General," he said to the empty room, "I'm so far down, it'd barely be a tumble now."

Later that afternoon, after sweeping out the cabin and ridding it of cobwebs, Rafe sat with his feet up on the porch rail, making a list of supplies. As he licked the tip of the lead pencil, he listened to the rising wind and to the distinct sound of an approaching horse. It wasn't long before he saw the sleek black mare and sunlight glinting on the vest of its rider. The local lawman. Rafe sighed as he stuck the pencil behind his ear, wondering what had taken him so long. It had been all of six hours since he'd been in town.

"You working this place for Con?" the man asked as he dismounted.

Rafe looked at the Colt snug against the wiry man's hip. "Yes, sir," he said as he eased his boots off the cross rail, then folded his list and stuck it in his shirt pocket.

"I'm the law around this part of the county. Name's Arlen Sears."

"Rafe Sugarman."

"Sugarman. Now where have I heard that name?" Sears pushed his hat back on his head. "You got kin around here?"

"Nope." Casual as his reply was, Rafe's whole body was tightening. He rolled his neck to ease the tension.

The lawman's gaze flicked over the cabin and then returned to Rafe. "Sounds familiar." He shrugged then. "What kind of deal did Con give you?"

"Shares," Rafe replied. "Sixty-forty."

Sears's thin lips edged sideways. "You're lucky he isn't taking seventy," he sneered. "'Course, he will be once he's got you furnishing out of his store, taking your cotton to his gin and putting your cash in his bank. Son of a bitch doesn't miss a trick."

Rafe didn't reply. He merely smiled affably at the constable and crossed his arms, waiting for the man to continue.

Arlen Sears strolled toward the porch and put a foot on the step. "The word around town is you've already made Miss Serena's acquaintance."

"In a manner of speaking," Rafe said.

The lawman snorted. "Don't go getting any ideas about her. She's a cold one. That's why she wears those shawls all the time. Woman's colder than ice on a pond."

Again, Rafe merely nodded. Sears was standing with the sun at his back, and it was hard to get a good fix on his shadowed face. It wasn't too difficult to pin down the man's sensibilities, though. Or his loyalties. "I appreciate the advice."

"Yeah. Well." The constable backed up and turned toward his black mare, then, with one bounce for heft, lofted into the saddle. Now he stared down at Rafe. "See that you stay on the right side of the law, Sugarman. We don't like troublemakers in Quinn County."

You don't *like*, period, mister, Rafe thought as he waved to his departing visitor. He sat back down, took the list from his pocket and the pencil from behind his ear, and added a few more items. Then he gazed out at the slant of the sun on the rolling green countryside.

Serena Quinn, unbidden and unwelcome, strayed into his thoughts.

The lawman was right about her daddy. Con Quinn didn't just drive a hard bargain; he caught a man up by his privates and squeezed—hard. But that was all right. If this were Sugarman County and Rafe were The Man, that's what he'd do, too. He respected Con Quinn, even when the man was giving him the proverbial shaft. Rafe had had no choice but to take it— grinning. For now, anyway.

Con Quinn was what he appeared to be. On the other hand, Miss Serena was like a flame quivering beneath a sheet of ice. He had felt that ice melt and turn to liquid heat when she was in his arms. Just briefly. Before she got a handle on her senses and tugged that blasted shawl around her.

For a moment he imagined her wrapped in a shawl, blue as her eyes, soft as her skin—and nothing else. He imagined her ripened body heating the silk where it draped around her shoulders, where it skimmed over her hips. He imagined . . .

He shifted abruptly in his chair, mouthed a quiet curse and went back to his list.

# Chapter Four

The candles were lit in the dining room and their flames danced in the high gloss of the cherrywood table. Esme, in pale watered silk, sat across from Serena, who had changed—grudgingly—from damp blue serge into dark green velveteen with a matching shawl.

Serena was running a finger beneath the starched ecru lace around her throat when she heard her father's footsteps coming down the stairs. She took in a deep breath, waiting. He'd taken his meals in his room for two months. Surely he wasn't . . .

His bulk in the doorway blocked the light from the vestibule lamps. "Evening, Sister. Evening, Sister Belle."

A little squeak of surprise broke from Esme's throat. "Daddy Quinn, we had no idea . . ."

"I can see that," he said, glowering at the table that was laid for two. "Uncle Peter!"

The servant immediately appeared in the door that led to the kitchen. "Yes, Mr. Con?"

"We're going to need another place set here, Uncle Peter. See to it, will you?"

The black man flashed a gap-toothed grin, then slipped back into the kitchen. In the meantime, Esme had jumped up and run to kiss her father-in-law. Con seated her, then yanked out his own chair at the head of the table.

"Aren't you glad to see me, Sister?" he asked Serena, skewering her with his dark eyes. "I haven't heard the first word out of you yet."

"I'm glad to see you, Daddy," she said. "Our suppers have been much too quiet lately."

"Seems like your whole life's been too quiet. I'm planning to change that." He was interrupted by Uncle Peter's trayful of china and silverware, so he sat back in silence.

Serena took the opportunity to stiffen her backbone. She had spoken the truth; she was glad to see him up and around, with his usual vigor and his habitual ax to grind. Unfortunately, Serena thought, it was her head on the block this evening.

Aunt Pete carried serving dishes from the kitchen, and as she placed a bowl on the table she leaned close to Serena and rasped in her ear. "We got my fancy roast and all these vegetables, but we ain't got no Mr. Pettigrew, I see."

Ignoring the remark, Serena turned toward her father. "What sort of changes did you have in mind, Daddy?"

Con lifted his fork, aimed it at her, and sighted down the handle. "Two by two, Serena. That's the way of the world." He glanced at Esme. "You listen, too, Sister Belle. You've been a widow...how many years now?''

"Eight," Esme said quietly.

He nodded, closing his eyes a moment as if picturing the son he'd lost to the Southern cause to which he, himself, had been relatively indifferent. War wasn't good for business, he had blustered. Five years after the bloodshed, Quinn County was still recovering, though Con had managed to keep out the carpetbaggers and the scalawags who were skimming the profits in other counties.

Now he slammed his big fist on the table. "Things are going to change around here. The past is past. I'm looking toward the future now.''

Serena reached out to keep her water goblet from tipping. "The future's all well and good, Daddy, but it'd be nice if we could get through the present without breaking the crystal.''

Esme laughed, but Con shot his daughter a dark look.

"Damn the crystal," he said. "It's people that matter. Men and women and children.''

"You're very philosophical this evening, Daddy Quinn," Esme observed. "Are you taking a new tonic?''

He smiled then, a slow, almost mystical smile. "I made the acquaintance of a young man today, Esme, who reminded me a whole lot of myself when I was young and feverish to succeed.''

Serena's heart stuttered, then resumed its normal rhythm. She knew immediately who her father was referring to. So, The Sugarman had charmed the old goat!

"He's a drifter, Daddy. I'm surprised you let him pull the wool over your eyes." Her confident tone faltered slightly then. "You aren't letting him sharecrop Chickapee Bend, are you?"

"I am."

She snorted. "Well, that's money thrown to the wind."

"What wind?" Esme asked. "Who's this you're discussing, Serena? Is somebody new in town?"

They both ignored the little blonde as their steely blue gazes locked.

"Drifter, is he? How many drifters do you know, daughter, who plant peach trees and cherry trees?"

"He told you that?" she asked.

"He did. He's going to Memphis and bringing back a wagonful of saplings."

Serena raised an eyebrow. "With money you loaned him, I suppose."

"I gave him a cash advance. An investment in the future."

"It'll be a miracle if you even see him again, then," she said indignantly.

Con Quinn tilted his head. "You're awful hot under your lace collar about this *insignificant drifter*, Sister."

She was, and she'd be damned if she'd lift her hand to give that collar a tug. Instead she took several thoughtful sips from her water goblet and retreated into a safe silence.

"Who are you two talking about?" Esme demanded.

"Hush," Serena hissed.

After forking in a good-sized piece of roast, Con chewed with deliberation, his eyes on Serena. Then he banged his fists on the tabletop again. "We're going to have a party. We're going to put on the biggest she-bang since you came out at the cotillion in Memphis."

Esme's eyes sparkled. "A party! Whatever's gotten into you, Daddy Quinn?"

"We've been living too quiet. It's time to stir things up a little, Sister Belle." He paused, slowly turning toward Serena. "And it's time you made your debut, Sister."

Serena nearly choked on a green bean. "I did that seven years ago, Daddy."

"For all the good it did you," he grumped. "You came out at that fancy ball, then you went right back in." He sighed now. "You were such a bright, blooming girl. Then you just closed up under those damn shawls."

When Serena didn't reply, Esme said, "It was the war, Daddy Quinn. Serena took it hard."

"Well, the war's over. And so is the past. We're talking about the future now."

"You're talking," Serena cut in, "pure silliness."

"Call it what you want, Serena," he replied. "We're going to put on a grand gala. Have people in from miles around. Have young people in."

"Young men." Serena sniffed.

Con Quinn's voice rose now, and the candle flames wavered as if a wind were blowing through the dining room. "Young men with warm blood flowing in their veins. Not pale, manicured specimens like John William Petticoat. Young men with vinegar and gusto." He paused dramatically. "Eligible men."

Esme tittered, but stopped when her father-in-law and Serena both glared at her.

"I don't care who you choose, Serena. Let it be the butcher or the baker or the confounded candlestick maker. But you will choose, you hear?"

Serena's eyes burned behind a sheen of tears. "I hear you, Daddy."

"Good," he boomed. "Smile, Sister. You're gonna be married before the summer's out."


Aunt Pete waddled across Serena's bedroom squatting to pick up discarded clothes, muttering all the while. "This house would be up to the rafters in castoffs if I didn't go 'round every night. Yes, it would."

Serena smiled into the mirror where she sat brushing her hair. "We'd be up to our ears in pantalets and petticoats if it weren't for you, Aunt Pete."

"Humph." She dropped her bundle by the door, then came back to grab the brush from Serena's hand and commenced to whisk it through her long hair. "You'd be tangled every which way, too, the way you goes about that."

Serena clenched her teeth and braced her neck against the hard pull of the boar bristles.

"You got anything you want to talk about, child?" Aunt Pete asked, looking in the mirror now, seeking Serena's eyes.

Glancing away, Serena shook her head. This woman had always been a refuge of sorts, but tonight there were so many emotions swirling inside her that Serena didn't know where or how to begin.

Aunt Pete's competent hands separated the thick auburn hair into three long hanks and began braiding them down Serena's back. "You lost a beau, Miz Serena, and you been threatened with a husband. Seems there's room for conversation somewhere in there."

"Seems to me you were listening at the kitchen door again," Serena snapped.

The rotund woman laughed. "Got to," she said. "How else am I going to know how to take care of all my Quinns? 'Specially my baby Serena."

"How else?" Serena murmured as she let her head drift back onto Aunt Pete's ample bosom. "What am I going to do? Whatever am I going to do?"

Hands on Serena's shoulders now, Aunt Pete said, "In all my thirty years with Mr. Con, I never did hear him sound so set on something as he is about you marrying."

"He wants grandchildren."

"He's a man. He wants to leave his mark on this earth. Your daddy's worked long and hard for what he's got, Miz Serena. He don't want it all to come to nothing." She chuckled softly. "Even that man of mine, little as he's got, glories in his grands. You've heard Uncle Peter go on about how Little Joab takes after him."

"Hester wanted to marry. She wanted Big Joab. He was the sun and all the stars to her."

Aunt Pete's reply was an indignant sniff. "I don't want to talk about that no-'count slave man my baby run off with. We're talking about you now, Miz Serena."

Equally indignant, Serena snapped, "Me and some stranger."

"You and whatever man you decide to share your life with," Aunt Pete replied. "That John William— he was a nice enough boy, but he wasn't for you. You're a big, strong, sharp-tongued girl. You need a man to match."

A vision of Rafe Sugarman ducking through the mercantile door flashed through Serena's mind, prompting a chill to race down her spine.

"What's wrong, baby?" Aunt Pete cooed.

"I don't want to marry anybody. I don't want to marry at all. Ever."

The black woman clucked her tongue and fussed with Serena's braid. "Such talk," she murmured.

"It's not just talk. I mean it."

Responding to the almost desperate note in Serena's voice, Aunt Pete clasped her by the shoulders and turned her around. She took Serena's chin in one hand, forcing their gazes to meet. "You ain't talking 'bout marriage at all, is you, Miss Serena? When you say marriage, what you mean is what goes with it."

Wrenching away, Serena stood and walked to the shuttered window. Undeterred, Aunt Pete followed. She slipped a solid arm around Serena's shoulders and whispered, "Is my baby still dwelling on that black night when them Yankees done you wrong?"

Serena flinched, her voice barely more than a breath. "I tried to forget. I even thought I could marry John William. We were friends. I trusted him. I knew he'd never . . . never do anything I didn't want."

"You don't know what you want, child. You don't even know what's to be wanted. All you know is the pain and shame of that dark night and those Yankee devils." Her voice dropped lower as she stroked Serena's hair. "That was seven years ago, honey. I told you that night what those cur dogs did to you didn't count for nothin'. Don't you recollect that? I told you to fold all those memories in one of your mama's silk hankies and bury them out back of the barn. You did it, too. I can still see you crying and digging, then stamping the dirt with your bare feet." Aunt Pete shook her head now. "You never said no more about it after that."

Serena stood, arms tightly clasped around her, lips pressed together, mute.

"It's no good carrying all that pain, honey. It only weighs you down. You want me to get another of Miz Quinn's hankies and we'll go a'burying again? Just you and me, out back, like before?"

A tiny smile flared on Serena's lips. "No. Thank you, Aunt Pete. I don't think all the silk hankies in Mississippi would help me." She threw her arms around the woman's solid warmth and buried her face in the damp folds of her neck.

"We got to do something, sweet child," Aunt Pete murmured as she stroked Serena's head. "Your daddy's right set on your marrying and giving him grands.''

Serena shivered again, then wept as she hadn't wept, hadn't allowed herself to weep, in seven years.

Long after Aunt Pete had tucked her into the high four-poster bed, Serena lay with her wet eyes wide open. Every time she tried to close them, it seemed, visions of that hellish night came back. Even now, staring at the ceiling, the ghosts kept returning.

It had been the autumn of '62. The Yankees were advancing into Mississippi from Tennessee. The boys in gray were rushing to meet them near Corinth. But that was north and east of Quinn County. Not close enough to lose a good night's sleep, her father had maintained.

And Con Quinn had indeed been sleeping, soundly, the night Serena had gone out to the barn to make sure the new Morgan foal was warm enough. She remembered the crispness of the air and how it had chilled her skin despite the wrapper she wore. She remembered the soft nickering of the horses as she'd entered the barn and the feel of the hay-strewn floor under her bare feet. With only moonlight through the hay doors to guide her, she had stepped cautiously toward the stall where the Morgan mare and her foal were bedded down.

Only she never got that far.

She shuddered now, beneath the pristine white sheet. Her lips moved, not in prayer, but offering one more curse for those blue-coated demons who had stripped her of her innocence, who had torn her and taunted her, then left her ripped and bleeding on the barn floor.

She had crawled like a wounded animal into the kitchen. Aunt Pete had bathed her and soothed her and told her what to do with the warm vinegar. "Don't nobody have to know, child. You and me, we're gonna wrap your ruination in a silk hankie and bury it. Just like it never happened. Just like that."

Just like that, Serena thought now. If only it were as simple as Aunt Pete claimed.

Then, as she pulled the covers closer, another voice—deep and dark as the bottom of a whiskey barrel—reverberated through her. *What is it you believe a few flimsy yards of fabric can protect you from, Shawl Lady?*

"Everything," she whispered in the darkness. "You."

## Chapter Five

It was shortly before noon the next day when Serena, stifling a yawn, looked hard at the clock behind the counter. She'd slept fitfully, if at all, the night before. But it wasn't lack of sleep that was worrying her now. It was Little Joab. He was more than three hours late. The ten-year-old had chores to see to at home before he came into town to work for her, but it wasn't like him to be this late. Lord only knew what was going on now that Big Joab was out of jail.

She reached into the pocket of her freshly pressed blue serge skirt, fingering the coin the child had given her yesterday. Rafe Sugarman's last nickel, it occurred to her as she quickly withdrew her hand. Well, not anymore, she thought, now that her father had advanced him a fistful of cash. Chances were good they'd all seen the last of The Sugarman.

When nobody came into the store during the next twenty minutes, Serena decided to lock up and pay a long-overdue call on Hester Inch. She walked home briskly, asked Uncle Peter to hitch up the buggy, and in no time at all she was heading west beneath a soft, butter-colored spring sun.

Her fingers worried the reins as she gazed at the sleek rump of the Morgan, the foal whose comfort had taken her out to the barn that night seven years ago.

"It's all your fault, Rebel," she chided him. Sighing then, she chided herself. She hadn't dwelt on her sorrow overmuch in the past years; now here she was getting all down in the mouth over something she couldn't change. But everything seemed awry suddenly with John William gone and her father making his outrageous demands.

It was her father's fault, she decided. Daddy and his quest for life eternal. Why couldn't he be satisfied leaving Quinn County as a memorial?

And, she thought, it was that impertinent drifter's fault, too. Not only had he somehow gotten her father all stirred up, but he'd stirred her up as well, bringing to the surface feelings Serena had successfully subdued for years. He'd made her think about being kissed. No, he'd made her *want* to be kissed. He'd breached her defenses as no one ever had. But then, no one had ever tried.

She was wondering what it was about Rafe Sugarman that had so quickly gotten under her skin when the Inch cabin came into sight. The little place was, without a doubt, the best-kept sharecropper's cabin in the county with its whitewashed walls and neat border of pink azaleas. Little wonder, since Hester Inch was Aunt Pete's daughter and had been brought up in the Quinn house surrounded by finery. All the porce-

lain and damask had meant nothing, though, once
Hester fell in love with Big Joab Inch, a runaway from
Silverwood Plantation near Natchez. Big Joab had
been heading north, but once he encountered Hester,
he never got beyond Quinn County.

He was a free man now. Well, Serena thought, that
was only true in the legal sense. He was too outspo-
ken for most, too "uppity." More than anything else,
he seemed to stick in the constable's craw like a fish
bone. That didn't make for an easy life—for Big Joab,
for Hester or for their children.

Hester ran out of the front door now, waving, with
Little Joab right on her heels. Like her son, she was
sapling thin. It wasn't from lack of food, however,
because Uncle Peter—at Con's insistence—made regular trips out here, laden with provisions from the
kitchen in the big house. Serena thought Hester was
just naturally nervous, and all that flitting and fluttering ate away at her flesh. Her hands were dancing
like dark butterflies now as Serena climbed down from
the buggy.

"I was worried about Little Joab," she said just
before Hester's thin arms encircled her.

"Lordy, it's good to see you, Serena."

Serena held back as she hugged the woman, not for
lack of affection but for fear of breaking her reedlike
spine. "I was worried," she said again, pulling back
from the embrace and holding Hester by the upper
arms to keep her still. "I thought Little Joab was
sick."

"Oh, I'm all right, Miz Serena. It's my daddy what—"

"Hush up, you hear, Little Joab?" Hester broke from Serena's grasp and pulled the boy into her skirt. "Miz Serena didn't come all this way to hear us moaning and groaning."

Little Joab stared at the ground. "She prob'ly come to give me what for 'bout that nickel," he muttered.

"I came," Serena announced, linking her arm through Hester's, "for a cup of coffee and some good conversation. Do you suppose I can find any around here?"

The smell of freshly brewed coffee filled the main room of the little cabin. Sunlight filtered through the starched gingham curtains and fell softly on the crib where a small bundle slept peacefully. Serena stood gazing down at the baby girl while Hester poured coffee.

"Flora's grown, Hester," she said softly. "And just look at all that hair."

"I told you that child wasn't going to be bald, Miz Serena." Hester put a mug of steaming coffee in her hand. "That baby just takes her own sweet time."

"You make it seem so easy." There was a wistful note in Serena's voice as she continued to gaze into the crib.

Hester laughed. "Babies? The only easy thing about babies is the getting of them."

Serena's smile thinned to a taut line as she turned and took a seat at the table in the center of the room. In light of her father's demands, babies and the getting of them wasn't something she wanted to discuss. "I imagine you're happy having Big Joab back," she said, changing the subject. "Think he can keep out of Arlen Sears's hair for a few months?"

"Already in his hair." Hester slid into a chair. "The constable was out here just after sunrise, wanting to know who stole Emery Todd's chickens."

Serena was shocked. "That's ridiculous," she exclaimed. "Emery's chickens are always wandering off. One of them's roosting in our barn right—"

Hester's hand flew up like an agitated sparrow, silencing Serena. "That man don't care about chickens, Miz Serena. Constable Sears just got it in for my man."

"Where's Big Joab now?"

"He took off soon as he heard the horse coming. Figured we'd all be better off if he and the constable didn't have a set-to."

Serena caught Hester's jittery hand and held it tight. "I wish there was something I could do."

Hester smiled and shrugged helplessly. "Everybody knows Arlen Sears is Mr. Con's man. And we all know Mr. Con don't sway easy. He's like a big old oak tree."

It was true, Serena thought bleakly. Once Con Quinn made up his mind—about people or events—it was made up. Her father had hired Sears primarily for his meanness. The man's hard glares were enough to keep the peace in town. But keeping the peace and harassing innocent citizens were entirely different matters, and she meant to let her father know.

The two women chatted for a while, letting their conversation turn to more pleasant subjects, like the baby who now suckled at Hester's breast. Serena was almost mesmerized by the intimate sight of mother and child. A kind of longing rose in her, lodging in her throat, but she swallowed hard and dismissed it. It was her father who ached for progeny, not her.

She left Hester with the promise that she would speak to Con about Arlen Sears, and left Little Joab with a gentle warning about his responsibilities at the store.

The Morgan trotted along smoothly, pausing—as if to ask which way—where the road forked south toward Chickapee Bend. Serena leaned forward, looking down the weed-choked path that led to the tenant cabin. Her brow crumpled and her teeth worried her lower lip.

He wasn't there. She was sure of that. Her father had given Rafe Sugarman a pocketful of greenbacks and a good excuse to beat it out of the county. Con Quinn had been conned, for once in his long, crafty life. There weren't going to be peach and cherry trees at Chickapee Bend. There'd just be, as always, a tumbledown cabin with a sagging front porch and dank corners to shelter critters.

Serena tugged on the reins and the Morgan turned down the weed-strewn path. It was Quinn property, she told herself. She had every right to check on it. And as firmly as she believed the man was gone, she found her eyes searching through the trees for evidence of his presence. A man that big couldn't very well hide.

He wasn't hiding, but rather standing bigger than life in the dooryard, legs spread like a colossus, sun gleaming like butter on his broad, bare back. She drew in her breath with a little gasp, then fidgeted with the reins, uncertain now whether to pull the buggy around and make a hasty retreat or to continue toward the cabin.

The decision was made for her when he turned—muscles rippling and tendons straining—and gazed at her steadily before raising his hand in a wave. For a moment she felt like a schoolgirl caught peeking through a knothole into the boys' coat closet, and color rushed to her face even as her hand lifted in a responsive greeting.

She snapped the reins then, reminding herself this was Quinn property and the person planted in the front yard was not a Greek statue but a Quinn employee. He had stayed one day, proving absolutely nothing except perhaps that he was tired of tramping.

"Out checking on the help, Miss Serena?"

He smoothed one big hand along the flank of her horse, then stood beside the buggy, half-naked, his mouth crooked in something closer to a dare than a smile.

"Actually," she replied, "I'm surprised to see you're still here."

Hard ropes of muscle twisted as he crossed his arms. "And not all that pleasantly surprised either. Guess you'd be a lot happier now if I was in the next county, counting your daddy's money and laughing out loud, instead of breaking my back trying to shore up these rotten porch boards." He angled his head toward the cabin.

"You do look busy," she said, thinking he looked beautiful and trying to dispel the thought.

Rafe laughed. "I look like a lathered ox." He reached up, took the reins from her lax hands and looped them around the brake handle. Then he clamped his hands around her waist. "Come on, Miss Serena Quinn. You came out here to snoop so you might just as well get to it." In one smooth motion he lifted her down from the buggy seat.

Too surprised to protest, Serena discovered her hands on slick, sun-warmed shoulders. Her head was swimming from the abrupt descent from the buggy and from the earthy scent of a man who'd been hard at work. She swayed when her feet met the ground and her lashes fluttered up to his face, but Rafe's sure hands steadied her and his slow smile oddly warmed her.

"I've got you," he assured her.

And for a moment, caught in that damp, shawling embrace, Serena felt more secure than ever before in her life. Safe. Oh, so safe. In the arms of a total stranger! She pulled away and stepped out of that beguiling grasp. Her hands jerked to the edges of her shawl to readjust it.

He simply stood there, gazing down at her almost studiously, as if trying to read her thoughts. Then he shrugged slightly and turned away.

"I'm going to put my shirt on, Miss Serena. Go on and have a look around."

She wanted to, but she was unable to take her eyes off those broad shoulders and the slick little pool of sweat where his spine met his belt line. The dark fabric of his trousers was darker still and damp at his waist. He picked up a dipper from a bucket on the porch, bent and poured a bright stream of water over his head, then shook it. Beads of golden, sun-struck water flew in all directions, then his dark curls sprang back to glossy life as Serena watched. The water coursed down his chest, briefly tamping the dark pelt of hair. He lifted his whiskey-colored eyes to hers, then held out the dipper.

"Thirsty?"

Serena heard herself swallow. Her throat felt dusty, but she shook her head. "No. No, thank you. I'll just peruse the place while you..." Cover up all that glorious, glistening skin, she thought. "While you make yourself decent, Mr. Sugarman."

He chuckled as he reached for the shirt that was draped over the porch rail. "Sorry if I offended your maiden sensibilities. I wasn't expecting callers. Not of the female persuasion anyway."

She sniffed and drew her shawl closer. "Don't flatter yourself that this is a social call. I'm merely looking out for my father's business interests."

"Well, have at it, Miss Serena." He stabbed his arms into the sleeves of the worn blue chambray shirt. "Anything you don't like, you just let me know."

Rafe yanked at his shirttails. Damn frustrating female. He had a full day of work cut out for himself and now here she came, all soft and defenseless one minute, all stiff and proper the next. She had looked at him with an unguarded yearning that had gotten his blood hot, then she'd closed up tighter than a tavern on the Sabbath.

Now she was moving around the yard, her spine stiff as a rod, her chin up and her elbows angled—like a general inspecting a regiment of ne'er-do-wells and stragglers. Right now Rafe thought he'd rather face a grim-lipped general than the rose-colored lips of Serena Quinn. He didn't need temptation now. Especially in the form of a woman who could get him booted out of the county by just crooking her little finger under her old man's nose. Quinn County wasn't exactly the Garden of Eden, and Con Quinn wasn't the Almighty Lord by a long stretch, but right at that moment Rafe felt a weak-kneed kinship with poor old Adam.

He swore under his breath as he buttoned his shirt and walked toward the prim and shawl-draped Eve.

"Well, Miss Quinn, does the place pass your inspection?"

The bottom-of-the-whiskey-barrel voice seemed to reverberate inside her. Serena turned slowly, and once again was surprised that she had to look up to encounter his gaze.

"I was just wondering where you intend to plant your orchard, Mr. Sugarman." She fully expected him to flinch, then fumble with a vague reply since she was sure he hadn't given a moment's thought to apples and cherries, but only to dollars and cents.

But he didn't so much as blink, and his reply was immediate and assured as he raised a hand to point to the rolling green ridge behind the cabin. "Right up there. There's a line of white pines that make a perfect windbreak and the ground's high enough so the river won't be much of a threat."

It was Serena who blinked. He meant it! There was purpose in his tone, along with an intense amber light in his eyes. With a single gesture of his big hand, he caressed the landscape, moving over each dip and rill with a lover's tenderness and care. Rafe Sugarman was in love with the land. Or, she thought, he was a consummate actor who had his answers ready before she had even formed the questions.

"How long will it take to bring in a worthwhile crop?" she inquired now, knowing the answer was years. Trees, after all, didn't grow like corn or cotton.

He scraped his fingertips along his jawline now, and Serena noticed all of a sudden that he'd shaved since she'd last seen him. Without whiskers his jaw appeared even stronger. There was a tiny cut close to his ear. She wondered if he had cursed when the blade nicked him. She wondered if it had hurt him, and found herself hoping it hadn't. Then she realized he had answered her question and she hadn't even heard his reply because she had become so intrigued by his chin.

Her lashes flitted up to his whiskey-warm eyes where amusement glinted now.

"I plan to put my roots down, too, Miss Serena, if that's what you're really asking."

"I wasn't..." she stammered.

"Yes, you were. You're wondering just what kind of an investment you can risk. Financial or otherwise." One dark eyebrow arced as a grin played at one edge of his mouth. "And you're not a lady who's partial to risks."

"On the contrary, Mr. Sugarman," she snapped. "I come from a long line of gamblers and risk takers. My grandfather put roots down here when the nearest neighbor was a Choctaw Indian. And after the Indians were gone and the land opened up, my father sank every penny he had into acreage, and he held on to it when everybody else was going broke."

Rafe laughed. "By hook or by crook, I'd imagine."

She sniffed. "What difference does it make? He held on."

"And what about you, Miss Serena?"

"Pardon me?"

"Other than going without your shawl once in a while, what have you risked? What've you held on to except for that flimsy piece of yard goods?"

Her eyes were hot and her hand clenched into a fist, which she shook beneath his nose. "Don't you dare talk to me about risk, Mr. Sugarman, when you don't have any notion who I am or what I am." She paused to take in a gulp of air, then let it out furiously. "How dare you say a word about holding on when it's obvious you've never held on to a thing in your life?"

Now his eyes lost their amused glint and his mouth hardened. "Well, I've tried, Miss Serena," he drawled. "And I'm still trying, if that means anything to you. You've got me pegged for a drifter who scratches the dirt awhile then disappears. You look at me and think you see a man who wants fast cash and nothing more." He crossed his arms now and widened his stance. "Maybe if you looked harder you'd see a man more like your daddy than you'd ever dream."

Serena tightened her eyes in an exaggerated squint now, as if indeed attempting to look harder. "You mean I'd see a hardheaded conniver? A man who'd deal with the devil himself and then leave poor old Lucifer scratching his head and wondering how in blazes he'd lost all but his red underwear in the bargain?"

"Maybe," Rafe replied. "If that's what it takes to get what I want."

She raised her chin into his face now. "And just what is it you want, Mr. Sugarman?"

"Do you want to hear the truth or just some polite and pleasant answer?"

He was smiling at her now, she thought, the way a snake charmer must smile at a snake. A beguiling expression not unlike the one her father wore just before he sealed a bargain. "The truth," she said. Then she lifted her chin a notch to add, "If you're capable of it."

"All right, then." His smile increased as he relaxed his stance, shifted his hips, then hooked both thumbs under the buckle of his belt. "I want what your daddy's got," he replied with cool certainty. "And that, Miss Serena, might even include you."

Serena was two miles down the road before she drew back on the reins and brought the buggy to a halt. She had made a perfect spectacle of herself, she knew, and the palm of her right hand still stung from its hard, quick contact with Rafe Sugarman's face. Her pride stung, too, for she had the distinct feeling that he had allowed her to strike him when he could have prevented the blow with a mere flick of his wrist. Afterward, he'd simply stood there, stone-cold still, not even rubbing the place where she'd hit him. She had, however, succeeded in removing the predatory grin from his face just before she'd picked up her skirts and stomped toward the buggy.

The nerve of the man! The reins shook in her hands and the horse started forward only to be yanked back in the traces again. The sheer, unmitigated gall! Well, he was right about one thing. He *was* more like her father than she'd ever dreamed. Only *dream* wasn't the word she would have chosen. Nightmare was more like it. It was bad enough that her father regarded her as an object to satisfy his personal dreams of posterity. Now, it seemed, the fly-by-night, Mr. Rafe Sugarman, deemed her nothing more than a rung on the ladder of his own overblown ambitions.

And just when she'd been swayed by the apparent seriousness of his intentions. When she'd been impressed—no, intensely moved—by his love of the land.

Worse, when she'd stood there in his enormous shadow, her heart picking up speed as she pondered his jawline and actually feeling sorry because he'd cut himself shaving. She had nearly reached up to touch the tiny wound, believing she could soothe it, wanting to try. She couldn't remember ever having felt such a simple, yet overpowering desire to touch, to heal.

"Too bad he didn't slit his throat," Serena snarled now, thumping back against the leather-tufted seat and gnawing on a cuticle. And as for his love of the land, let him love it all he wanted. It still wasn't his. It was Quinn land, and it always would be.

No, not always, she thought. It wouldn't be Quinn land unless there were Quinns to claim it after she was gone. A next generation to stave off ambitious predators like Rafe Sugarman, wolves who prowled the county, biting off an acre here and a parcel there until there wasn't a square inch left.

She closed her eyes and clenched her teeth until the pain spiked through her jaw. It was the Yankees' fault—all of it. If the Quinns had no future, it was because the Yankees had obliterated half that future when they killed Con, Jr., at Shiloh. Then they'd tainted what hope was left for a Quinn dynasty when they'd attacked her that night in the barn.

She'd been bright as a butterfly then, just opening her wings, anticipating life, eager for love and all its manifestations. After the Yankees, her anticipation had withered to caution and her eagerness had turned to dread. The butterfly had closed up as surely as if it had returned to its cocoon. She had become The Shawl Lady, a spinsterish figure if ever there was one.

Serena sat forward, stiffening her spine. She had no choice but to marry in order for the Quinns to survive. Her father—damn him—was right. But she'd marry on her own terms and in her own sweet time. She wasn't going to pair up with the first man her father dragged into the house by the scruff of the neck. Maybe it would be the third man. Maybe the thirtieth man. Or the three hundredth man. She didn't know.

But she did know one thing, she thought as she snapped the reins and the buggy jolted forward. Whatever man it was, it wasn't going to be The Sugarman. By God, she'd take a Yankee first.

## Chapter Six

The big house was warmed by the flames of myriad candles. Uncle Peter had shoved the settees and armchairs back to the walls, and Aunt Pete—with her rugged mop and waxed cloths—had worked the floors to a high gloss. There were flowers everywhere, in vases, in cut glass bowls, in plain crockery covered with silk. Unable to import enough fresh flowers from Memphis, Con Quinn had sent Uncle Peter and Little Joab out to dig up young redbuds, which stood now in linen-covered buckets, arching their delicate purple limbs from every corner, only occasionally catching on a gentleman's sleeve or snagging a lady's hair. There was music—three fiddles and a fife. There was champagne and whiskey punch. The dining room table nearly sagged under the weight of smoked hams and fresh turkeys and tray after tray of oysters.

It was, Serena thought as she gazed down from the ribbon-festooned staircase, excessive. But then, her father never did anything halfway. If two were good, he seemed to believe, then three were better. But a dozen! Now that made a statement. She was glad he had had only a mere two weeks to plan this gaudy affair. Heaven only knew what another two weeks might have wrought. Peacock feathers and pink bunting, she supposed as she continued down the stairs where Con Quinn, master of the broad stroke, awaited her, glowering.

"The party's down here, Sister." He flicked his dark eyes up the curve of the stairs toward her bedroom. "Ain't nothing going on up there . . . yet."

For the sake of the festivities, she ignored his rather crude, suggestive remark, but her smile was brittle when she replied, "I didn't think you'd mind if I powdered my shiny nose, Daddy. After all, I am on display here."

"Indeed you are." He stepped back, taking her in from the auburn curls piled atop her head to the satin roses that dotted the hem of her skirt. As his gaze swept back toward her face, his dark eyes paused on the folds of her shawl. "Why are you always hiding yourself, Serena?" he groused. "God gave you a fine, sturdy body. God, with a little help from your mama and me. Why, a person would think you were ashamed of that."

"I'm chilly, Daddy." Her remark was curt to the point of rudeness, but it seemed to mollify him nevertheless, and he grasped her elbow and propelled her toward the dancing couples in the living room.

"Dance, Sister," he commanded. "That'll heat your blood."

Rafe sat with one hip on the Quinns' veranda rail, one leg cocked and the other extended to support his weight. He held a cut glass tumbler of whiskey punch in his hand. Hester Inch, who was dressed in a starched apron over a prim black dress, had sneaked it to him. He sipped the sticky-sweet mixture now, wishing the woman had just slipped him a bottle instead.

"Mr. Con sure knows how to put on a shindig, don't he, Sugarman?" Little Joab's big eyes were shining. The boy had spent a furious hour tending buggies and horses when the guests arrived, but he was resting now, leaning his whip-thin body against the railing, trying hard to imitate Rafe's pose. "Just look at all that...that splendor."

"Splendor, huh?" Rafe chuckled as he gave the boy's head an affectionate rub with his knuckles. "You like that, do you, Little Joab?"

The boy sighed. "I sure do."

Rafe sighed now, remembering twenty years ago how he'd stood just like Little Joab, a poor kid looking in lighted windows, getting a taste and a glimmer of the way rich folks carried on, learning—for better or worse—to want.

Thinking back, though, it hadn't been the fancy clothes or the light-catching jewels or the tables laden with silver that had impressed him. It had been The Man, Dr. Daniel Merriweather, who had stood in the center of all that splendor, unmoving, like the sun in the center of the swirling planets. The men competed for his ear; the women vied for his eye. And Daniel

Merriweather just shone there, taking it in as naturally as breath, absorbing it the way the earth takes in the rain, as if it were the natural scheme of things. His rightful place. His due.

It had been a heady vision for the son of the town drunk, a man who garnered laughter and jeers rather than respect, a man whose rightful place was crumpled in a doorway or passed out in somebody's privy. When Scruff Sugarman died—his neck snapped from a loose-limbed tumble down the tavern stairs—his wife and children stood dry-eyed witness as the Baptist preacher said a few quick words before they lowered the pine box into the earth.

On the other hand, when Daniel Merriweather died, the whole county came and shed tears enough to float an ark. But that was after Rafe had come back from the war, and he hadn't been welcome in the church or at the graveyard. It didn't matter, he thought now. He had no longer had any respect to pay to the dearly departed Dr. Merriweather.

He lifted the tumbler to his lips, then cursed before taking a healthy swallow. Twenty years and he was still standing on the outside looking in. Not that this was exactly where he wanted to be tonight, but he'd needed cash and the Widow Fairfax had needed somebody to hitch up her wagon and drive her to the Quinns'. It had seemed a good idea at the time, but now Rafe was questioning his judgment.

He'd been questioning his judgment for the past two weeks, ever since Serena Quinn had cracked the flat of her hand across his cheek. He'd figured he had two choices—either seek her out and apologize for his blunt remark, or avoid her like the plague. By choosing the latter, he'd been forced to buy his supplies over in Slidell, where a stranger had as much chance of buying on credit as a pig had of sprouting wings. He didn't want to use the money Con Quinn had advanced him, so he'd done odd jobs around town, hoping like hell Serena didn't happen along when he was weeding Mrs. Fairfax's vegetable patch or mucking out old Hiram Wells's stable. Her contempt for his brashness was one thing. He could handle that. It even gave him a perverse kind of satisfaction. But he didn't think he could handle her disdain—touched with disappointment, perhaps?—if she saw him doing boys' work at ten cents an hour.

Pride, he thought. Damn stubborn pride. It was what had brought him back to Mississippi. It was what kept him here, what kept him from changing his name when that seemed the wisest and most logical thing to do. And it was pride perhaps that spurred him to plant a long-term fruit crop rather than a quick season's growth.

He and his damn pride had made the trip to Memphis in a borrowed wagon and brought back peach and cherry trees, two dozen each. When he'd returned yesterday his disposition had been as mulish as the pair of jennies pulling his wagon. He'd saved back just enough cash with the intention of spending it in a fancy house, putting out the fires that Serena had ignited in him. But when the time came to actually pay his money and make his choice, Rafe had turned on his heel and walked out, then wandered up and down Beale Street for hours, cursing himself and Serena both.

"That Shawl Lady sure is all got up tonight, ain't she, Sugarman?" Little Joab's voice broke into Rafe's thoughts as if the boy had been reading his mind.

"Yeah," he replied, gazing through the window instead of looking down at the boy, who sighed loudly now.

"Miz Serena puts me in mind of a birthday cake all slathered with white frosting and then pink roses stuck on around the bottom."

Rafe laughed. Leave it to a ten-year-old to describe a woman in terms of food. To Rafe she looked like what she was—a beautiful woman in an alluring white dress. Hell! On second thought, she did look good enough to eat. But she wouldn't taste like birthday cake. Her smooth skin would have a slight tang of salt. The depths of her mouth would taste like honey.

His groin tightened at the thought, and he shifted on the veranda rail before downing the last of the whiskey punch in an attempt to replace the imaginary taste of Miss Serena Quinn with the very real taste of liquor.

The chime of the clock was barely audible, but through the din of conversation and laughter, over the strains of three fiddles and a fife, Serena counted eleven strikes as she sat in a corner, attempting invisibility behind several large sprays of redbud. The back of her dress was damp from clammy hands. Her toes hurt from being stepped on. Her face ached from smiling.

She had probably danced with every eligible man in Quinn County, not to mention several adjacent counties. She had even danced with the man who had carted the flowers down from Memphis and then had been invited to stay over for the festivities. She had, she thought, put on her best dress, not to mention her best face, for this party, and had put forth her best efforts in conversation and choreography, suffering bad jokes along with trampled feet. Now she was just plain tired, and all she wanted to do was escape her father's eagle eye for a while.

From the sidelines now, Serena watched while other couples danced. Without exception, the women were much shorter than their partners. Her gaze came to rest on her sister-in-law, dancing in the arms of Arlen Sears. Esme looked so tiny, breakable as spun glass. The constable smiled down on her protectively, and for a moment Serena envied that and heartily wished she could inspire the same chivalrous behavior. It seemed to confer a kind of power on the tiny blonde, a power Serena had never noticed before and certainly had never experienced herself.

Then, as she watched, that possessiveness took on darker overtones as Arlen Sears moved the hand he had planted on Esme's tiny waist. It curved around her delicate rib cage then, the thumb nudging up just beneath Esme's breast. The little blonde's eyes widened in shock and her curls shook vehemently as her mouth flattened in disapproval. Serena would have expected a red-faced, apologetic Sears to remove his hand immediately. His face grew red, all right, but it seemed to come from anger rather than embarrassment. He did remove his hand, Serena noticed, but only after he had given little Esme a punishing pinch.

It was all Serena could do to remain in her quiet corner. She wanted to jerk her sister-in-law out of the lawman's grasp and then give him the tongue-lashing of his life. But just as Serena was about to stride out on the dance floor, Esme's expression resumed its gaiety and Sears was once more looking down at her with adoration, as if she were fragile as a snowflake in his arms. They exchanged such warm glances then that it made Serena question her own eyes, or at the very least her perceptions. Perhaps what she had viewed as a subtle but nevertheless brutal show of power had not even taken place. Or maybe the incident was something else entirely.

Perhaps, she thought, she had quaffed just a bit too much champagne and breathed in too much smoky air to see things clearly. Most definitely, she decided, she could use a breath of fresh air. Con Quinn was deep in conversation now with his back to her, so she rose quickly from her corner chair and stole out the front door.

Out on the veranda, she took in a deep, cleansing draft of the crisp evening air. It was laced with dogwood and hyacinth, cool and heady as a glass of champagne. She let her breath out with an audible sigh.

"Tired of dancing, Miss Serena?"

Her head snapped left at the sound of the deep voice. Without thinking, she hugged her shawl a little closer as she spoke. "I guess I was," she confessed. "I'm not particularly fond of dancing."

Rafe was quiet a moment as his lazy gaze took her in from head to hem. "Doesn't surprise me," he drawled.

"Why is that, Mr. Sugarman?" Her eyes blazed in the glow of the carriage lamps that flanked the front door. She hadn't laid eyes on this man in nearly two weeks, and the first thing he did was insult her. "Do you think only dainty, graceful creatures enjoy being twirled on the dance floor?"

His mouth curved in amusement as he angled his hip off the rail. "No, ma'am."

"Well, what, then?" she snapped.

He walked toward her now. "I've been hanging around out here with nothing to do but look in the window. I was watching you, Miss Serena. You might even say I was studying you."

"Really. And how did you arrive at the conclusion that I don't care to dance? If you were studying me, you surely saw that I spent a good two hours doing precisely that."

"What I concluded was there isn't a man in that room who knows how to hold you."

Serena had been staring out into the yard, but now her eyes returned to his face. He was right! One of the reasons she had retreated from the dance floor was that she had felt her partners were pushing her around like a broom rather than leading her through schottisches and waltzes. She had done her best to compensate for the awkwardness, though, and now the knowledge that Rafe Sugarman had not just noticed it, but had studied it, was mortifying.

Still, she wasn't going to give him the satisfaction of agreeing with him. She sniffed indignantly. "What makes you such a terpsichorean expert?"

He came two steps closer now. Close enough for the tips of his boots to disappear beneath the hem of her skirt. "I didn't claim to be an expert, Miss Serena. Not at dancing, anyway. But I guarantee you I could hold you better than any of those gentlemen inside. Here." He had her shawl off her before Serena could even blink. Then one big arm circled her waist while his hand clasped hers.

"What do you think you're doing?"

"Proving my point." Rafe drew her closer.

With her free hand Serena pushed against his chest only to encounter—as she had that day in the rain—a solid and unyielding wall. "This is ridiculous," she snapped when her efforts proved useless.

Not ridiculous, Rafe thought. Foolish if not downright suicidal. But the sight of Serena Quinn in other men's arms all evening long had taken a hard toll on his body. Then, when she was so close, his good sense had deserted him. He simply had to have her in his arms. No woman had ever felt so good, so absolutely right.

He stared down at her bared shoulders, rigid now with resistance, and at the defiant set of her mouth. There had to be hundreds, even thousands, of willing females in the state of Mississippi. He'd encountered his share of them, too. But there wasn't a woman who had ever pulled him closer while she was pushing him away, who had beckoned him irresistibly and despite his better sense.

"Stop staring down my dress," she hissed now.

Rafe flexed his arm, drawing her closer so there was no room between them now. "Better?" he growled.

Heaven help her, it was better with her breasts crushed against him and his arm hard at her back. His warm breath was ruffling her hair now. His lips just touched her temple with a moist heat that shimmered through her and pooled deep within her.

"You feel so good, Serena," he murmured. "Just right."

"Yes," she whispered as a kind of lethargy swept through her. She wasn't sure she was standing on her own. It seemed as if her bones had turned to feathers, and Rafe Sugarman was supporting her effortlessly.

A small, insistent voice in the back of her head tried to tell her that yes wasn't what she meant at all. But yes was what she felt. And delicate. And divine. She tipped her head back and drank in his intense, lamplit gaze, feeling suddenly drunk with the kind of power she had witnessed earlier with Esme.

Her lips parted slightly. Rafe couldn't tell if it was in surprise or in an effort to take in more air. About all he knew that moment was that those lips were the most inviting he'd ever seen and he was aching to taste them. He did, dipping his head and laying claim to them, softly, so softly. Then he raised his head, gazing at her, entranced by the glistening his kiss had left on her mouth, the heaviness of her lids, the smoldering heat in her eyes.

He thought right then there was nothing else in the world he wanted to do so much as kiss her again, then lose himself so deeply within her he wouldn't know or care whether he was in Quinn County, Mississippi, or on the moon. It was the piercing intensity of that knowledge, like lightning slicing through his brain, that made him straighten up. The fact was he did care where he was and if he didn't watch every step, and regretfully, every kiss, he wouldn't be here long.

When she came to her senses, Rafe thought, she'd haul off and slap him the way she had before. He was hoping she would, hoping she would attack him directly rather than surreptitiously by putting notions in her father's head. But her eyes were still glazed and it didn't look as if a return to her senses was imminent. Rafe sighed, deciding he'd have to help her along a little, even if it did earn him another crack across his jaw.

"You're welcome to slap me now, Miss Serena," he said as he eased his arms from around her. He cocked his head playfully and gave her a grin to match. "I wonder if you'd mind doing it on the right side this time just so I can keep my face even."

It was chilly outside his arms. The feathery lightness she'd experienced evaporated, and her bones, once again, felt heavy as lead pipes. Her flesh felt cumbersome now. In a matter of seconds she'd gone from sleek Thoroughbred to plodding dray horse.

Rafe Sugarman had kissed her, then quit—obviously disappointed.

She reached for the shawl he'd flung over the railing, snapped it open, then tugged it around her shoulders and pulled it tight. "You're not worth the effort, Mr. Sugarman. Slap yourself if you're so inclined."

Serena turned her back on him and strode briskly into the house.

Con Quinn caught her by the arm as she came through the door. "Hold on there, Sister. You're rushing in like the whole outdoors is on fire."

It is, she thought. Or it had been before the flames had fizzled out in a disappointing kiss. Her face was burning with shame now, but she prayed her father would think it was merely the flush of excitement. Serena summoned up a smile. "Actually, it's cool outside, Daddy. I was out getting a breath of fresh air."

He raised an eyebrow. "Is that what you call it, Sister? I happened to be looking out the window and it appeared to me that you were getting yourself kissed."

She opened her mouth, ready to deny it, but no words would come.

Her father studied her face, then a slow smile worked across his lips. "Left you speechless, did it, Serena?"

Once again she tried to reply but was, indeed, speechless. It wasn't the kiss that had done it, she told herself. It was the fact that her father had witnessed it.

He cupped her elbow in his hand, drawing her closer. "I must be slipping in my old age," he said with a sigh. "The one man who sparks your interest is sitting on my front porch instead of waltzing in my parlor. I should have figured that. Damn."

"You're talking nonsense," she snapped, jerking out of his grasp.

"Is he the one you want, Sister?" He withdrew a cigar from his breast pocket and planted it between his teeth, eyeing Serena all the while.

She answered his insistent gaze with as much coolness as she could muster. "Daddy, the last time I saw that look in your eye was when you were bidding on a prize stallion."

Con Quinn struck a match now and touched it to the tip of his cigar. He squinted against the rising smoke. "Could be, Sister. Could be."

## Chapter Seven

At breakfast the next morning, Esme chattered and chirped like a brightly colored finch. Her appetite, however, more closely resembled a vulture's as she forked in her second helping of ham and eggs. Across the table, Serena sullenly rearranged her own first helping on her plate, hoping to avoid Aunt Pete's disapproval. She was hiding a substantial portion of her scrambled eggs under a slice of ham when her father's voice boomed in the doorway.

"Morning, daughters." He yanked out his chair and settled himself at the head of the table, looking more like a man taking charge of a meeting than sitting down to breakfast.

Esme swallowed, then smiled brightly. "Morning, Daddy Quinn. I thought you'd sleep in after such a late night."

"I tried, Sister Belle, but between the racket Aunt Pete was making and your most animated conversation down here in the dining room, I seem to have failed."

The little blonde blushed apologetically, then bit off a corner of a triangle of toast while her father-in-law shifted his gaze to Serena.

"I don't believe I've heard you say a word, Sister." He looked at her plate. "Lost your appetite as well as your tongue?"

Serena put down her fork and folded her napkin. If her father hounded her on the subject of marriage this morning, she thought, her temper was what she was going to lose. "Neither, Daddy. You look well rested after so little sleep."

Con sat back to allow Uncle Peter to place a plate heaped with ham and eggs before him. "As a matter of fact," he said, leaning forward once more and taking a deep breath of the steam rising from his breakfast, "I slept very little. I spent the night thinking about my daughters and their happiness." He paused auspiciously. "Or lack of it."

Serena braced her spine against the chair back and flattened her feet on the floor, then relaxed slightly when her father directed his next words to Esme.

"Arlen Sears." He pronounced the name, then forked in a good-sized portion of food, studying Esme's face as he chewed. "I believe that was the sole name on your dance card last night, Sister Belle."

"I believe you're right," Esme said brightly.

His eyes narrowed now. "One question. Does he treat you right? I mean, has he been conducting himself as a gentleman with you?"

Serena recalled the incident the night before when Esme had discouraged the constable's advancing hand. Now, as her sister-in-law effusively praised Sears's behavior, Serena also thought she saw a slight tremor in Esme's hands along with a kind of hectic brilliance in her eyes. Esme's afraid, she thought suddenly. No, that couldn't be right. More likely she was just nervous and overwrought after so little sleep. And she *was* defending the man with a vengeance.

Con appeared to believe her. "All right, Esme. No need to go on. I merely asked because I employed Constable Sears based on his reputation for…well…"

"Meanness?" Serena suggested, earning herself a withering glance from the head of the table.

"Physical efficiency in carrying out his duties," Con continued. "I'd be disappointed if that efficiency carried over into his personal relationships."

"Well, Arlen's been a perfect gentleman, Daddy Quinn, so you don't have any worries on that score," Esme said.

Liar, Serena thought, but the thought vanished as soon as her father turned his gaze on her and said, "Your turn, Sister." She squared her shoulders then.

"All right, Daddy. Have at me."

He snorted and ate a few more bites, presumably allowing Serena ample time to squirm.

"Rafe Sugarman," Con said then. "I trust that name rings one or two bells."

"Not wedding bells," Serena replied hotly. She shot up from her chair, then jammed it back beneath the table. "Now, if you'll excuse me, Daddy, I have work waiting for me at the store." She grabbed her cup and saucer and strode into the kitchen before her father could say another word.

Aunt Pete was sitting in her rocking chair in a corner of the kitchen, holding Little Joab on her lap. His arms were strung around her neck while his thin legs were nearly invisible in the deep, swishing folds of her skirt.

Serena set her cup and saucer on the table. "What's wrong, Aunt Pete?"

"This sweet child just needed his gran to hold him for a while," she crooned as she continued to rock and stroke the boy's head.

"It's my daddy, Miz Serena," Little Joab sobbed. "That lawman's trying to run him off again."

Hands on her hips now, Serena cursed through her teeth. "I've had just about enough from Mr. Arlen Sears. Is he out at your place now, Little Joab?"

The boy shook his head. "No, ma'am. Least, I don't think so. He's out beating the bushes for my daddy. Said he going to throw him in jail and toss the key away this time."

"Over my dead body," Serena snapped. "There's not going to be any throwing or tossing if I have any say-so. I'm going upstairs for my bonnet and gloves, Aunt Pete. Please tell Uncle Peter to have the buggy ready for me."

"You oughtn't to be messing in this, Miz Serena," Aunt Pete cautioned. She clasped Little Joab's head closer to her bosom then and covered one of his ears with her hand. "Hester went and bought herself a life of trouble when she married that no-'count runaway.

Now he's still running. Seems like that's all Big Joab
knows how to do.''

"When has he ever had a choice, Aunt Pete?"

Hester Inch paced back and forth in front of the
little cabin. Baby Flora was draped over her shoulder
like a ten-pound sack of flour, which Hester alter-
nately patted or smoothed.

"It's no good staying here, Miz Serena," she said,
turning on her heel and retracing her own footsteps.

"You leave and you'll break your mama's heart,"
Serena answered from her perch on the porch rail. "I
won't let that happen. Hester, will you stand still, for
pity's sake? You're wearing a rut in the yard, plus
you're making me dizzy."

The thin woman ignored her and continued pacing,
patting the baby in time with her steps, muttering to
herself now.

"You're not leaving Quinn County, and that's
that." Serena took off her gloves and slapped them
across the palm of one hand. "If anybody's leaving,
it's going to be Arlen Sears."

"Ha!" snorted Hester in midstride.

"I'll talk to Daddy again and—"

Hester came to a standstill now. "I hate to tell you
this, Miz Serena, but your daddy doesn't listen. 'Specially not to women. Most 'specially not to women.
You go telling him to fire Arlen Sears, and your daddy's going to clasp that lawman to his bosom like a
long-lost son." She snorted again, shifted Flora to her
other shoulder, and resumed her pacing.

She was probably right, Serena thought dejectedly. And she wasn't exactly in her father's good graces at the moment. Furthermore, to ask such a favor from him now would require that she do one in return, and it didn't take a genius to know what that favor would be. She could already hear him bargaining. *All right, Sister. It pains me, but I'll dismiss Mr. Sears.* He'd pause then to lift a weighty brow before continuing. *I'll give him his walking papers on your wedding day.*

Despite her love for Hester and her concern for the woman's happiness and welfare, Serena couldn't do that. Not yet, anyway. She chewed doggedly on a thumbnail, watching Hester trek from one end of the porch to the other.

"I suppose hiding out is the best course for Big Joab now," Serena said at last.

"That's what I told you," Hester grumbled.

Sighing, Serena slid off the porch rail. "What can I do to help?"

Hester had a simple and direct answer to Serena's question. "Mustard plaster." Then the woman went on to explain that Big Joab was coming down with the grippe and had been forced to flee the cabin before Hester could concoct a remedy.

"I daren't take it to him myself," she explained. "I know that lawman's watching. He said he'd be keeping an eye out. Him or one of his redneck deputies. But nobody would follow you, Miz Serena."

Hester gave her directions, and an hour later Serena was trudging through a thicket, carrying half a ham along with a mustard plaster. She found Big Joab just where Hester had said he would be—in a half-collapsed duck blind on a secluded stretch of river-bank.

Big Joab Inch was six feet of hard muscle. His skin was glossy and rich as coffee, and when he smiled it always reminded Serena of cream skimming the surface of a thick, rich brew. But now, when he saw her coming through the dense undergrowth, Big Joab wasn't smiling. He looked fit to be tied.

"Aw, Miz Serena, what you doin' out here?" he groaned. "It ain't safe."

"Safer for me than for Hester." Serena placed the ham in Big Joab's open hands, then plopped the mustard plaster on top. She gazed around, frowning. "You can't stay out here, Big Joab. You'll get eaten alive by mosquitoes."

"Got to," he said. Then he angled his head toward the western sky. "Anyway, a storm's coming in. That'll keep the skeeters down for a while."

Serena cast a worried glance up over the trees where the sky had turned a threatening green. The color seemed to darken as she watched, and she could feel her heart start hammering even though not a single drop of rain had fallen.

"I need to get back." There was a shakiness in her voice that she quickly tried to disguise by laughing. "Do you suppose that Morgan of mine can outrun a twister, Big Joab?"

The man was squatting down now, stashing the ham and the plaster under a bed of leaves in a corner of the duck blind. "You ain't scared of storms, is you?"

Again, she forced a laugh. "Me? No, I..." Her voice failed her then as the nearby trees began to rustle and the first raindrops splatted on the ground and on the crown of her bonnet.

Big Joab stood up. "I'll take you home, Miz Serena."

Relief swept through her, only to dissolve as she realized the danger lying in wait for Hester's husband. No matter how frightened she was, she couldn't permit him to take such a risk. She drew herself up and squared her shoulders. "You'll do no such thing, Mr. Inch." She held her hand out, palm up. "I'm not afraid of a few little raindrops. Anyway, it'll get the smell of that awful old mustard plaster off me."

Before he could give her an argument, Serena swung around and headed for the thicket. "You take care, Big Joab, you hear?" she called over her shoulder. Then the wind picked up and a long roll of thunder shook the ground, and if Big Joab answered, his voice was lost to the storm and the thunder of her own heartbeat as she began running toward the Morgan.

Rafe emerged from the woods, a cane fishing pole over one shoulder and one hand clapped to his head in an effort to keep his hat on in the rising wind. He recognized the shiny black buggy immediately. The Morgan, well trained as it was, was rearing back in the traces now. One good thunderclap and both the Morgan and the buggy would be gone, he thought.

He dropped the fishing pole on the ground and quickly stowed his hat under the seat before he grabbed a handful of bridle. "Whoa, fella," he said, smoothing his other hand over the horse's rain-damp shoulder while he searched the leather-tufted seat for any clue as to which Quinn had driven the horse and carriage out here in the middle of nowhere with a storm boiling up and just about to spill over. He sincerely doubted if Con Quinn would have had business out this way, and he was willing to bet little Miss Esme never went anywhere in inclement weather. Which left one other Quinn, the one who would probably shake her fist at thunder and dare a tornado to cross her path if she wanted to get somewhere.

"Damn," Rafe muttered as he led the nervous horse toward a good-sized mulberry bush and secured the reins. He should have known this wasn't going to be his day the minute he opened his eyes this morning and was greeted by the black-rimmed, insolent stare of the former tenant of his cabin. From the light streaming into the room, it was evident the raccoon had made short work of the newspaper rigged up over the window. When Rafe had tossed a boot, the critter hadn't even had the decency to run. It had lumbered to the window, lugged itself up on the sill, then calmly licked a paw before exiting, tearing what was left of the newspaper.

After that auspicious beginning to his day, he should have assumed the fish wouldn't be biting. But like a hopeful fool, he'd dug up worms anyway, then sat on the riverbank for a good two hours, swatting at mosquitoes and choking on gnats, which he'd finally concluded were all he was going to get for breakfast this day. Naturally, then, it had started raining.

Now he was standing tall as a lightning rod in a clearing with a panicky horse, and rather than showing a sane man's concern for his own hide, he was worrying about the soft alabaster skin of Miss Serena Quinn. And, despite his better judgment, he was about to go crashing through the brush to find her.

But he didn't have to. It was as if his luck had finally curved around some invisible bend when the woman in his thoughts came crashing out of the thicket—dress ripped, wet to the skin, red hair dripping like liquid fire, and scared as any human being he'd ever seen.

Something told him it wasn't just the storm that made her eyes round and white as dinner plates, that tightened her lush mouth thin as a wire, that finally drove her legs from under her when she emerged from the brush, then left her in a puddle of skirts on the ground.

Rafe was beside her in an instant. And an instant after that a blue bolt of lightning ripped down the trunk of a nearby oak while thunder shook the ground beneath them. He was stunned for a second, momentarily deaf, and for a heartbeat he was back in the mire and the gore of battle, gritting his teeth against the urge to moan and stiffening his legs against the need to run. He knelt there dazed until something hit him like a cannonball—a soft, wet, whimpering cannonball burrowing into his chest.

"Yankees," she moaned. "Don't let them. Oh, don't let them."

"Serry," he whispered as he gathered his legs beneath him and rose with her in his arms. "I won't let anything hurt you, Serry. I promise you that."

The flares of lightning quickened and closed in around them, familiar as muzzle flashes and cannon fire against a sky as dark as night, as he walked toward the buggy. It was as if the storm had swept him back in time to a nameless battlefield where two invisible armies clashed, and he swore for a moment he could hear men and horses screaming through the rolling din of the thunder and the fierce howling of the wind in the trees.

Serena's wet arms clung to his neck and her face pressed into his shoulder. "Yankees," she kept moaning as if she, too, had been swept into the raging battle.

Holding tight to his precious burden, Rafe stood still a moment. He raised his face to the fierce heavens, letting the rain slash at him and the wind tear at his skin while Serena's mournful cries filled his ears and weighted his heart.

Overhead, hot blue filaments twisted across the sky. Rafe cursed them. "If you wanted the Mississippi Yank so bad," he roared, "you should have taken me sooner. It's too late now. It's too damn late."

# Chapter Eight

Serena huddled on the cot, exactly where Rafe had put her down after he'd carried her into the cabin. Outside, the storm was still raging. Rain had soaked the window papers, and it slanted through the one uncovered window, pooling on the rough planks of the floor. With every crash of thunder, the glass chimneys chattered and trembled on their lamps. Serena, too, was trembling as she watched Rafe Sugarman. Watched him the way a cold, wet, frightened dog kept an eye on the human being who had brought him inside. For the moment, the huge man was her lifeline, her sole security, and she was afraid to look away for fear he would disappear. On the other hand, looking at him wasn't doing much to quiet her nerves.

He was hunkered down in front of the fireplace now, coaxing a blaze. Every once in a while rain dripped from his dark curls and sizzled when it struck the grate. When the logs caught, he turned on his haunches, his massive forearms resting on his knees, his head tilted quizzically in Serena's direction.

Just then the wind gusted and rain shot farther into the room from the unprotected window. Thunder boomed again, and Serena scuttled deeper into a corner of the cot, closing her eyes tight and clutching her wet shawl. She heard him mutter an oath, and then the floorboards shuddered beneath his tread as he moved around the cabin. Finally, the cot creaked as he sat beside her.

"Here. You'll catch your death if you stay in those wet clothes."

She started, from the abruptness of his tone and then again when something plopped into her lap. Opening her eyes a fraction, she could see a neatly folded chambray shirt atop a pair of denim pants. His. "I can't..."

He stood, and in one fell swoop Serena found herself standing, too, or more exactly wobbling while his hands gripped her upper arms. When her footing was relatively secure, he let go to pick up the clothes that had slid to the floor. He tossed them onto the cot.

When he turned and started for the door, Serena reached out and grabbed Rafe's wet sleeve. She let go quickly, afraid he would stay, terrified he would go. "P-please..." she stammered.

His voice was soft now, and he stepped closer, lifting a hand to cradle her chin. "I'm not leaving, Miss Serena. I'm just going to tend to your horse and buggy, and to batten down what I can against what's left of this storm." His fingertip traced the curve of her cheek. "You get out of those soggy skirts now, you hear? I'll knock good and loud before I come back in."

She nodded and then drew in a wavering breath. "I . . . this isn't like me. Not in the least. I'm not some skittish little girl, Mr. Sugarman. Believe me." Her face grew hot with embarrassment. Serena turned away, only to be coaxed back by a firm hand.

His eyes reflected the amber light of the fire. They were just as warm as they homed in on hers. "It's all right, you know," he whispered.

Her teeth dragged over her lower lip before she responded. "What?"

"To let go, Shawl Lady. To take somebody's hand." He did just that, bringing it to his lips. "To let somebody take yours."

Her hand, nested in his, looked no bigger than a doll's. It was pale and delicate as porcelain. Her fingers warmed to his lingering kiss, and her heart surged with pleasure and with a sweet sensation which she couldn't really describe but could only define as peace. Utter peace. The thunder was still rattling the lamps and reverberating off the hills, but now it didn't seem a threat so much as an excuse to remain here. With him. With her hand lost in his and her heart taking up the rhythm of the thunder and her blood running fast and hot as lightning.

He squeezed her hand before he let it go. Then he was striding out the door, dipping his head and angling his shoulders to clear the frame. When he pulled the door closed behind him, Serena just stood there,

as swamped on the inside now as she was on the outside.

Let go? She didn't know how to begin.


Rafe practically ripped the Morgan from the har-
ness, then dragged the nervous beast to the lean-to
beside the cabin, where he tethered him tightly. He
squinted through the rain then, trying to survey the
damage. A hickory limb had come down on the water
trough and the chicken coop had lost a board or two,
but since he didn't have any chickens it didn't matter
all that much.

As near as he could tell when he glanced up the hill
behind the cabin, his orchard was still vertical. Young,
supple trees could withstand a storm far better than
their older, more brittle counterparts. Young men, too,
he thought glumly. Suddenly he was feeling old—battered and bruised by the elements, which had never
before done much more than inconvenience him.

It wasn't the storm, he thought as he crossed the
muddy yard to the porch. And it wasn't the bloodred
mist of the war that the storm had stirred up in his
brain. It was Serena Quinn. The woman was worse
than weather the way she blew hot and cold, the way
she shone like noontime, then chilled and darkened
like the sun slipping down behind a distant hill. Far
worse than weather. She was beginning to pervade his
every breath, to slip like a drowsy fog into his dreams.

Now she had him standing out in a driving rain, like
as not to get fried by a bolt of lightning. Rafe shook

his head. No. Chances were slim that he'd get struck twice, and she'd already sliced him pretty good.

He sat on the porch steps, arms draped over his knees, staring out at the gray curtain of rain, allowing her more than enough time to get out of her wet clothes. Water leaked through the rotten boards over his head, but Rafe was oblivious to it as images of cool, wet cotton gliding over delicate ribs filled his thoughts. Damp curls clinging to the curve of her neck. Silk sliding down long, endless legs.

He shook his head hard enough for water to spray from his sopping hair, trying to clear his head, damning weather of every sort, cursing every element over which he had no control. And it seemed to Rafe right then that he'd abandoned control since the day he'd crossed into Quinn County.

Hell, it had been raining then, too, when he'd picked her up so she didn't blind him with her confounded umbrella. Then she'd gone and blinded him anyway with the flames that burned beneath her cool surface. At the very least she'd put blinkers on him so he couldn't see anything but her.

Well, it was time to tear those blinkers off, to concentrate on the forest instead of a single beguiling tree—the pretty live oak with its constant shawl of Spanish moss. He had to be more careful, Rafe told himself. His damn heart was getting in the way of his head, and if he didn't watch out he'd lose not only his heart and his head but the last frail vestiges of his hopes and dreams. There was also the distinct and highly distasteful possibility that he'd lose his life.

* * *

Serena perched on the edge of the cot, having just rolled up the second long denim pant leg, craving a pier glass. For a woman who could pass a mirror without a second glance—let alone a first—it was a novel and rather unsettling desire. Just what she wanted to see, she wasn't sure. But she felt different somehow and needed a reflection to confirm it.

Her wet clothes were draped over two chairs a safe distance from the fire. She had discarded them with more relish than she'd ever dreamed—unbuttoning, untying and tugging while keeping one eye on the cabin door and the other eye on the neatly folded pile of clothes. She couldn't wait to have them next to her skin. When she'd gotten as far as her chemise and cotton drawers, Serena stood motionless for a moment in the center of the room. The many layers of shawl and dress and petticoats had succeeded in keeping her underclothes dry. There was no need to take them off. No need except her own surprising desire to feel the soft blue chambray on her breasts and the rough denim rubbing on her thighs.

She stood on one bare foot and then the other, chewed her lower lip then traded that for a thumbnail, before she quickly, almost furtively, whisked off the white cotton garments and slid into Rafe Sugarman's clothes.

The shirt smelled like pure sunshine. It made her want to laugh for joy and sheer silliness the way the shoulders sloped off her own and the sleeves billowed and cascaded over her hands. The pants were a differ-

ent story. Except for the fact that the legs were a mile
too long, her hips filled out the fabric so it was almost snug. She was accustomed to the tight restraint
of corsets, but this was a totally new experience. Like
being caressed rather than squeezed. She wiggled her
bottom. Little wonder, she thought, most men walked
with a swagger. It wasn't attitude at all. It was just
their pants! She strutted toward the cot just to prove
to herself how good it felt, then she sat and rolled up
the pant legs, feeling silly and carefree for the first
time in years.

She was perched there for some time, wishing for a
mirror, before Serena noticed her underclothes right
where she had dropped them in the center of the room.
"Well, that won't do at all," she said as she rose and
swaggered toward them. She was bending over to pick
them up when a brisk knock sounded on the door.

The doorknob froze to his hand as Rafe stood on
the threshold staring at snug denim and the flare of a
pair of hips he'd never quite been able to conjure up
in his imagination. Now that same imagination was
running rampant and his heart felt like a bomb at the
center of a hundred sizzling fuses. He swallowed hard
as if that could put out the fires.

Serena whirled around then to face him. Holy hellfire. His big shirt didn't quite whirl with her, expos-
ing one perfect curve of breast before she tugged the
errant shirtfront around her. Her eyes were huge as a
startled doe's and her mouth was open, a perfect, mute
O.

His gaze shifted to the fluttering fabric in her hands, and when he realized the nature of the frills and ruffles, he felt a cold sweat glaze his skin and begin to trickle down his sides. Rafe knew right then he had to defend what little control he had left. Like most men, in order to defend himself, he attacked.

"That was a fool thing to do, going out into the woods all by yourself with a storm brewing up. What the hell were you doing, anyway, other than making trouble for me?"

Her eyes narrowed and her vulnerable mouth thinned to a steely line. "I don't have to answer to you for my whereabouts," she snapped. "And, believe it or not, Mr. Sugarman, I didn't ask for your help."

"Yes, you did," he growled, stalking past her and taking up a wide-legged stance in front of the fire. He held his hands out to the flames, but when he saw how badly they were shaking Rafe quickly shoved them into his pockets. He wanted to sit but her clothes were flung over every available chair. It was his cabin, he thought. A man ought to be able to sit down in his own damn place. Especially when his knees felt like jelly.

"You're right," she said. "I did."

Rafe nearly jumped into the fire at the sound of her voice so close behind him. He leaned his head on the rough planking that served as a mantel while she continued.

"Not in actual words, however, but I'm sure my distress must have called out to you as it would to any gentleman."

The little twist she put on the word *gentleman* clearly implied she didn't consider him to be in that category.

"You're welcome," he growled.

"I beg your pardon?"

"I said you're welcome."

"I wasn't exactly thanking you, Mr. Sugarman."

He lifted his head from the mantel, sighed and turned toward her. How much worse could looking at her be when his imagination already had her peeled down to sweet skin and nothing else? At least now, he noticed with some relief, she had his shirt buttoned up and was no longer waving her underclothes at him. They had in fact disappeared, but not knowing where they were wasn't the problem. It was knowing where they *weren't*.

Rafe sighed again. "You don't have to thank me. I just happened along, Miss Serena. Guess we just kind of blew into each other like two ships in a storm."

"I guess we did," she agreed, somewhat mollified now after his sudden and wholly unexpected attack. Serena knew very well if Rafe hadn't rescued her, she'd probably be half-dead by now or else completely dead, skewered to the ground by a bolt of lightning. But she'd be damned if she was going to thank such an irritating, ill-mannered man. She couldn't for the life of her figure out what she'd done to set him on her like a crazed hound.

A crazed, very wet hound, she observed now. His wet shirt was molded to the curves of his chest. His dark eyelashes were tipped with beads of rain. He made a kind of squishing sound each time he moved.

"You're dripping all over the floor," she observed.

He looked for a moment as if he were going to explode in another irascible fit, but then his mouth slanted into a rather sheepish grin. "Yes, ma'am."

"Perhaps you should get into some dry clothes, Mr. Sugarman."

"Well, I would," he drawled, "but I don't believe we'd both fit."

Serena blinked. "These are your only spare clothes?"

Her hands fluttered up to the top buttons of the shirt as if impelled to start undoing them right then. Rafe stifled a groan as he reached to stop her.

"It's all right," he assured her. "I'm just going to plant myself in front of the fire. That'll dry me off right quick. But first I'm going to warm up my insides with some brandy. Care for a taste, Miss Serena?" He walked toward the pine cupboard on the far side of the fireplace. "Might help take your mind off the thunder," he added as he opened the cupboard door.

As if on cue, a loud thunderclap rattled through the cabin. Amazed, Serena realized she'd completely forgotten the storm that had brought her here in the first place. She seemed to have forgotten everything except the man who was now pouring brandy into two tin cups. The man who stood soaking wet while his dry clothes were currently caressing every inch of her skin.

He put a cup in her hand, then proceeded to the fireplace where he folded his long legs beneath him and lowered himself to the hearth. He lifted his cup toward her. "Down the hatch, Shawl Lady."

Serena took a sip. The brandy traveled down her throat like liquid flame. A shiver worked up her spine. It was definitely the brandy, she knew, but the way the flames were glossing Rafe Sugarman's dark hair and the way his head was tilted just so and the way he was looking at her right now...

"Good gracious," she said, forcing a laugh. "I'd nearly forgotten about the storm." In fact, she thought, she had become totally oblivious to her surroundings ever since he'd walked back into the cabin. She let her gaze travel around the room now, as much to observe as to seek out a distraction. The cupboard door was open, so Serena went to close it.

Rafe's leather suitcase lay sideways on the top shelf. She studied it a moment, then said, "Perhaps there are some more dry clothes in your grip. Shall I look?" Her hand was already on the handle when his voice boomed like thunder.

"Don't. Leave it alone."

"But I—"

He was on his feet in a second, and a second after that he was slamming the cupboard closed after jerking back Serena's hand. She uttered a tiny squeak of surprise as she stepped away from him.

Rafe swore and ripped his fingers through his damp hair. "I'm sorry." He reached for her hand. "It's just that... I didn't mean to..."

Serena wrenched free of his grasp, turned on her heel and stomped to the cot. "I was only trying to help," she snapped as she plopped down. She shot him a scalding look, then stared out the window, ignoring him.

"I'm sorry." he managed to say as he settled in front of the fire with his back to her now.

If there was anything Serena Quinn hated, it was a quick apology. Once her dander was up, it stayed up. Now was no exception. "You needn't have manhandled me," she growled at the broad expanse of his back. Then she snagged her lower lip between her teeth and watched as that back grew even more gigantic as he took in several deep breaths.

"Are you working yourself up to a slap again, Shawl Lady?" he asked almost wearily. "'Cause if you are, you'll have to come over here. I'm just about too waterlogged to move." Then he sneezed.

"Bless you," Serena said automatically, then wished she hadn't. She did want to slap him, and it galled her that he seemed to be able to read her thoughts when she hadn't a clue what was going on inside his head. Other than sneezes.

He did it again, and this time she remained silent.... Well, for as long as she could, considering the turmoil inside her.

"That's what you get for sitting around in wet clothes," she told him.

He took a slow sip of his brandy, then mumbled into the depths of the cup, "Next time it storms, I'll keep that in mind." That, and manage to be miles away

from wherever you are, lady, he thought, taking another swallow of liquor, wishing he felt its effects
rather than her effects. He twisted around to look out
the window. "Rain's letting up a little."

She murmured noncommittally.

A silence welled up between them, broken only by
the slow and deep cadence of the thunder and an occasional crack of a log on the grate. Rafe continued to
stare into the flames, berating himself for the way he'd
flown off the handle when she went for his suitcase.
Hell, she'd just been trying to help and he'd hurt her
feelings—if not her hand. The way he saw it at the
moment, it wouldn't make a whole hell of a lot of
difference whether she hated him now or later.

Not that she was overly fond of him at the moment. Still, if she weren't interested, he doubted she'd
be coiled over there on the cot like a rattlesnake about
to strike at his back.

"Just what is it you want, Mr. Sugarman?" It
wasn't the casual tone of a shopkeeper inquiring about
a purchase. Her voice was low and serious, tightly
woven with suspicion. Her question caught him off
guard, and caused him to shake his head in dismay
because right that minute there was nothing more in
the world he wanted than to uncoil her, to touch her
and to coax a yielding warmth from the cool contain-
ment of her body.

"I suppose you're asking about my long-term plans
and expectations," he replied.

"Assuming you have any."

Rafe shifted slightly, resting his chin on his shoulder, inspecting her with a single eye. He'd been wrong to envision her as a rattlesnake. Right now, in spite of her stern expression, she looked about as dangerous as a toddler who'd just been yanked out of a creek, rubbed shiny and dry, and then wrapped up in big clothes.

He could tell her now—the truth, all of it—and then watch her bright, curious eyes go cold with disdain, the way they would have if he'd let her go ahead and open his suitcase. Bright blue eyes melting then, chilling to ice the way his mother's had.

*What's that?*

*It's my uniform, Ma.*

*Traitor!* She'd slapped him so hard it had brought tears to his eyes.

No, Rafe thought now. The tears had already been there. His mother's stinging blow had simply loosened them.

"Well?" Serena asked him now.

He dragged in a deep breath. One truth was as good as another, he thought. "I want you, Serena," he said, then watched her blue eyes widen and her stern expression falter and slacken with surprise.

"Not that I'm going to do anything about it, mind you," he continued, turning fully toward her now, his forearms draped over his knees. "So I guess you might say my long-term plans are inconclusive and my expectations are hanging fire, so to speak."

Her voice was little more than breath. "Nobody's ever..."

"Told you they wanted you?" he finished for her. "It doesn't mean nobody's ever felt it. I imagine you just scared every poor fool off, Miss Serena, before he could ever get the words out of his mouth." He grinned. "Now, me. I'm a bigger fool than most, and I don't scare all that easy."

"You don't even know me." Her shocked breathlessness was edging slowly toward testiness.

"You didn't ask me what I knew," he countered. "You asked me what I wanted." Rafe shrugged now. "Doesn't matter. I could have told you the moon. My hopes of getting it are about the same. Don't ask questions if you don't want to hear the answers, Miss Serena."

She was quiet a long time, hugging his shirt about her now as if it were a shawl, staring at her fingernails while she worried her lower lip with her teeth. Rafe didn't have a clue what was going on behind those half-closed eyes of hers. Maybe she was brewing up a storm of her own. Maybe she was taking all those buried passions of hers and burying them deeper inside so she couldn't reach them even if she wanted to.

He had told her the truth, he thought, even if it wasn't his only truth. He wanted her in a way he couldn't even explain to himself—for what she was, for what she represented, and right this aching minute for the way the soft chambray of his shirt was slipping over her shoulder and the snug denim grazed the curve of her hip as she unwound her long, elegant legs to stand and walk to the window.

She leaned out and the wind ran like a lover's fingers through the wild tangle of her hair. "The storm's passing on," she said quietly.

Just as quietly, Rafe said, "They always do, Shawl Lady. I'll take you home now."

Serena turned, leaned her hip against the window-sill and crossed her arms. "Thank you for telling me the truth," she said, trying to communicate her sincerity while keeping a firm hold on her traitorous heartbeat. Her whole body had been betraying her ever since he'd walked into the cabin. Her mind, however, was still loyal and lucid. "It's very flattering. I hope it won't dash your male pride when I tell you that I'm not interested in your attentions, Mr. Sugarman. In the future, assuming you remain in Quinn County, I hope you'll direct them elsewhere."

He stood, or rather unwound, and rose in a smooth, almost lazy display of wet clothes over solid muscle. "My pride's been kicked a whole lot worse, Miss Serena. I'll survive."

"I'm glad to hear that." She thrust herself away from the sill, gathered up her damp clothes, then headed for the door, telling herself she *was* glad to hear it, and was well rid of this unsettling complication in her life. Now if she could just handle all the other complications with a similar ease.

Con Quinn peered out the upstairs window, his eyelids half shut against the rising smoke from his cigar. "Who's that ragamuffin clambering down from my buggy, Uncle Peter?"

The dour servant stopped brushing his employer's blue cutaway coat and walked to join him at the window. "Sure do look like Miss Serena, Mr. Con."

"Uh-huh," Con said as if to himself. "And who's that with her?"

Uncle Peter pressed his wrinkled forehead to the window glass. "That'd be that Sugarman fellow, I reckon. Don't know nobody else that big." He walked back to the open wardrobe and resumed his brushing.

Con remained at the window, staring down through a haze of cigar smoke. "You're half right, Uncle Peter. That is my daughter looking like a ragpicker's child. But that other. Now, that's not a man at all. What I see down there is a prize stallion. A stud come to the Quinn County auction. That's what he is, all right. And I just might make myself a bid."

Shaking his grizzled head, Uncle Peter kept brushing as he muttered, "You'll be trading with the devil, like as not."

Con Quinn laughed. He contemplated the fat ash on the end of his cigar for a moment, then looked out the window once more. "Well, it won't be the first time I've done that, will it? Fact is, Uncle Peter, it might just be the last, and that makes it all the more urgent."

## Chapter Nine

Yesterday's storm had swept northeast, leaving a swath of sapphire sky over Quinn County. The air was crystalline and clear. The earth was a vibrant green. Rafe could almost hear the grass growing and the sap rising in his orchard on the hill.

Or he could have, he thought, if it weren't for the sonorous voice of Con Quinn, who was currently striding around the cabin's yard like an inspector general. The Man had shown up just as Rafe had been finishing his morning coffee. Uncle Peter had helped him out of the buggy, then climbed back in to continue on to his daughter's cabin down the road.

"You go on about your business, Sugarman," Con had grunted, shooing him away with a meaty hand. "I'm just gonna meander around."

An hour later the man was still meandering, pausing every now and then to tug at a fence post or pull a weed or just to stand cross armed and spread legged, staring at Rafe.

And it was driving Rafe stark raving, around-the-bend, utterly mad. He'd intended to spend the morning repairing the damage the storm had done to the water trough. Since he didn't have a washtub, the trough was the only decent-sized place he could manage to take a hot bath. He wasn't a cooper, but he figured, with green lumber and plenty of pitch, he could at least elevate the tub's condition to a slow leak.

But with the old man wandering around, Rafe had spent the bulk of the past hour hammering his own thumb. He'd just done it again. He slammed the hammer onto the ground now and jammed his mangled finger into his mouth, stifling a vicious oath.

"Tar would do a sight better than pine pitch," Con observed as he brought his meanderings to a halt at the foot of the trough and stared down at its weathered boards.

Rafe plucked his thumb from his mouth just long enough to grunt, "Yeah, well . . ."

The curtness of his reply seemed to have no effect on Con, who swept his arms across the yard in a grand gesture. "The place looks good, Sugarman. A lot better than the last time I saw it. You propped up that old porch. Cleared out most of the scrub over there by the lean-to, and you even—"

"I know what I've done, Mr. Quinn." Rafe held his hands out, palm up. "I've got the blisters to prove it." Then he hooked his thumbs over his belt and shifted his stance. "You didn't come out here to check on a few rotten porch boards and a pile of weeds, so why don't you get to the point."

That point, Rafe suspected, was a sharp one. And it could probably be summed up in a single word—daughter—and a single command—hands off. For a bleak minute, he wished Serena Quinn didn't exist.

It didn't surprise Rafe a bit that Con Quinn hadn't even winced at the directness of his words. He was surprised, however, to see a slow smile spread across the man's lips. It reminded him a little of a spark inching along a fuse.

"I like you, Sugarman," Con drawled, dark eyes narrowing in a leisurely perusal of Rafe's face. "You remind me of myself in my prime. Quick tongued. Hot tempered. Full of piss and vinegar."

Rafe grinned. "I don't see that your gray hairs have changed you all that much."

"Some. You can't see my aches and pains. You can't weigh the heaviness in my heart."

"True enough," Rafe agreed, distinctly unhappy to hear the word *heart* enter the conversation, for he knew the old man wasn't talking about the blood-pumping organ lodged in that barrel of his chest.

With some effort, Con raised a boot up on the edge of the trough then leaned forward, arms braced on his knee. "You're a plain talker, Sugarman. You say what's on your mind. So do I." He twisted his face up to Rafe's, squinting against the morning sun. "I want you to come to work for me."

Rafe jerked his thumb toward the cabin and the hill beyond. "I'm already working for you, in case you hadn't noticed. Sixty-forty, I believe, was the figure. Are you angling for seventy now?"

"I'm not talking about scratching weeds," Con grunted. "I mean in town. You get yourself some decent clothes and come work for me in my mercantile, and—"

"Whoa now. Just a minute, old man. You've already got somebody working there." He cocked his head quizzically. "Or did you forget that redheaded, shawl-wrapped daughter of yours? I don't think Miss Serena's going to take too kindly to the notion of having me sharing her turf."

"It's my turf," Con boomed, "and I'll damn well do what I want with it."

Rafe shook his head. "Well, it's my head, Mr. Quinn, and I'd just as soon keep it right here on my shoulders. Thanks all the same."

"Nobody tells me no, Sugarman."

"Somebody just did." Rafe swiped his hammer from the ground and turned for the cabin. He was taking the porch steps in one long stride when Con called out.

"I want you to marry my daughter."

The hammer clattered to the porch boards. Rafe stood still. He could feel Con Quinn's eyes drilling two holes in his back, practically feel the man's hot breath on his neck despite the distance between them. He had an overwhelming urge to strike the palm of his hand to his ear to clear his senses. Surely he hadn't heard...

"I said I want you to marry my daughter."

Rafe turned slowly. "Either you're plain crazy or I'm not hearing you right."

"You heard me right. And I'm no crazier than any other man with an old-maid daughter under his roof. An old-maid daughter who's had a glint in her eye ever since you happened along, Sugarman."

Far from glinting, Rafe's eyes were smoldering now. "You don't know the first thing about me, Quinn, yet you're ready to put your daughter in my bed?"

The old man winced then, and even from the porch Rafe could see his face turn a chalky color. Good! He hoped his guts were twisting with shame. He wished they'd churn up and strangle him from the inside so he didn't have to fight his own urge to do it. Disgusted, Rafe turned and mounted the steps, only to have Con Quinn call out to his back.

"You're wrong, Sugarman. I do know the first thing about you. That and a whole lot more."

Rafe drew up, his hand poised inches from the doorknob. Hell, his breath was snagging in his chest now and his mouth suddenly felt dry as cotton. His voice throbbed in his throat, a deep rumble. "What do you know, old man?"

Then he stood there, trying to breathe, listening to the wet grass whisper beneath Con Quinn's boots as he crossed the yard. The porch boards groaned under the man's great weight, and the roof trembled as he leaned against a rickety column.

"I know your type, Sugarman," he said to Rafe's back. "You've got a reach that far exceeds your grasp. You have ambitions, expectations. You want a leg up in this world, but so far, every time you try to climb, the ground just sinks another inch or two beneath your feet. You can't quite get a purchase, can you? And that ground gets a little more slippery every time you try. And you keep getting a little older, a tad slower, a fraction less agile than you were the year before.''

The old man paused. Rafe heard a match pop and flare under a fingernail. A moment later the dead match landed beside his boot and he smelled cigar smoke.

He turned to find Con Quinn grinning at him like a tomcat with a mouse in its jaws.

''You correct me if I'm wrong, boy,'' the old man said almost affably.

Correct him! Hell, Rafe thought, he'd have been hard put to describe himself half that well. ''You been reading my mail?'' he asked, only half in jest.

''No. I've been looking in a mirror and seeing myself when I was a hungry, young pup.'' He took a long, thoughtful pull on the big cigar, then exhaled a thick cloud of smoke as he picked a fleck of tobacco from his lip. '''Course, I didn't have anybody around back then to give me a thimbleful of advice, much less a boost.''

''Yeah, well, things were easier back then,'' Rafe cut in.

''Maybe.'' Con shrugged. ''Maybe not. The way I see it, a man makes his own luck. He grabs what he can when he can.''

Rafe crossed his arms now, spreading his legs wide, shifting his weight. ''And you want me to grab Miss Serena.'' His tongue rasped contemptuously against his teeth. "What the hell kind of father are you, Quinn?"

Ignoring the insult as well as the question, Con drew again on his cigar while his gaze roamed the property, coming to rest at last on the damaged water trough. "She used to be a bright, happy girl. Used to laugh from sunup to sunset. Do you believe that? 'Serena,' I'd say, 'what are you laughing about?' And she'd always say, 'Well, I don't rightly know, Daddy. I guess I just felt like it.'"

Con's voice thickened as he spoke, and Rafe thought he detected a sheen of tears over those dark, wily eyes, though he supposed it could have been the cigar smoke.

"But she stopped laughing when the war came along. Her brother died. She took it hard. Wrapped herself up in a shawl like an old maid and never laughed again." He rubbed a knuckle in one eye. "You've never seen her without one of those damn shawls, have you, Sugarman?"

A vision of soft chambray and snug denim filled Rafe's head, but it wasn't a memory he wanted to share. "No. Can't say as I have. Miss Serena keeps herself pretty well under wraps."

"A shawl's a mighty poor substitute for a pair of arms." Con Quinn's tone was wistful, almost warm. Then, as if to roughen it up again, he cleared his throat. "Marry her, Sugarman. I'll make it worth your while."

He'd been moved by the sudden tenderness in Quinn's voice, had even thought for a minute the old man had Serena's best interests at heart. But the reality was that even if he prized his daughter's happiness above all else, Con Quinn still believed it was his to bargain with. He'd been wheeling and dealing so long it was in his blood, even where his daughter was concerned.

His heart was pumping in his chest now, nearly making him light-headed. He tried to keep his face an impassive mask, tried to keep a level tone as he asked, "Why me?"

"Why not? You're young. You're strong. It would appear you're unattached. I saw you kissing my daughter the other night on my veranda so I'm assuming you don't find her all that unattractive. Best of all, Sugarman, you want what I've got." Con encompassed the property with a sweep of an arm. "This is hardscrabble. Small potatoes. I'll give you a thousand acres for every grandchild you give me."

The devil couldn't have put it better, Rafe thought. And through the sunstruck haze of smoke, that's what the old man looked like right then. God help him, how he longed to reach out and grasp the hand that offered him his every dream. Instead, he turned and walked into the cabin. In less than a minute he was back, dropping his suitcase at Con Quinn's feet.

"You take a look in there and then tell me if you still want me for a son-in-law," he growled.

For the first time that morning, Con looked baffled. "What's..."

Rafe stabbed a finger at the case. "Open it."

Blinking then and with some difficulty, Con squatted down. He muttered around his clenched cigar as he began slipping the leather straps through the buckles. "What've you got in here you think is going to shock me so bad, boy? Huh? Maybe a silver tea service you lifted from an unsuspecting but very grateful widow? Or a couple thousand you stole from a bank somewhere?" He was chuckling as he opened the case. Then he fell silent as the sunlight glinted on the gold buttons of the dark blue uniform and lit up the embossed letters on the belt buckle—U.S.

Rafe was measuring his every breath, bidding himself take air in and let it out again. His hands were fisted at his sides. "Isn't exactly what you were bargaining for, is it, Quinn?"

Shunting the cigar to a corner of his mouth, Con angled his head up. "This is yours, I take it."

"That's right," Rafe answered through clenched teeth. "Mine. Bought and paid for with a couple of quarts of my blood."

Con grunted, then slapped the case shut. "That's the past." He grabbed the porch rail and struggled to his feet. "I'm talking about the future, Sugarman."

"You're talking about it with a Mississippi Yank," Rafe countered. "You're crazier than I thought."

"And you're more honest than I gave you credit for, boy. I like that." Con leaned back against the porch rail. "What'd you think I was going to do when I saw that blue uniform? Faint dead away? Get apoplectic? Have myself some kind of conniption fit?"

"It's what everybody else does. Or worse," Rafe flung back. "Why shouldn't you?"

Con studied the ash on the end of his cigar a moment. His forehead furrowed over eyebrows that nearly overlapped. Then he flicked the ash away and raised his eyes to Rafe's. "I didn't get where I am by looking back over my shoulder. That's why. And you, if you've got a shred of sense, won't look back, either." He jabbed his cigar toward the suitcase. "You burn that. Or bury it. Do it now. I'll help you dig."

"No, sir."

"Damn fool," Con snapped. "What're you going to do with it except get your neck stretched?"

Rafe's answer was immediate and firm, the same answer he'd given Ulysses S. Grant five years before. "I'm going to wear that uniform in a parade when I'm ninety years old. Right here in Mississippi. I'm going to hold my head high and wave to my great-grandchildren who'll be standing on the sidewalk, shoulder to shoulder with the great-grandchildren of slaves." He shrugged then. "'Course, I've got to get through the next sixty years."

Con arched an eyebrow. "You figure you can?"

A roguish smile cut across the younger man's lips. "What do you think?"

"I think my daughter's gonna be a widow right quick. And I think you best keep that blue soldier suit out of her sight. She's none too partial to Yanks."

"You're counting your chickens a little early, aren't you, old man?" Rafe crossed his arms. "I don't recall accepting your offer."

"You will, son." Con lumbered off the porch now. "You will. Oh, you'll stew about it. You'll probably spend the rest of the day and most of the night turning my proposition this way and that, like a diamond held up to the light. You'll get yourself all mired in dilemmas and ethical considerations. I suspect you might even get good and drunk." He paused, a smile tilting his mouth. "Then you'll show up bright and early at my mercantile, ready to go to work."

"You sure about that?"

"Am I sure?" Con Quinn took out his pocket watch, checked the time, then turned his gaze toward the road where his buggy suddenly careened around a bend, the Morgan's hooves eating up the ground while Uncle Peter leaned forward and twitched a whip over its back.

"Right on time." Con thumbed his watch back into his pocket. Then he grinned over his shoulder at Rafe. "Yeah, son," he drawled. "I guess I'm sure."

Smack in the middle of his orchard, Rafe lay on his back, contemplating the sky. The moon reminded him of a big pearl button, and he'd consumed enough brandy so it didn't strike him as all that odd that the black velvet sky was held in place by a single button. Stranger things had happened, after all.

Like what had happened today. The old man had offered him not just the moon but the sun and stars, as well. Then, just as Con Quinn had predicted, Rafe had spent the rest of the day "mired in dilemmas and ethical considerations." His mood had swung wildly from joy to despair; his face had changed from grinning to scowling so many times it was about worn out. Right now his mouth felt lopsided, as loose and noncommittal as a string.

What amazed him most was that he had actually considered turning the old man down.

He crooked his arms under his head now and crossed one ankle over the other, ignoring the dew that was soaking through the back of his clothes. The moon wasn't so much a button anymore as it was a face—her face. Rafe knew that because just below the moon, silvery clouds shawled over a pair of invisible shoulders.

Beautiful, he thought, and beyond his wildest dreams. Only not anymore; he wasn't dreaming anymore. He had only to reach out and take her because the old man was offering her on a silver platter. Even now his fingers twitched as they cradled his head.

"I'd be a fool to turn him down," he said to the serene countenance of the moon, imagining it was Serena herself, watching as a wisp of cloud rose like a curious eyebrow on the smooth surface.

"No, it's not the land anymore or the power that goes along with it. It used to be. That was all I ever wanted from the minute I learned what wanting was. I wanted to be like your daddy. I wanted to be The Man."

He edged up on an elbow now, reached for a tall weed and planted it in the corner of his mouth before returning his gaze to the sky. "Not anymore," he whispered. "I just want to be your man, Serry."

If nothing else, he thought as he lay back down, these past five hardscrabble years had taught him patience. He'd been born with persistence. Now he was going to put the two traits together to win The Shawl Lady.

He couldn't take her gift-wrapped the way her daddy offered. She'd come to him. She had to come to him, had to let that shawl slide willingly from her smooth white shoulders.

The vision made him smile. Rafe cocked his arms back under his head, admitting it didn't hurt a bit that that vision came trailing acre after acre of Mississippi green in her wake.

## Chapter Ten

Serena was late and it was all Rafe Sugarman's fault. It didn't matter that she hadn't laid eyes on him since he'd driven her home after the storm. It didn't even seem to matter that she'd blocked him out of her every waking thought, because the man had taken up residence in her dreams. The past two nights she'd sat bolt upright in her bed—damp, shivering, dazed—knowing she'd been dreaming but sure that he had touched her all the same.

And the worst part of it was that she hadn't stopped him, but rather encouraged him—begged him, even—for more. More of those soul-shattering kisses. More of his big hands over more and more of her skin. Both nights, then, she had lain there, wide-eyed and outraged, baffled and betrayed by her very own body, bemused that asleep she could crave what she so feared when awake.

Now he wasn't just ruining her sleep, he was ruining her life by making her late opening the store. All she needed was Myra Wells or Mary Ann Stanton left cooling her heels on the sidewalk and then letting Con Quinn know about it in no uncertain terms. Her father would yank her out of the mercantile so fast her head would spin. Lord knew he was just looking for an excuse to do it.

Serena hiked up her skirt a notch in order to walk faster. Then, as she gathered speed and rounded the corner by the bank, she collided head-on with Mary Ann Stanton. The jolt set both women's straw hats aslant on their heads. Mary Ann was quick to resettle hers atop her thick, honey-colored curls.

"Good Lord, Serena, you nearly killed me coming around that corner the way you did."

"I'm sorry. It's just that I'm running late, and..." Serena sighed. The truth was she'd been thinking about Rafe Sugarman and she hadn't been paying the slightest attention to where she was going. Mary Ann was barely bigger than a minute. It was a pure miracle she hadn't broken half her bones. "I am sorry," Serena repeated. "Why don't you come along with me to the mercantile and I'll make amends by showing you the new bolts of silk that just came in from New York City?"

"I've already seen them," she said. "As a matter of fact, I purchased one entire bolt. Your helper is delivering it this afternoon."

Serena frowned, wondering how the store managed to open without her, then trying to figure out how four-foot-tall Little Joab was going to manage to get a five-foot-long bolt of silk all the way to Stantons'. "It might not be delivered till close to suppertime,

Mary Ann. My helper might require a bit of assistance," she warned.

The little woman raised an eyebrow then and her voice took on an uncharacteristic sultriness when she replied, "Oh, honey, I doubt that. I truly do."

On that peculiar note, she left Serena standing there, hat still askew and her shawl all out of kilter on her shoulders.

And that was how Serena looked when she marched through the open door of the mercantile to see her father leaning against the counter, smiling to beat the band, and her new helper up to his armpits in women.

By four o'clock Serena's head hurt so badly she wondered if she hadn't inadvertently jabbed a hat pin into her skull. Con Quinn had slunk away before she'd had a chance to speak with him that morning, leaving her in the middle of what amounted to a circus.

No, that wasn't quite true. She'd been on the fringes of the circus; the center had been reserved for that silver-tongued snake oil salesman, Rafe Sugarman.

It was quiet now, though, thank suppertime and the Almighty. Everybody had gone home. Well—almost everybody.

The snake oil salesman was still there, rolling up a bolt of silk, looking smug and altogether pleased with himself. Unable to bear the sight, Serena put her head in her hands.

If he made any noise at all coming around the counter, she didn't hear it. She felt him, though—first the heat emanating from him, then the warm spread of his fingers on her collarbone and his thumbs kneading the tight muscles of her shoulders.

"It's been a long day," he said quietly. "You look tired, Serena."

She raised her head a fraction, keeping her eyes closed, unwilling to forgo the warm sensations he was stirring in her. As in her dreams, she seemed unable to resist the touch that terrified her. She felt weak—of body and of will. Floating. Her eyes shot open in the hope of finding something, anything, to anchor her. Instead, she shrugged his hands from her shoulders and moved away, adjusting the shawl those hands had brushed aside.

"It's time to lock up, Mr. Sugarman," she said stiffly. "I'm assuming you and my father have worked out some kind of arrangement and that you'll be back to help tomorrow. If that's the case, you'll be needing a key." She opened the cash box and poked through the bills and coins in search of the spare.

"No need to look," he said. "I already have it. Your daddy—"

"Has already taken care of it," she finished for him as she slapped the lid down on the metal box. "Well, then, there's nothing left for me to do but bid you good-evening." Serena stuffed the cash box in a drawer, slammed it, then started around the counter for the door.

"I'll walk you home, Miss Serena."

"That won't be necessary." She jammed her hat on her head, then stabbed the long pins through the straw.

"Well, I'm going that way, anyway, so I might as well—"

"Chickapee Bend is west, Mr. Sugarman," she reminded him. "My house is south of town."

"Yes, ma'am. And supper's at six-thirty sharp, or so your father told me."

She raised her hands in a gesture of helplessness, then let them drop to her sides. Her father had obviously decided to insert this big oaf into every nook and cranny of her existence in the mistaken hope that proximity would lead to fondness. Well, she had news for him. He could chain her to the man and she still wouldn't consent to marry him.

The thought of such close, enforced contact sent a shimmering rush of heat through her, which only made her angrier. Not only did she have to fight her father and this grinning fool, but she had to contend with her own mutinous body.

She drew that body up stiffly now and redirected the heat into a glare as she reached for a broom and tossed it toward him. "In that case, Mr. Sugarman, you can just work a little longer and earn your supper. I'll thank you to lock up after sweeping." Saying that, Serena walked out the door.

Little Miss Esme was all aflutter. As soon as Rafe had arrived, she'd tugged him up the staircase, down the hall and into a room where she'd pulled half a dozen shirts out of a drawer, held them up to his chest, then tossed them aside with a sigh. Now she was kneeling on the floor and rooting through a camelback trunk in the hopes of finding at least one item of clothing that would fit him.

Rafe leaned a hip on the windowsill, feeling more and more like a wild bull shunted into a pen with a delicate dairy cow. Not that the little blonde wasn't pretty or working herself into a dither trying to be helpful, but she made him feel clumsy and obstreperous and ... well ... enormous.

She was holding up a brocade vest now, sizing him up across the room, then sighing again and dropping the garment back into the trunk. "Oh, dear. I guess my memories of my husband's girth have expanded over the years." Her hands fluttered on the billowy pool of her silk skirt. "Con must have been a rather small man."

"Probably not, Miss Esme. I'm just a little taller and a tad broader than most." She looked so despondent, so disappointed that Rafe wished he could shrink to accommodate her. "Here. Hand me those suspenders. They should fit, and if they don't, I'll just squinch down a little to make sure they do."

With a laugh, she tossed the gray suspenders across the room. "I know you think I'm foolish, Mr. Sugarman. It's just that...well, it's been so long since we've had a supper guest and I wanted to try to make everything perfect. For Serena and her new beau."

The word brought him up short, and Rafe quit tugging on the suspenders.

Esme laughed again. "It's not exactly a secret. I'd say your feelings are written all over your face, Mr.

Sugarman. In bright pink letters now, as a matter of fact.''

His cheeks indeed felt as if they'd been touched by a branding iron. For a minute Rafe felt like a sixteen-year-old kid caught wearing his heart on his sleeve. And for a minute he felt adrift, lost in a sea of emotions he couldn't comprehend. If his heartfelt intentions were so obvious to Miss Esme, why not to Serena? Was it possible The Shawl Lady would never, ever come around? And what, then, would he do with his heart and with the rest of his life?

As if understanding his befuddlement, Esme said quietly, "Give her time. My sister-in-law's not as chilly as she pretends underneath that everpresent wrap of hers. At least she wasn't before the war. Then… I just don't know. She changed. We all changed, I guess, but Serena more than most.''

Rafe gave up on the suspenders, which lacked the stretch of a full six inches to reach his waist. He handed them back to Esme. "What do you suppose changed her?''

Esme shrugged as she placed the suspenders in the trunk, then slowly let the lid down. "I don't know. I lost my husband, but even I realize that life continues. Sometimes I think Serena just plain gave up on happiness back then. I've tried to ask her, but she won't discuss it. Any reference to the war sets her teeth on edge.'' The blonde rolled her eyes. "The mere mention of the word *Yankee* sends her into a fit. You'd do well to avoid the subject entirely, Mr. Sugarman.''

Rafe smiled halfheartedly. "I appreciate the advice, Miss Esme." And now you don't happen to have a straight razor I can borrow to slit my own throat? he added to himself.

"I like a man with a hearty appetite." Con Quinn slapped the palm of his hand on the table. His gaze moved from Rafe's empty plate to Serena's. "Are you watching your waistline, Sister, or have you suddenly developed a distaste for Aunt Pete's cooking?"

That just about did it, Serena thought as she balled her linen napkin in her fist and used every ounce of restraint she possessed to keep from throwing it in her father's face. She'd had it up to her eyebrows with their good fellowship while they were both shoveling in roast pork and mashed potatoes as if all the pigs and potatoes on the face of the earth were going to disappear that very night.

How he expected her to eat when she could barely swallow was beyond her. Not only that, but every time she moved a foot beneath the table she encountered one of *his* feet, as if it were lying in wait for her. Then he'd made it a point to brush her fingertips every time he passed the butter or the corn bread or the pickle relish, and had had the gall to sit there as if nothing had happened while her own hand burned as if he'd held a lit match to it.

Her jawbone was clamped so tight she could barely speak. "I'm just not hungry, Daddy," she said, then endured one of his hell-hot stares.

Fire, she thought suddenly, was the answer. She'd been using icy looks and cool indifference as her weapons, and they obviously hadn't hit their mark. Maybe it was time to fight fire with fire. She summoned up a smile—as fetching as she could manage. She aimed it at her father first, then turned it on the beast with the hearty appetite at the foot of the table.

"Perhaps you'd like to join me on the veranda for a brandy, Mr. Sugarman?"

She batted her eyes in an attempt to nail down the impression of the limpid, honey-toned Southern belle, and she heard her father's sharp intake of breath as well as saw the quick rise and fall of the beast's broad chest.

He smiled, tilting his head, bathing her with the whiskey warmth of his eyes. "I'd like that, Miss Serena." He folded his napkin then, placed it beside his plate, and rose....

He rose, or rather unfurled from the chair in such a fluid motion that Serena couldn't turn her eyes away. He towered over the table, making it seem like a piece of dollhouse furniture and making her feel raggedy-limbed as a doll and very sorry she'd opened her mouth to do anything but put a fork in it.

By the time Serena had punched her skirts through the front door and taken a seat on the veranda, she had once more managed to stoke the fire inside her. Now that she had him alone, she was going to scald The Sugarman with her temper. By the time she was finished with him, he'd be sorry he'd ever heard of Quinn County, much less crossed its borders.

\* \* \*

Rafe edged back on the veranda rail, then tipped his head trying to catch a glimpse of the moon. He was almost shocked to see its smooth, expressionless face. He wouldn't have been at all surprised had it been scowling, or crinkling up its alabaster brow or gnashing its pearly teeth. Serena Quinn's face had a whole catalog of expressions, all of which had been displayed at supper. Along with one more, he thought now. That come-hither look she'd given him when she'd invited him out here on the porch.

Her daddy had fallen for it like a ton of bricks. The old man had promptly whisked Miss Esme off to the parlor, hollering over his shoulder for Uncle Peter to produce two brandies and take them out to the youngsters on the porch.

Well, Rafe was no youngster. And Miss Serena was no siren, despite the way she'd flapped her eyelashes and added a little smoke to her voice. She had a plan, but he'd be damned if he could figure it out.

He shifted around on the railing to discover her, all prim and starchy and shawl wrapped, in a fan-backed chair. Uncle Peter came out the front door carrying two brandy snifters on a silver tray. Serena took hers with a languid grace, although Rafe couldn't help but notice how her hand was shaking or how she was trying to disguise it by quickly lifting her other hand to anchor the glass.

In contrast, his own hand was rock steady when the white-jacketed servant offered the tray and its remaining snifter to him.

"Thank you, Peter," Rafe said. "How's that grandson of yours doing? I haven't seen him in a couple days."

"Oh, he's all right, Mr. Sugarman. He's just keeping his head low for a while and staying home to help his mama." Uncle Peter turned toward Serena. "Will you be wanting anything else now, Miz Serena?"

She shook her head, and the elderly servant nodded and disappeared through the door.

Rafe sighed. "Well, the last time you and I were out here, Miss Serena, you were escaping from the dance floor." He swirled the brandy in the glass, then took a swallow. "I'm trying to figure out now just whether you're running *from* or running *to.*"

"Neither one, Mr. Sugarman." She lifted her chin and met his gaze. "As you can see quite plainly, I'm not running at all. I'm sitting here enjoying this fine spring night."

"Your feet may not be moving, lady, but you're running, just the same." He slid off the rail and moved toward her. "That's all you've done since the day we met. Why are you so afraid of me?"

"I'm not," Serena insisted. She clenched her fingers around the snifter, feeling defensive. Just when she'd been ready to flay him alive, he'd picked up the whip and turned it on her. "I'm not the least bit afraid of you. Why ever would I be?" Her gaze fled to the safety of the hem of her skirt. Not all that safe now as the tips of his boots punctured her field of vision.

A deep chuckle rumbled in his chest. "Maybe because I'm big as a draft horse. Maybe because I'm the first man to come along who makes you feel small and defenseless, and you don't quite know how to handle that. Or maybe because I'm the first man who's made you *feel,* period."

"What I feel, Mr. Sugarman, is angry. You have no right to plant yourself in my life the way you've done. First it was the mercantile. Then my dining room. Lord only knows what you're planning next."

Rafe drew in his breath and released it slowly while he let her remark pass. The logical progression, of course, was her bedroom and that was indeed his plan. When she was ready.

"Your father offered me a job. I took it. Then he offered me supper. I accepted his invitation. I haven't planted myself anywhere, Miss Serena." He lifted a foot and displayed the worn sole of his boot. "Look. No roots."

She stared at the weathered brown leather, at the caked mud near the heel. A little bit of Quinn County that had attached itself to Rafe Sugarman. Her county—her heritage—to keep and hand on to her children, or to lose, bit by bit, year by year. All she had to do was choose a husband. Why not this big-booted, draft horse of a man?

Because he was partly right, she thought. He did make her feel small and defenseless. But he was wrong that it was the first time in her life she'd felt that way. Seven years ago she hadn't only *felt* defenseless, she'd *been* defenseless against the Yankees. Never again. If she had to choose a man, it would be one who didn't addle her brain and turn her very own body against her. A man who wouldn't be able to strip her of all those defenses she'd struggled so hard to rebuild.

"Your boots are muddy," she said, infusing her voice with as much indignation as she could, hoping to shame him if she couldn't discourage him.

He winced. Serena didn't see it so much as feel it. She knew her cruel remark had been a physical blow, a punch that left him momentarily breathless and in pain. Immediately, her heart regretted it, but her head wouldn't let her take it back. She had meant to hurt him—albeit in her own defense—and she had.

"It's spring, Miss Serena," he said at last. "I've been working in your wet fields."

Rafe swigged the last of his brandy, almost wishing it were hemlock instead, wishing for once in his life that—as Con Quinn had so aptly put it—his reach didn't exceed his grasp. Was that how she truly summed him up? A pair of dirty boots, stomping through her existence, sullying it?

He balanced his glass on the veranda rail, then forced those boots to walk down the steps. His throat was so thick he couldn't even say good-night.

"Mr. Sugarman," she called. Then, when he didn't alter his stride, she cried out, "Rafe!"

He halted for a second and stood looking down where the moon should have been shining like a silver buckle on polished leather. Only it wasn't. And maybe it never would. He lifted his shoulders in a shrug, a show of casualness that cost his soul.

"Good night, Shawl Lady."

## Chapter Eleven

Rafe was there in the mercantile the next morning when Serena arrived. That didn't surprise her. Nor did the fact that he was once again encircled by females, elbowing one another out of the way in order to stand closer. What did surprise her, though, was catching a glimpse of glossy boots through the welter of skirts that surrounded him. And what shamed her was that he had caught her looking, and instead of winking or grinning irreverently over the heads of his bevy of belles, he had looked away as if that moment were painful.

For the rest of the week, without ever really coming right out and saying the words, Serena tried to apologize. If she'd intended to knock the stuffing out of him, she'd done a bang-up job. But that hadn't been her intention. She'd merely wanted to discourage him, to keep him at a safe distance. Now that he was distant, she found she missed those irritating grins and the whiskey glimmer in his eyes. He tiptoed around her in his shiny boots, and she found she missed the stomping and even—dammit—the mud.

Most of all, though—and heaven help her—she missed his warm attention. Not that he was ignoring her exactly, but his replies were brief, businesslike and painfully polite. She had brought a basket lunch on Tuesday. He'd thanked her kindly and declined to share it with her. On Wednesday, instead of asking Rafe to sweep, she'd started in on the back room herself, and when he'd taken the broom away from her, he'd been oh, so careful not to touch her hands. Each evening he would walk her up the hill, always a pace or two behind her, tip his hat and then continue on his way.

"Are you doing this on purpose?" she shouted at him one evening just as he was about to leave her.

Rafe had already gone several paces beyond the brick walk. He turned, regarding her as if she'd been speaking in a foreign tongue. "Doing what, Miss Serena?"

She had opened her mouth then and nothing had come out. She'd stood there like a wide-eyed mute while he had shoved his hat back a notch on his head and drawled. "Maybe you ought to take a day off. You're looking a bit frayed at the edges."

Serena had found her voice then, but it came out more like a screech. "So you can be alone with your harem? I think not, Mr. Sugarman." She had done an abrupt about-face then and stomped toward the house.

The store, meanwhile, was thriving. Her father was delighted with the week's receipts when Serena dumped the cash box on his desk at the bank.

"I knew that young man would turn things around in this town," Con said, gnawing his cigar while he counted the bills and looked extremely pleased with himself. "I knew he'd do a helluva job."

"If you like snake charmers," Serena sneered.

Continuing his counting, without missing a bill or a beat, Con replied, "Well, daughter, I guess it would depend on which snake was on the receiving end of the charm, now, wouldn't it?"

The belles of Quinn County weren't the only ones who were making the mercantile their second home. The constable had taken to dropping in with annoying frequency. Serena dreaded seeing his lean, angular form sidling through the front door every day and loitering by the cracker barrel as he helped himself to its contents with no regard for the crumbs at his feet and no intention of paying for them.

She had complained to her father, but he had dismissed it. "A perquisite of Sears's job, Sister, and a small price to pay for law and order."

What bothered Serena most was the way Arlen Sears treated Rafe. When the lawman wasn't eyeing him from a distance, he was standing smack in front of him, poking a finger in Rafe's chest while he quizzed him and warned him to watch his step. The daily scenes reminded Serena of a banty rooster pecking at a hibernating bear. Rafe endured the inquisitions with a cool politeness and an almost sleepy indifference that Serena didn't believe for a minute. The man was boiling under the superficial layer of frost, and she could feel it all the way across the store. Today more than ever before.

In an attempt to cool the situation down, Serena walked around the counter and inserted herself between the two men. With her back to Rafe, she leveled her double-barreled gaze on the constable.

"Surely you've got something better to do than hound innocent citizens, Arlen."

"I don't know that he's all that innocent, Miss Serena," the lawman replied. "Seems to me he's got a lot to hide, otherwise he'd answer my questions." He pointed his chin over her shoulder toward Rafe. "What about that, Sugarman?"

There was no reply from behind her, but there was heat. A solid wall of heat. It was like standing in front of a furnace or at the gates of hell.

The constable was poking his finger again, and Serena slapped it aside.

"Leave him alone, Arlen. Quit hounding him."

Sears's lips shifted sideways in a smirk, bringing Serena's blood to a boil. She was just about to smack that greasy expression off his face when two hands clamped around her waist and her feet left the ground and she was being swept back behind the counter.

"I'd appreciate your staying out of this, Serry," Rafe growled in her ear as he set her down with enough force to rattle her teeth. Damn feisty female! Sears was about as dangerous as a flea and a hundred times as irritating, but Serena was going to turn him into a rabid bloodhound. That was the last thing Rafe needed, he thought as he strode back around the counter toward the cracker barrel where the constable was fingering his gun belt and looking as if he wanted to pin Serena's alabaster hide up on his office wall.

Then, just as Rafe was about to lay into the man, Miss Esme came through the front door. Sears's gun hand went to the brim of his hat, and his smirk ratcheted up into a smile as he pushed past Rafe to greet the little blonde.

"Aren't you sweet, Arlen," she exclaimed, offering her cheek for a kiss. "Good morning, Serena. Good morning, Mr. Sugarman."

Rafe couldn't decide if she smelled like verbena or orange blossoms as she wafted toward him in a swirl of organza. The scent was powerful, though, whatever it was. She lifted on tiptoe, then whispered in his ear, "How goes the courting, Mr. Sugarman?"

His reply was an exaggerated roll of his eyes toward the ceiling and the firmament beyond, after which Esme patted his arm and murmured, "Courage."

"I'll thank you not to be whispering things in my store, Esme," Serena said indignantly, glaring over the counter. "Or distracting the help."

The two of them looked like a pair of Roman conspirators, Serena thought. A side glance at Arlen Sears revealed that his mood had turned surly once more and she shivered to imagine the consequences for her little sister-in-law, or, for that matter, for Rafe.

"I was just asking Mr. Sugarman if his ears were burning this morning," Esme said brightly. "The ladies in my sewing circle couldn't seem to talk about anyone else."

Her own ears were burning, Serena thought, but it wasn't from idle chatter. Her face was hot and her stomach in knots at the idea of a gaggle of females discussing the man she . . . well . . . employed. "Don't you have anything better to do than gossip, Sister Belle?" she snapped.

Esme just smiled and moved in a swish of silk toward the door, where Arlen Sears promptly grasped her elbow.

"I'll see you home, Miss Esme," he said sharply. Over his shoulder he muttered to Rafe, "And I'll see you later, Sugarman."

Serena was about to vault over the counter when she saw the brusque way the constable ushered her sister-in-law out the door, but Rafe reached the door before she could even react.

"Stay here if you want, Miss Esme," he called out.

Esme declined, but there was a note of false bravado in her voice that Serena heard clearly. From the way Rafe walked back into the store, she knew he had heard it, too. His face was taut and his eyes were dark and stormy as he took up his broom once more.

"What?" Serena asked. "What are you thinking?"

But a sudden and not wholly unexpected flock of females chose that moment to descend on the mercantile, and Rafe didn't get a chance to reply.

\* \* \*

Serena had escaped to the quiet and the solitude of the backroom, where she sat at a rolltop desk writing orders. In the week since Rafe had started working there, the mercantile had run out of white cotton thread. The Sugarman's ardent admirers had felt obliged to make a purchase each time they visited, and white thread was a cheap and sensible choice. Seemed as if it was the only sensible thing those silly women had done, Serena thought.

She brought the tip of the pen to her mouth now, her teeth rediscovering the notch they had previously worn into the wood. Silliness. It was pure silliness. If the women of Quinn County wanted to behave like fools, let them do it where she wasn't forced to witness it, hour after hour, day after day. Let them tramp out to Chickapee Bend and hang around his cabin like ants around a jam jar.

Sinking her teeth deeper into the writing implement, Serena wondered if that were the case. Maybe the women already did. Maybe Rafe wasn't sleeping alone on that cot, with his feet dangling over the end and the wood frame creaking and the canvas sagging under his solid weight. Maybe...

Maybe she should stop thinking about things she didn't care about. If Rafe Sugarman was sparking every female in the county, it didn't make any difference to her. It pleased her, in fact. Maybe he'd quit bothering her.

He had quit, though. The tip of the pen snapped under the pressure of her teeth. Startled, Serena spat it out onto the desktop, brushed it aside and continued with her order.

She was writing furiously when she became aware of a presence behind her—a large presence, a warm one seeming to increase the temperature in the already stifling back room.

"Everybody's gone," Rafe said.

Serena let out a deep breath as she swiveled around in her chair. Not only was he taking up half the space back here, she thought, with those massive shoulders and that wall of a chest, he was using up all the good air, leaving only heat for her to inhale.

"You might as well go, too," she said with a stiff, proprietary air.

"I'll wait." He leaned against the doorframe and crossed his arms. "Don't let me distract you, Miss Serena."

"You won't, I assure you." Serena stabbed her feet at the floor, swinging the chair around, not so much to get back to her order writing as to escape the grin that flared across his mouth and instantly touched off a spark within her. She dipped the nib of the pen into the inkwell, shook off the excess, then proceeded to write with such a vengeance that she scribbled right through the page.

"Damn!" she muttered, then swung the chair around again intending to blast the man for making her ruin half an afternoon's work. But just as she turned to face him, Little Joab raced into the room.

The little boy was panting and his dark face shone with sweat. Words tumbled out of his mouth even as he was struggling to catch his breath. "Mama says come quick, Miz Serena. She says if you can't come, then to let me have a gun."

Serena jumped out of her chair, but before she could reach the boy, Rafe was kneeling beside him with one big arm around his frail shoulders.

"You take a few deep swallows of air, son, and then you start at the beginning."

In a panic, the child shook his head. "There ain't no time. My mama's in trouble. Whole gang of rednecks say they're gonna hurt her if she don't tell them where my daddy is."

Serena gasped. "Run up to the house, Little Joab, and tell your grandpa I said to get the buggy ready for me. Then you bring it back here. Don't tell Uncle Peter what's going on, or your grandma, either. I don't want them getting mixed up in this." She reached out and cupped the boy's chin. "You hear me?"

"Yes'm."

"All right, then. Hurry on up the hill, then. I'll have the store locked up by the time you're back."

The boy's big eyes sought Rafe's then, as if for approval.

"Hurry, Little Joab," Serena urged. "You do what I tell you."

It was only when Rafe nodded, however, that Little Joab took off running. The boy's hesitation and the man's interference irked Serena, but she swallowed her irritation as she moved quickly into the front of the store, where she swooped around the counter and lifted a rifle from its pegs on the wall.

"I suppose you know how to use that," Rafe said.

Serena ignored him as she pawed through a drawer in search of cartridges.

"I suppose you're prepared to use it," he added, coming around to her side of the counter. "On a human being. A neighbor, more likely than not. Is that how your daddy handles things, Miss Serena?"

She stood there with the box of cartridges in one hand, the other just touching the smooth walnut butt of the carbine, feeling foolish suddenly because she didn't even know how to load the gun, much less shoot it. Even if she did, she was sure she couldn't point it at a living creature and pull the trigger. Not even on the confounded beast who was standing beside her right now. The beast who had just pointed out that her father had never once resorted to a gun himself to tackle the county's problems.

He took the box from her lax hand, opened it and began loading the rifle. "We'll just stash it under the buggy seat, just in case."

"We?"

He smiled as he thumbed the last cartridge into the breech. "I've already decided not to waste my breath trying to get you to stay here, Miss Serena. So the only choice that leaves me is to go with you." Then, as he snapped the rifle shut, his smile, too, snapped into a taut, thin line.

Little Joab clung to the seat between them as the Morgan raced the three miles to the Inch cabin. Serena had given up trying to keep her hat on. The jolting buggy had loosened the coils of her hair till there wasn't a curl left in which to anchor a hat pin. She shoved the hat under the seat, beside the loaded rifle.

Like Rafe, she had decided there wasn't time to argue, so she had agreed to let him accompany her and Little Joab. Well—it had been more like agreeing to let a tornado take the path it wanted. The closer they got to the Inch place, though, the more she was regretting her decision.

Quinn County, after all, wasn't just her home. It was her problem. And after her father was gone, it would be hers exclusively. She needed to learn how to take care of it the way he had all these years. She needed to know how to hire and fire, how to settle disputes and disagreements, how to take charge. That was one of the reasons Serena hadn't sent Little Joab running to the bank to get help. She wanted to begin now, today, taking her place as his successor.

Rattling along in the buggy, Serena wondered what her father would do to put out the fire that was burning at Hester's. He wouldn't do it with a gun, as Rafe had been quick to remind her. He would use his commanding presence alone, and draw upon the deep respect the residents of Quinn County had for him. Or, for the ones who didn't respect him, he'd play on their fear of his displeasure. Somehow, Serena thought, she'd have to do that, too.

Reaching out her hand to give Little Joab's leg a reassuring pat, she let her glance stray to Rafe Sugarman's powerful hands as they rested on his thighs. His grip on the reins was relaxed. Trouble didn't seem to bother him, she thought. Still, she couldn't understand why he was racing into this particular trouble. Surely he must have some notion of how dangerous it was for strangers to get mixed up in Quinn County business.

The ruffians bothering Hester Inch would at least figure Con Quinn's daughter had a right to protest. Not Rafe, though. A stranger didn't have any rights. Just trouble.

She let her gaze drift to his face. His jaw was firm but not clenched. His mouth tilted up at the corners slightly. His expression wasn't that of a man rushing headlong into trouble, but a Sunday picnicker heading out into the countryside.

Well, if he was fool enough to stick his nose into local problems, then let him worry about it. And if he was under the impression that her father's obvious regard for him made him a full-fledged member of the community, he was in for a rude awakening. Above all else, she thought, she didn't need his help.

"When we get there, I'd appreciate it if you'd wait in the buggy, Mr. Sugarman." She clasped her hands in her lap, preparing for his stubborn refusal.

It jolted her as much as the speeding buggy when he replied, so quietly, "All right." Her eyes flitted to his face where that damn half smile still flirted with his lips.

"It's your party, Miss Serena." One of those whiskey brown eyes winked. "Give 'em hell."

"I intend to." Serena tried to return his smile then but her lips felt wooden and her mouth was dry with fear. She patted Little Joab's leg again, murmuring, "Your mama's going to be fine, honey. You'll see."

The child glanced up to Rafe, again as if for confirmation, but Serena took his chin in a firm hand and directed his gaze back to her. Fine thing, she thought, if she couldn't even convince a little boy of her abilities. "I'm going to see to this, honey. Me. What's my last name, Little Joab?"

"It's Quinn, Miz Serena."

"That's right," she said. "And don't you forget it."

Don't you forget it, Serena, she told herself as the Inch cabin came into sight and she counted six men scattered around the front yard. Four of them were digging up the shrubbery and hacking at the porch rails with axes. The other two were feeding azalea branches and whitewashed boards to a roaring bonfire. Hester was walking back and forth on the porch, screaming and flourishing a cast-iron skillet.

Serena was out of the buggy almost before the wheels stopped turning.

"Bobby Witherspoon! Tate Prewitt! I'd like to know just what you think you're doing!"

The two men by the bonfire dropped the branches in their hands. The younger one scraped his hat off, gaping at Serena as she stormed across the yard.

"Miz Serena," he gulped as she swept past him, bearing down on the man whose back was still toward her as he pried up an azalea by its roots.

"You give me that shovel, Joe Sweeney. You give it to me this minute if you know what's good for you. Or else."

The man swung around, looking confused, as if he didn't know whether to doff his low-crowned hat or hand over the shovel. But Serena made the decision for him, grabbing the tool and brandishing it like a pike. She sent him scurrying toward the bonfire, then wrestled her skirts and her weapon up the steps onto the porch.

Hester's eyes were as big and dark as the skillet in her hand. "They're hunting Big Joab, Miz Serena. They're gonna tear my house down lessen I tell them."

"Nobody's going to do any tearing down, Hester," Serena said firmly.

The black woman let out a sigh. "How many folks you got coming?"

"It's just me. I'm going to take care of this."

Hester's big eyes widened even more. "Just you! Oh, Lord, we're in a fine mess now."

"I'll handle it," Serena retorted as Hester merely stared at her in disbelief.

Little Joab came running up and buried his face in his mother's skirts. Hester held the frying pan in one hand in order to stroke his head. "It's all right, baby. It's all right." She rolled her eyes in Serena's direction. "Our cavalry done come. All one of her."

The men had gathered near the bonfire, muttering, stabbing the tips of their boots into the ground. Joe Sweeney, his hat in his hand now, stepped toward the porch. He screwed up his pockmarked face. "Our business ain't with you, Miz Serena. It's with her." He shot his sharp chin toward Hester. "Her man made off with my lop-eared mule this morning."

"Did not," Little Joab yelled, briefly leaving the refuge of his mother's skirt.

Serena squared her shoulders. "I don't see any mule around here, Joe. Lop-eared or otherwise."

"That's 'cause Big Joab's got him out in the woods somewheres," Tate Prewitt shouted from the edge of the fire. "And we're not leaving till we find out just where."

"That's right," the others echoed, moving toward the porch now.

"We got no quarrel with you, Miz Serena. Why don't you just go on back to town like a good girl." Joe Sweeney stepped closer to the porch, bracing his arms on the rail, twisting his hat in his hands.

"I'm staying. In case you've forgotten, Joe, you're the one who's trespassing on Quinn property," she informed him sharply. "And in case you've mistaken me for someone else, let me remind you that my name is Quinn. I'm asking you to leave. Right now."

The man gave her a cold, reptilian stare as he sucked on a tooth and continued to work the brim of his hat through his fingers. "You ain't your old man," he said through clenched teeth. "And we ain't leaving."

Serena wasn't sure which remark made her see red—whether it was the man's indifference to her authority or his refusal to leave or a combination of both. But her temper exploded like a bomb inside her, and before she knew it she was swinging the shovel at his head.

Joe Sweeney merely ducked, then dropped his hat and grasped the shovel, twisting it out of her hand.

"You're gonna be sorry you did that, lady," he snarled as he raised the implement over his head, ready to bring it down on her, hard.

A single shot rang out, shattering the wooden handle Sweeney held in his fists, sending the metal blade clattering to the ground. The men behind him dived for cover while the stunned Sweeney just stood there, wielding a one-foot length of wood.

# Chapter Twelve

The men on the ground scuttled out of Rafe's way as he strode across the yard toward the porch. The rifle was cradled innocently in his arms now, but the tension in his body and the look in his eye warned that further violence was a mere provocation away. Joe Sweeney dropped the shattered shovel and backed away toward his cohorts.

In the blink of an eye, Rafe shifted the rifle and reached for Little Joab, hiking the boy up onto his hip. "Get to the buggy," he commanded the two women on the porch.

Hester complied immediately. She disappeared into the cabin, returning in a second with baby Flora in her arms. "Bless you, Sugarman," she breathed as she rushed past him.

Serena, however, was not so quick to comply. Now that the immediate danger was over, her knees had solidified and her heart had begun beating again. "You didn't have to do that. I was handling it," she snapped.

"Let's go." Rafe yanked her off the porch and pulled her toward the buggy.

The rednecks had gotten their feet beneath them by now and were regrouping around the fire, muttering and casting hot glances toward the man who had sent them scrambling.

"I was handling it," Serena said again when they reached the buggy.

Rafe tossed Little Joab up onto Hester's lap then stashed the rifle before he turned to Serena. "You were about to get your head handled right off your pretty neck," he fumed. Then his hands clamped at her waist and Serena found her feet leaving the ground and her backside making abrupt contact with the leather seat.

He stalked around to the opposite side of the buggy.

At the bonfire, Joe Sweeney raised a fist into the air and called out, "You get rid of them damn women and then we'll take this up man-style."

Rafe ignored the threat as he hoisted himself onto the seat. Little Joab handed him the reins.

"You in for it now, Sugarman," the boy warned.

By that evening, Serena's combativeness had all but withered away. Little Joab, it seemed, had taken great delight in telling Mr. Con about how The Sugarman had shot a shovel clean in half while rescuing them from certain death, how he had whipped the Morgan into a lather driving them back to town, and how Miz Serena had almost strangled him with her shawl when he'd lifted her out of the buggy. Her father had then spent half the night raking Serena over the coals of his displeasure, stabbing his cigar in her direction and blowing smoke like a dragon. Serena had gritted her teeth and withstood the heat, nursing her own ire, until her father had concluded his tirade by shouting, "I hope you're happy with yourself, Sister. Whatever happens now is on your head."

She had sniffed with righteous indignation. "What could possibly happen? Hester and her children will be safe as long as they stay here, and I really don't imagine Joe Sweeney's going to be coming after me with a bigger shovel, do you, Daddy?"

He had given her a flat stare then, a look full of dismay and even a touch of pity. When he'd finally spoken again, Con's voice had been tired and had lacked its normal bluster. "I didn't mean you, Sister. I meant him. Tell me something. Have you ever seen six wild-eyed dogs bring down a bear?"

The image and its human counterpart had sent shivers rippling over her skin. "N-no," she'd stammered.

Her father had turned his stare out the window then, muttering, "You best get down on your knees and pray you won't, Serena Quinn."

She didn't get down on her knees, but she did pray that her father was wrong and that Rafe Sugarman wouldn't have to suffer for coming to her assistance. She had not, however, Serena stubbornly reminded the Almighty, asked for his help in the first place.

It surprised her the next morning to find the store still locked when she arrived, its interior chilly and dim, its empty spaces emptier somehow without

Rafe's enormous presence. She told herself she shouldn't be surprised. After all, she'd warned her father that the man was unreliable. Didn't his absence this morning prove that? She didn't know why he was absent, but she didn't care. The fact spoke for itself, loud and clear.

The morning dragged on, and Serena kept finding herself looking from the clock to the front door and back. The women who entered so hopefully left quickly once they discovered the object of their visit wasn't there.

"Aren't you worried, Serena?" Mary Ann Stanton had asked. The question had earned her one of Serena's blackest looks.

"Seems to me he's the one who should be worried about keeping his job," she'd replied.

By ten o'clock, when Rafe still hadn't shown up, she pronounced him a no-account fly-by-night, just as she'd suspected. By eleven, her anger had cooled to curiosity. And by noon, Serena was quite frankly alarmed by Rafe's absence. Her father's words began to sound with each advancing tick of the clock. *Have you ever seen six wild-eyed dogs bring down a bear?*

She must have murmured the words aloud, because Little Joab put down his feather duster and came to stand by her side. He raised his big glossy eyes to hers.

"What we gonna do, Shawl Lady?"

The clock kept ticking behind her. *Whatever happens now is on your head.*

"It's too pretty a day to stay inside, Little Joab. Let's you and I take a ride out to Chickapee Bend."

\* \* \*

Rafe inched down into the trough, his naked body displacing more and more of the tepid water until it began to trickle over the edge. By his calculations— considering the slow leak at the bottom of the trough and the liquid that sloshed over the top each time he moved—he'd be sitting in a teacup's worth of water in about two hours.

He stifled a moan as the water level worked up his torn back, then closed his eyes and leaned his head back on the lip of the trough. He tried to recall the last time he'd hurt this badly but couldn't because re- membered pain wasn't real. Only this. Only now. Sweet Lord, the pain tore through him. It ripped up along his spine and neck, threatening to explode through his skull.

Life had somehow come full circle, he thought mo- rosely. A whipping was what had set him on this path in the first place, only he hadn't been the victim then. He'd been a mute witness. Ten years old, choking on rage and tears and trying not to vomit, while he watched Dr. Daniel Merriweather's overseer lay open the sleek black skin of a field hand. The incident had burned itself into Rafe's young brain and, if anything had destined him to wear blue rather than gray, it was that. Not a cool political decision, but a hot rage that had been branded on his soul.

Twenty years later he could still envision it. The slave had bitten through his lip rather than cry out. Rafe ran his tongue along the laceration on the inside of his cheek now, tasting again his own blood, returning from past visions to present pain.

If there was any consolation, it was the knowledge that it was his back and not Serena's. It was his pain and not hers. Not that he expected her to be grateful. Hell, if he had his way she'd never even know. Most of all, he didn't want her to know what a fool he'd been to let his guard down the way he had the night before.

They'd come, as he had known they would, to tear off a little piece of the man who'd shamed and embarrassed them in front of two women and a child. But they'd waited till long after dark, when lack of sleep was wearing him away at the edges, dragging his eyelids down and dulling his reflexes. Six. He'd faced those odds before. But when they came, there were ten. Too many. Too damn many.

If he'd had half a brain, Rafe thought, he'd have taken off for the river at sunset and settled in with Big Joab Inch, sharing a bottle with the former slave, both of them getting drunk as skunks in the remote safety of the duck blind. But it hadn't been his brain that had prevented him from fleeing. It had been his heart.

His brain—half or otherwise—and his good sense urged him to give it up and move on. God knew he had before, from county to county till he'd etched a zigzag path across the map of Mississippi. But never before had his heart compelled him to stay.

Now he was paying the price, he thought glumly, biting down on a curse as he shifted his body in the trough. The hell of it was the beating he'd taken last night had been for personal reasons—just a small taste of what was in store when those reasons became political.

The sun, high overhead, knifed through his closed lids. Rafe jerked awake, first cursing the white-hot light that had awakened him, then the depleted water level in the trough, and finally—fiercely—the black buggy that was fast approaching his cabin. By the time it occurred to his pain-clouded, sleep-drenched brain to make a quick dash for the cabin and his clothes, the vehicle was parked solidly in his path and Serena was yanking on the brake.

He slid down as far as he could in the leaking trough, hoping to keep her from discovering the raw stripes on his back. As for the rest of him...Rafe cast a woeful glance toward his barely concealed groin and the solid evidence that, in pain or not, his body still craved Miss Serena Quinn. He grinned crookedly then—the first time he'd done anything but wince or grimace since the whip bit into him. If nothing else, his amorous condition would distract her from the rest of him if it didn't send her flying back to town in a snit of grand proportions.

It was the grin that set off the fireworks in Serena. She had run the Morgan flat out, her fears increasing with every mile. When she had seen Rafe's big body all slung out in the water trough her first reaction had been relief. A flood of relief that had rushed through her like a warm tide, and she had thanked God he was all right. But then she had seen that arrogant grin swag across his mouth and her relief turned instantly to ire. How dare he not show up for work, make her worry and eat her heart out for five miles while he was lazing around, happy as a damn pig in a puddle of mud?

Nearly blinded by her anger, Serena marched across the yard, intent on violence. She was going to do whatever she had to, whatever was required to eradicate that mocking grin that seemed to say, "I knew you'd come. I knew I could get you to care. I win. You lose."

When she reached the water trough, though, and when her hot gaze swept over every solid, wet inch of her intended victim, Serena's fury melted to confusion. "Oh, for pity's sake," she hissed as she whirled around so she was no longer facing him. "You're stark naked."

"I wasn't expecting company, Miss Serena," he drawled.

Serena glared at the ground, her anger coming back to life now that she wasn't looking at him. "I'm not company, Mr. Sugarman. I'm your employer come to fire you. Only... only I can't very well do that while you're..." His image rushed through her head in a swirl of wet, dark chest hair, hard curves of muscle and corded flesh where the water lapped. The shocking display of his masculinity should have terrified her, but instead had sent a sizzle of desire along every nerve. "While you're..." She struggled for a word other than beautiful.

"Wet?" he suggested.

"Exactly," she said with a sniff. She wrenched off her shawl and dropped it on the ground behind her. "You may dry yourself off with this while I go inside and find something appropriate for you to wear when I fire you."

Rafe was watching the way her red hair tumbled over her shoulders, reaching almost to where her waist nipped in. Without the shawl, she always seemed smaller and more vulnerable, which, he supposed, was the whole point of wearing it. But she wasn't now. He was studying her intently—the way her hair gleamed in the midday sun and the way her skirt swayed as she walked purposefully toward the cabin—concentrating so completely on how she was moving rather than where, that it was only when she slammed the cabin door that reality struck him.

First she was going to discover the bloody shreds of his shirt and know precisely what had happened to him. Then—worse—she was going to make a beeline for the cupboard and his suitcase in search of other clothes.

Ignoring the pain that screamed across his back, Rafe reached for the shawl and rose out of the water with a rough curse.

It took Serena's eyes a moment to adjust to the dimness. The windows were both papered over now, allowing only a suffused yellow light into the cabin. She didn't need perfect vision, however, to locate the shirt that had been discarded on the floor beside the cot. Clucking her tongue, she whisked it up, then looked around for a pair of pants.

The chambray fabric she remembered as soft when she had worn it felt oddly stiff now as she touched it, and when her fingers encountered the slashes, Serena gasped and looked down. The shirt was in tatters and caked with blood. In her shock, she opened her hands and let it flutter to the floor.

The opening door cut a broad swath of bright light through the cabin. Serena stood mute in the glare.

Rafe was still dripping as he crossed the threshold with Serena's shawl draped around his lower torso. All she could think of was a Roman god—Neptune, perhaps—who'd left his mythical realm to suddenly appear in Quinn County. His gaze lowered to the shirt on the floor and then swung back up to her face. It was a questioning gaze mixed with pain and puzzlement and stubborn pride.

"They hurt you," she said softly.

"No. Hell, it was just—" Rafe broke off his denial as she stepped toward him. There was care and comfort in her eyes and her lips quivered as she reached out both hands to lay them on his arms. He stood absolutely still beneath her warm touch, wanting her comfort now almost as much as he wanted the rest of her.

"It's all my fault," she whispered, taking another tentative step forward, pressing her cheek against his damp chest. "I'm sorry. I'm so sorry,"

Rafe brushed his lips over her hair, fitting his own cheek to the crown of her head. "It doesn't matter,

Serry." And it didn't. If it had to be the brutality of
the whip that brought her to him, so be it. She had
come, close as his own skin, real as the beat of his
heart and the heat of his need—at last.

# Chapter Thirteen

Intending to give comfort, Serena found herself comforted instead by the sheer size of the man, by his solid warmth and by the soft touch of his lips over her hair as he murmured her name. Her arms slid around him seeking to be closer still, then she heard his rough intake of breath and felt him wince when her fingertips encountered the raw slashes on his broad back. She ached suddenly as if it were her own flesh that had been torn open. A deep, primal ache that seemed to fuse her body and perhaps even her soul with Rafe's. She hurt with him, for him, and for herself all in the same overwhelming instant. She was no longer sure where he began and she left off, where the boundaries were between their bodies or their beings.

Her own sense of self seemed to shatter then, along with her sense of self-preservation. How strange, she thought, that she wasn't afraid. How natural it seemed to let his huge, callused hand caress her neck, to feel the press of his fingertips on her surging pulse, to respond to the gentle but insistent pressure of his thumb as it urged her chin up for his kiss.

His lips brushed gently across hers, less kiss than question. *Yes* bubbled in her throat, but her dazed lips were unable to shape the word, so she could only whimper. But it was answer enough for Rafe. His mouth slanted over hers hungrily as his big hands slid down to cup her bottom through the folds of her skirt, bringing her hard against him.

Serena's head was swimming, and her senses were drowning in the wet possessiveness of the kiss and the surge of his hips against hers. She felt a panicky urge to fight for air, but all of a sudden Rafe seemed to be breathing for her, filling her with sustenance and sheer heat. Her body sagged within the circle of his arms, allowing his strength alone to sustain her just as his breath alone seemed to be keeping her alive.

Then he groaned against her mouth, and Serena realized she had been clutching, as if for dear life, at his back. She pulled away, averting her face.

"I'm—I'm sorry. I don't know how to do this," she stammered.

He cradled her chin in the palm of his hand, gently drawing her gaze back to his own. "Hush, love. You don't need to know anything. Just feel." Once more his head dipped and his mouth sought hers, this time just sampling each corner, the quivering seam.

Quick little footsteps sounded on the porch boards then. "Lordy, Sugarman. They done whupped you something awful," Little Joab exclaimed.

With a sigh, Rafe raised his head. The moment had slipped out of his grasp, just as Serena was slipping out of his arms now and stepping back, gaining some control over the mental capacities he had hoped to obliterate. Still, he was grateful to the child for breaking the spell and allowing him to regain his own badly eroded control. The pain Serena had made him forget returned with a vengeance now.

He looked down at the boy, grinning as best he could to mask his discomfort. "It's probably time for you to see The Shawl Lady back to town, son."

The boy glanced to the paisley fabric draped around Rafe's hips. "I hope you ain't thinking of giving that back to Miz Serena right here and now."

"He most certainly is not," Serena cut in. "But Mr. Sugarman is quite right about your returning to town, Little Joab. I don't want to add to your mama's worries any more than I have to."

"Yes, ma'am," the boy answered obediently.

"And don't you stop for anything," Serena told him. "Or anyone."

"Ain't you coming with me?" Little Joab asked.

It hadn't occurred to Serena until the boy questioned her that that was indeed what she was intending. The knowledge took her by surprise, and a sidelong glance at Rafe told her he was just as surprised by the news as she was. She could feel her face growing hot under his now-curious inspection.

"Mr. Sugarman needs tending to, Little Joab. You run and fetch my handbag from the buggy. I believe I have a jar of wintergreen salve in there."

Little Joab made a face. "That smelly stuff you kept slathering on that blister of mine?" He nudged Rafe's leg. "You best get while the gettin's good, Sugarman. That salve don't just smell bad, it stings like a whole hive of bees."

Serena turned the boy's shoulders toward the door. "It cured you, though, didn't it? Now scoot." As she watched him skip down the stairs, out of habit Serena reached to clasp her shawl about her shoulders. Her fingers fluttered briefly over her upper arms then dropped to her side when she recalled just where that shawl was.

"You don't need it, you know," Rafe said quietly, his fingertips grazing along her arm.

"What?"

"Your protection, Shawl Lady. You're safe with me."

His touch was gentle as a breeze, and yet it provoked a whirlwind of desire in Serena. She shivered. "I'm not sure I know what safety is anymore," she admitted.

"Yes, you do. Otherwise you wouldn't stay."

"Perhaps you're right." She lifted her eyes to his now, feeling the full impact of their warmth. Their whiskey color worked into her bloodstream as surely as if she'd just drunk half a bottle of hundred-proof liquor. She wasn't thinking clearly anymore, Serena knew. Along with safety, she'd abandoned her good sense. A nagging part of her desperately wanted to retrieve both—before it was too late.

At the same time, though, she just wanted to stand there drinking him in—from his whiskey eyes to his long, corded legs. She cleared her throat. "I imagine I'd feel a good deal safer if you were dressed." It wasn't true, though, she thought. Clothes were not the issue anymore. Rafe Sugarman could be wearing seventeen layers of cotton and wool and she'd still be aware only of that powerful, purely male body.

He walked to the cot where a pair of trousers lay on the floor. All the while Serena's eyes followed him. He didn't walk so much as move with a sculpted grace. Like a hip-draped statue of a Roman god come down from its pedestal. She felt awkward in comparison. As clumsy and fluttery as a girl on Christmas morning when first laying eyes on a shawl-wrapped gift.

"Serry."

His husky voice broke her trance. Serena's eyes snapped to Rafe's face, where a grin flickered like candle flame.

He held the dark trousers up. "I'd love for you to watch, darlin', but..."

She turned, mortified by her own obvious desires, grateful for the dim interior light that hid her crimson face. What was she doing? Whatever was she thinking, assuming she was thinking at all?

Little Joab came through the door then, carrying her handbag. "Here you go, Miz Serena."

The weight and texture of the crocheted bag the boy plopped into her hands brought her back to reality. What she was doing, Serena reminded herself sharply, was taking care of the man who'd been hurt because of her actions. No more, no less. She stuck her hand in the bag, happy when her fingers touched the jar of salve.

When she withdrew it, Little Joab scrunched up his face. "Too bad for you, Sugarman," he said. "She done found that awful stuff."

"Hush," Serena told him. "I want you to take the buggy back to the house, Little Joab. Then I want you to find Mr. Con. He's probably still at the bank. Tell him where I am. And tell him not to worry." As if he would, Serena added to herself. Her father would be rubbing his hands together so hard and with such glee that his palms would probably shoot off sparks and set fire to all the papers on his desk.

"Yes, ma'am. I'll tell Mr. Con he's not supposed to worry." The child narrowed his eyes and rubbed his chin. "What'll I tell him if he asks me when you're coming back?"

"Well, I'm not exactly—"

"Tomorrow." Rafe was standing close behind her now, and his deep voice reverberated through Serena. There was a certainty in his tone that brooked no questioning. He continued in the same sure fashion. "You tell Mr. Con that Miz Serena's with me now, Little Joab."

The boy nodded, seemingly satisfied that he had all the proper answers now and that he wouldn't catch it for being the bearer of bad news. He turned then and skipped off the porch toward the buggy.

Serena's heart beat a fast tattoo as she stood watching the black buggy disappear down the road. The little jar of salve was growing warm from the heat of her clenched hand, and The Sugarman was still standing close behind her. So close she could feel his breath shiver the hair atop her head.

It occurred to her that she had made a momentous decision, and that her head hadn't been involved in the process at all. Just her heart. The heart that was currently stuck in her throat like a piece of day-old corn bread.

Rafe sucked in his breath, pressed his lips together, and still couldn't keep from yelling out a curse. Serena had insisted on doing her ministrations out on the sunlit porch. He was sitting on the top step and she was squatting behind him, applying what felt like lit matches to his flesh. Hell, the whipping itself hadn't hurt this badly.

"Don't be such a baby," she told him, clucking her tongue and proceeding to touch yet another red-hot poker to his skin.

This time he swallowed the oath, trying to concentrate on her touch rather than the pain it induced.

"It isn't quite as bad as I first thought," she told him now. "The skin's only broken where the lashes crisscrossed. The rest are just nasty welts."

Rafe relaxed his clenched teeth long enough to mutter, "That's a comfort to hear, Miz Serena. Are you about done torturing me now?"

"Nearly. I'm not enjoying this any more than you are, you know, but it's necessary if you want these wounds to heal properly." She traced a searing path along his lower back, then sighed. "There. That ought to do it. For now, anyway. I'll repeat the treatment in a few hours. It wasn't all that bad, was it?"

"No, ma'am," he muttered. "I'll be looking forward to it."

Her fingertips touched the scar at his belt line. "How in the world did you get this, Rafe? It looks like somebody dug a bullet out of you." She explored the rough scar tissue where it dipped below his waist. "Dug it out with a trowel, too, from the feel of it," she added.

Now that some of the fire had gone out of his back, he sat up straighter. "Probably did. Army surgeons aren't too proud to make use of the first available tool." As soon as the words were out of his mouth, Rafe wished he could take them back. The war was the last subject he wanted to discuss, especially with Serena. Judging from her silence then, it wasn't her favorite subject, either.

She withdrew her hand while she took in an audible, almost weary breath. "I suppose you took part in the rebellion."

"Along with just about every other man my age," he said, "but that's history, Serena."

Again, the silence—as if she didn't agree. "Where were you shot?" she asked at last.

He angled his hand back to his waist at the same time as he turned his head to wink at her. "Right there."

But Serena was in no mood to laugh. "I meant what battle," she said sternly.

Not now, Rafe thought. It's too soon. She was here, but she wasn't his yet. He wouldn't lie to her, though. "Iuka," he replied quietly, truthfully. "In '62."

She nodded. "Yes, '62. I remember it well."

"Not as well as I do," he said brusquely. "Let's talk about something else." Please.

She lowered her eyes, drawing in her lower lip.

"Serry, I'm sorry." He angled one leg around, sitting now so he was fully facing her. "I didn't mean—"

"No. Don't apologize. I understand. Let's do discuss something else." As if in search of new subject matter, her gaze flitted to his leg where a patch of bare ankle was exposed. A patch of scarred skin. "Aha!" she exclaimed. "Don't tell me. Let me guess. That's from straying too close to a bonfire when you were a boy."

Rafe clamped his hand over his ankle. "Something like that." More like a brush with hot tar when the good and patriotic citizens of another county decided they could no longer tolerate the Mississippi Yank in their midst. He nearly told her then. It wasn't fair to let her believe he was something he wasn't, to lead her astray toward more acceptable conclusions. The words were piling up in his throat, nearly choking him, when she covered his hand with hers.

"I wish I could erase every scar," she said softly. "Especially the ones I caused." Her blue eyes shimmered with tears then, and when she blinked them back, her lashes grew wet.

Rafe cupped her chin in his hand. "Don't waste your tears on the past, Serry." He angled his thumb to catch the drop of moisture sliding down her cheek. "Let's not look back when we've got so much ahead of us."

"Us." Serena repeated the word as if testing the feel of it on her tongue. It felt new and strange, but, oh, so right. As right as Rafe's hand moving to the back of her neck and his other hand joining it to hold her poised for his kiss.

"No more tears," he whispered against her lips just before his mouth took hers.

This time there was no teasing preamble, no delicate-as-butterfly-wings beginning, no quizzical brushing of his lips over hers. This time he took her mouth by storm, and his kiss had all of the white-hot sizzle of lightning, the shuddering force of thunder. She swayed as if caught in the powerful vortex of a tornado.

It wasn't what Serena had ever imagined a kiss could be. Her experience had been limited to John William, whose lips—at their most passionate—had merely scraped hers. The sensation, if any, had been confined to her mouth alone. A kiss, to Serena's way of thinking, was like a dry handshake, both in feel and intent.

But this...this stunning intimacy...was no handshake. It was more like an earthquake. And it wasn't confined to her lips. Sweet sensations flowed to every part of her. Her heart was turning cartwheels while her stomach melted and seeped downward, pooling in her hidden depths. It wasn't a kiss at all, she thought, dazedly. It was a fierce possession.

And when his bold tongue breached the barrier of her teeth, it wasn't an invasion so much as an invitation to surrender. Which she did.

Rafe was aware of the moment Serena melted like butter in sunshine. One minute he'd been kissing a woman who was willing but wire tight; the next minute she didn't have a bone in her body. She was passion incarnate as he had sensed she would be from the first moment he laid eyes on her. It moved him now in a deep, primitive way, knowing he was the one who had stirred those banked coals in her just as she was igniting identical fires in him.

Without breaking the kiss, Rafe hauled her onto his lap. Ah, God, he thought, she felt like a warm kitten. Her little claws worked sensuously on his arms, and a contented purr was throbbing deep in her throat.

He splayed one hand over her delicate rib cage, feeling the rapid beating of her heart, rejoicing in the quickening he had instilled. Then he took the firm weight of one breast in the palm of his hand, thumb moving to tease its center through layers of cotton and silk.

Her arms slid around his neck then, and if she felt boneless before, she seemed even more so now, fitting closer against him, closing whatever spaces remained. Like mist filling in every dip in a landscape. Like fog, making it impossible for him to see anything but her, or feel anything but her. Making him feel so much it was all but impossible to think.

*Too soon.* The words sounded in the back of his brain with the insistence of a foghorn. *Too soon, Yank.* If he took her before she knew the truth, Serena would never forgive him. To love her now would be to lose her. He knew that instinctively, and the knowledge battled with his other instincts—the primitive ones that bid him claim her here and now.

With a groan to mask a curse, he tore his mouth from hers, clasped his hands at her waist and moved her off his lap. Just to make sure his warm little kitten didn't climb back, Rafe stood.

Serena blinked up at him, confusion dulling the blue of her eyes, disappointment dragging down the corners of her mouth. It touched Rafe's heart, but when he spoke there was only gruffness in his tone.

"Maybe your staying here wasn't such a good idea, Serena." He ripped his fingers through his hair. "Too damn much opportunity for us to get into trouble."

It hadn't felt like trouble, she thought as she sat gazing up at him. With the sun just behind his head, Rafe's face was dark, and she couldn't see his expression, much less read it. He sounded so angry, and she couldn't for the life of her imagine why.

For her part, Serena felt as if someone had just pulled the plug in the bathtub, leaving her high and dry and...not quite clean. Dear Lord, was that it? Was Rafe able to tell somehow just by kissing her that her innocence was long gone? Had the Yankees left some sort of stamp on her that she'd been unaware of all these years? Oh, God, if that were true, could Rafe ever understand, or would he simply shunt her aside as he had a moment ago like so much soiled merchandise?

"What?" she blurted out. "I don't understand." She'd been about to add "What did I do wrong?" but choked the question back because she couldn't bear the answer.

Rather than answer, he walked across the yard and snatched up a wooden bucket lying near the water trough, then came back to stand like some fierce colossus before her.

"I'm going down to the river," he told her, shaking the bucket as if it were an explanation.

It wasn't. "Why?" Much to Serena's dismay, her voice was thin as a porcelain teacup. And dammit, like a teacup, it cracked.

Whether Rafe heard it or not, she wasn't sure. He had already turned his back and was walking away, as if he couldn't get too far from her too fast.

Rafe didn't break his stride when he reached the riverbank, nor did he pause to roll up his pant legs. He walked right out to the center of the stream, dragged the wooden bucket through the chilly water and dumped it over his head. For all the good it did, he thought glumly as he settled himself on the mossy bank. It wasn't his head that needed to be cooled off. His head, in fact, had behaved with near-stupefying restraint, considering how the rest of him had responded to Serena's passionate acquiescence.

Eyes closed, he hung that head forward now, shaking it in slow dismay, baffled that he had had her—all warm and purring in his arms, all of her starch turned to liquid heat, all of her his for the taking—then promptly walked away.

Because he had a secret? Two secrets, really. The past that kept trailing him like a black dog and the bright future Con Quinn had promised him. Hell, there had to be thousands of men who'd bedded women while keeping secrets worse than his. And she hadn't exactly been asking for any heartfelt declarations while she was curling around him like a warm fog. She'd been asking for his body, pure and simple. Well, not all that pure. Not simple, either, with his conscience getting in the way.

*Tell her,* the voice in the back of his head nagged.

Then there was the other voice, this one reminiscent of Con's stentorian rumble. *Don't be a fool all your life, Sugarman. You wed her, then bed her and plant your seed deep in this fine daughter of Mississippi. If the details of your less-than-glorious past should one day come to light…well…it'll just be too damn late, won't it?*

Rafe raised his head and stared at the sun-dappled river. Con Quinn's river, twisting through the county like the man's signature.

"You old serpent," he muttered. "I can't do that to her. My blood's not cold enough."

But Rafe's blood did run cold as ice a second later when he heard Serena's terrified screams.

## Chapter Fourteen

Rafe paused only long enough to assess the odds. There were four of them—boys—no doubt following in their fathers' footsteps of the night before. Young roughnecks come to score whatever flesh their elders had left untouched. They'd come for him, but they'd found Serena instead.

Serena's flesh—petal white where they'd ripped her dress from her shoulders, long alabaster legs exposed—clawed at by rough hands.

Rafe crashed out of the brush, roaring like a wounded bear. Three of the boys took off immediately. The fourth fumbled with his loosened trousers as he stumbled backward. But not fast enough to escape the fist that flattened his nose against his face and dropped him to his knees.

Hands fisted like rocks, Rafe stood over him, dragging in air, trying to see through the red mist of violence that was blinding him, willing himself not to kill the boy. He didn't know if he could stop, or even if he wanted to.

On hands and knees, the boy crept backward, leaving a trail of bright red blood from his broken nose.

"Get out of here," Rafe growled, "while you still can. Next time, by God, I'll finish it."

Sobbing now, the boy struggled to his feet and hurried toward the road.

Rafe took in one more deep breath as if to cleanse his body and soul of brutality before going to Serena. She was still on the ground, curled on her side now. Gently, he slipped her skirt down to cover her legs.

"Oh, no. Don't," she moaned.

He stroked her tangled hair back from her face, softening his voice to a whisper. "You're safe, honey. You're safe now."

She shrank from his touch, curling her body tighter, squeezing her eyes closed.

"Serry, nobody's going to hurt you." He slid his arms around her, absorbed her struggles, then held her close, murmuring at her ear. "Trust me, love. Nobody will ever hurt you like that. I won't let it happen."

She went absolutely still in his embrace. Not even breathing for a moment. Then she drew in just enough air to sustain a fragile whisper. "You're too late. Dear God, you're seven years too late."

The truth came pouring out of her then with a flood of tears and a rush of words. Like a river too long dammed suddenly bursting all restraints. The night. The barn. The drunken soldiers—three of them— who'd dragged her into a stall, who'd taken turns with her. Who'd taken her innocence, and when that was gone, who'd taken a good chunk of her soul, then left her bruised and bleeding and used up with only fear in her heart and threads of blue wool under her broken fingernails.

Rafe sat in the yard, cradling Serena in his arms, rocking her as if she were a little girl who'd just awakened screaming from a nightmare. But it hadn't been a nightmare, and as he tried to give her gentle comfort he didn't feel gentle at all but wounded himself. Enraged.

She seemed boneless again, but this time like a broken doll when he carried her into the cabin and laid her on the cot. He knelt in silence on the floor beside her, at a loss in the face of her despair, feeling clumsy in his own welter of rage and anguish while he cursed himself for not having sensed the truth. Con had hinted at it. Little Esme had practically painted him a picture. Serena herself had provided ample clues, forever burrowing into the protective depths of her shawls.

*Something happened. Serena changed. She just plain gave up on happiness.*

Seven years ago. Where had he been then? Rafe didn't have to search his brain too hard to recall. Grant had been rolling like a dark blue tide down from Tennessee, and his Mississippi Yank had been with him. The Federal troops had taken a few good lickings while they advanced, but for the most part they gave worse than they got. He couldn't remember any activity in Quinn County, though. He knew he'd never been closer than fifteen or twenty miles. But somebody in blue had.

No wonder she couldn't bear to have anybody even mention the word *Yankee*.

No wonder that flame of hers, once brutalized, had buried itself under layers of ice and yards of fabric. The wonder was it hadn't burned out. But it hadn't. Rafe knew that, for he had touched it, tasted it and felt it burning him.

He looked at her now, wondering if these fresh tears would finally douse that fragile flame, wondering what he could say or do to coax it back to life. For all his size and strength, Rafe felt helpless now. The rage that coursed through him was a useless, choking emotion. Seven years ago such rage would have prompted him to murder those men with his bare hands, but, as Serena had said, he was too late.

Leaning forward, he kissed the wet, salty corner of her mouth. His voice was thick, as if her tears were his own. "Tell me what to do, Serry. Tell me how to make it right, how to take away your pain."

She opened her eyes then. They were blue as the skies over Quinn County. Huge and glossy with tears. Innocent, so damn innocent in spite of the brutal past. With an exhausted sigh she levered herself up, then lifted trembling hands to scrub her wet cheeks.

"You were right about those shawls of mine," she said, hugging her arms around her now. "I guess I figured they were the next best thing to armor. What a silly notion."

"Not so silly if they made you feel better," he murmured. "Maybe they helped you feel more secure."

Serena shook her head wanly. "I always thought I was doing right by avoiding men. I never wanted..." Her voice trailed off for a moment. "It wasn't so difficult. But now..."

"Now?" Rafe's voice was a low-pitched echo.

"Now there's you," she whispered as her wet eyes lifted to his. "Teach me how to stop being so afraid, Rafe. Please."

"Oh, baby." His heart welled up in his throat.

Her hand lifted, trembling fingers fanning out against his cheek. "Please. Teach me. Show me how..."

"Shh." He stilled her moist lips with his own. It was a kiss meant merely to quiet her, to suffice until he could clear his head enough to think of an answer, and clear his throat enough to utter it when it occurred. Then he sighed with rough frustration. "I'm not much of a teacher, darlin'. I'm, uh, more what you might call a doer."

"Oh." Disappointment sank in her stomach like a rock. It was obvious Rafe was in no hurry to make love to her. And why should he be? Serena thought. After all, she was behaving more and more like a big, gawky girl without any artful wiles to entice him. He undoubtedly found her fears and her lack of experience less than appealing. Or perhaps it wasn't the lack at all, but rather the ugly fact that she was experienced. Ruined, to be more precise.

Her fingers twisted in the folds of her skirt now. "I understand your reluctance. I truly do."

She didn't understand it at all, Rafe thought. But he couldn't take her under false pretenses. False colors, more exactly. Blue. Not gray. He was just too much of a coward at the moment to blurt out the truth. Instead, he tipped her chin up.

"These things need a bit of preamble, Serry." He slid his thumb along her lower lip, trying to coax a smile from her while at the same time attempting to come up with something, anything, to console her. "And anyway, loving's not all that great on an empty stomach. We probably ought to have a bite of supper first." He sat back on his heels. "What do you say we explore some of your more genteel domestic skills? Can you cook?"

"I can put up strawberry jam," she answered almost defensively. Then she sighed. "The bald truth is I always wreaked such havoc in her kitchen that Aunt Pete banished me years ago. And that last batch of jam was ... well ... slightly off."

He raised an eyebrow. "Off?"

"Seems I used salt instead of sugar." Serena shrugged. "They're both white."

At the very least she anticipated a scowl from Rafe. Men, after all, expected women to be accomplished in the culinary arts. Particularly if they had no talents elsewhere. Instead, he grinned with delight and reached for her hands to pull her up from the cot.

"Well, now, I think we've stumbled onto at least one thing I can safely teach you, darlin'," he said as he pointed her toward the cupboard.

Serena was burning the hell out of the bacon. Still, Rafe decided that was preferable to sizzling him. She was having a tussle with the corn bread now, tipping the bowl over the skillet, frowning when the batter failed to pour out.

"Put a tad more water in it," he suggested as he reached for another tin can from the burlap sack on the floor.

Serena blew a strand of hair up off her forehead. "Maybe we should trade jobs. You be the cook and I'll be the bell maker."

For the past hour, while overseeing Serena's cooking, Rafe had been punching holes in empty tins, rigging them with stone-and-twine clappers, then stringing them together.

"You're too late," he told her now, lifting a homemade bell and giving it a shake. The resultant clang was loud if not exactly musical. He grinned. "Now we'll hear any uninvited guests long before they arrive."

When he saw her forehead crease with worry, Rafe immediately regretted his words. "It's just a precaution," he said quickly. "I don't expect them to come back." Not tonight, anyway, he added to himself. Otherwise he wouldn't have let her stay. Those old boys would simmer for a few days before they boiled over again and came looking for him.

The tin bells clattered when he stood.

Serena laughed. "You sound like a herd of cows."

Rafe moved behind her, looping the strand around her waist. "I ought to just leave them right here." He bent to whisper at her ear. "Then I'd always know where you are."

Again she laughed. "Rings on my fingers and bells on my toes?" Then she turned, lifting her gaze to his face. Rafe watched the color of her eyes deepen to a midnight blue. Her lips parted slightly as she struggled to catch her breath.

He felt his own body react instantly. How the hell did she do that to him with just a look? he wondered bleakly. And how, in the name of sanity, was he going to be able to maintain his long enough to tell her all the things he needed to before he made love to her? And then, once he'd told her, why in the world would she ever want anything to do with, much less share a bed with, a down-and-out Yankee?

The cans jangled as he jerked them away from around her waist. "I best string these up before it gets dark," he said in a voice as rough as sandpaper. Seeing the passionate flame in her eyes flicker to disappointment, he kissed the tip of her nose. "And you best take that bacon off the fire, Serry, before you burn your daddy's cabin down."

Rafe came back inside the cabin after stringing the final line of his musical picket. Serena, egg basket hooked over her arm, waved to him from his refurbished newly populated chicken coop, then continued

her search for eggs. He didn't mind having the cabin
to himself a little while. He could even ignore the thin
veil of smoke that hung in the air, same as he had ignored the skillet of blackened corn bread out on the
porch. Hell, he didn't care if she couldn't boil water.
Not when she could boil his blood with a single look.
And his blood was definitely hot. Still, he had every
intention of telling her about his past before they made
love.

It was only fair. More important, it was the right
thing to do. And if he did it right, Serena would understand his reasons for turning his back on the Confederacy and taking up the Northern cause. Yankee,
yes. But not one of *those* Yankees. She'd see that.
He'd make her see it.

She had left his spare shirt—his only shirt now—
folded neatly on the cot. Rafe reached for it, then
stopped, his gaze flicking to the cupboard where his
suitcase was stowed. It occurred to him that perhaps
showing her would accomplish more than mere telling. Maybe, he thought, if somebody in blue touched
her with tenderness and love, it would heal her more
than mere words ever could. Maybe...

He crossed the cabin with grim determination, and
his hand was on the handle of the leather case just as
the cans he'd fastened to the door clattered against the
wood. He twisted his head. Serena stood framed in the
doorway. Light from the setting sun cast a golden glow
about her. It lit up her long, loose hair like flames.
Other flames, more fierce, licked along every nerve in
Rafe's body at the sight of her.

He'd thought he'd known what wanting was until that moment. He'd thought, despite his hard luck, he was still the master of his hopes and dreams and, yes, even his passions. But he wasn't. Not anymore. He couldn't even control his own unhinged jaw right now, or his rubbery knees, or the heart that was about to punch right through his ribs. He let go of the handle, let go of the past, stretching out his hand to his future instead.

Serena stood there, almost unable to breathe for the sensation of fullness in her chest. Rafe had looked at her with desire before, but this... It was like lightning snapping across the room, twining around her like a hot blue rope, holding her in place while at the same time tugging her toward him.

Her fingers loosened on the egg basket, letting it fall, and she made no effort to save the single egg she'd uncovered in the coop. It broke with a splat that she barely acknowledged because all her senses were trained on the man who was moving toward her now.

He was moving slowly. Relentlessly. His warm whiskey eyes were glittering. As the distance between them shortened, the hot blue rope binding her grew tighter, hotter still.

"I can't breathe," she said when his arms moved around her, gathering her against his hard, warm chest.

He took her chin in the V of one big hand, tipping her face up. "I'll teach you how." His mouth covered hers then, hungrily, and it didn't take long for Serena to realize that she didn't really need to breathe, for

Rafe's breath was sustaining her just as his heartbeat, against her own, seemed to be tutoring her in new, quicker rhythms. Still, whether it was the cadence of passion or panic, Serena wasn't sure.

Tin cans chattered at her back as Rafe reached behind her and pulled the door closed. She heard the bolt shoot home and felt darkness pour over her, all while his slow mouth never left hers.

Safe. She felt so safe suddenly, locked in the warm cabin, locked in Rafe Sugarman's warm embrace.

A big, slow hand sought the button at her collar and he murmured against her lips. "I'm going to touch you, Serry, and you're going to like it. You're not going to want me to stop." He slid the button through and moved to the next. "But that's all you have to say, darlin', and I will."

As his fingers slipped another button, something fluttered in Serena's stomach. She couldn't quite identify the winged emotion. Another button eased through. Rafe's fingertips skimmed her flesh, and the thing with wings stirred restlessly inside her. Her lips fashioned a sound against his. "Don't..."

He lifted his head, his hand hovering at the next button, his voice thick with desire. "What, love?"

"D-don't stop," she breathed. "I'm not afraid."

Rafe chuckled softly. "Yes, you are. You're scared as hell, Shawl Lady, but you're going to learn that you don't have to be. You're in control, Serena. You're holding my reins. I'll do what you want. Only what you want."

"I don't know what I want." Her voice broke into shards of nervous laughter. "And I can't think when you kiss me, Rafe."

"You're not supposed to think, darlin'," he whispered huskily. "Just feel."

Her gaze lifted to his for a moment, then fluttered back down. "I feel like I'm melting. And...dizzy...."

When she swayed, he lifted her into his arms and carried her toward the cot, where he bent and yanked the mattress to the floor. A sorry bed for their first time, he thought, but a sight more reliable than the wobbly cot. Someday he'd find the biggest, oldest live oak in Quinn County and he'd make her the finest bed in all of Mississippi. He'd carve their names on the headboard. Their children would be born there. And their grandchildren.

Now, though, there was only the floor. He lowered her there and slowly, gently, slid her dress from her shoulders and eased her arms from the long sleeves. His heart beat harder with each pale inch of flesh he uncovered.

"Your hands are shaking," Serena whispered. He was afraid, too, she thought incredulously. Of her! She reached out her own trembling hand to caress the hard curve of his upper arm, the arm that could lift her as if she weighed no more than a child. Her lashes fluttered up to his face. What she glimpsed there, in the hooded warmth of his eyes, in the tautness of his full lips and the muscle that clenched in his cheek, Serena recognized as a fierce combination of both desire and restraint.

She knew then that what Rafe had told her was true. She was in control. She did indeed hold the reins, and this huge, hard-carved, glorious male animal was hers, and all of him held in abeyance, awaiting... her. Her commands. Her whims. Her assent, or, if she chose, her rejection.

A feeling unlike any she had ever known encompassed her heart. Warmth. Pleasure. Power. And something more. Something that had no name and all names. Love.

"Let me," she said, slipping her hands beneath his where they were fumbling with the ribbons and tapes of her skirts. With her newfound confidence, Serena made short work of the fastenings, then slid out of the voluminous layers of fabric and tossed them aside. In just her thin cotton chemise and pantalets now, she fought the urge to hug her arms around herself.

"Look at you, Serry," Rafe said softly, fitting his big hands to her rib cage, thumbs snug just beneath her breasts. "You're just a little bit of a thing without all those ruffles and pleats." He dipped his head, and as his lips warmed the hollow of her neck, his hands moved slowly to take the weight of both breasts in his open palms. "Ah, Serry, you fill my hands, darlin', the way you fill my heart."

Her eyes drifted closed then and Serena gave herself up to stunning sensations she had never known before—the warmth of a mouth that whispered as it kissed, the sheer heat of two slow hands that lit up her skin everywhere they touched, the sweet ache deep inside her.

She moaned his name with what little breath he left her. "Sugarman."

His response came coupled with a kiss, a deep drink of her that sapped her at the same time it set her on fire. She didn't even know then how those hands managed to ease away her remaining clothes, and she had no awareness of Rafe taking off his own. The kiss that consumed her was never broken until he lifted his head.

"Serena, open your eyes."

She did. To a pair of glittering, whiskey-colored eyes that intoxicated her while they seemed to absorb her very soul. To a face that no longer showed the soft edges of restraint, but was all hard planes and sharp angles now.

Those amber eyes closed a moment, calling to mind a great, sleek cat. And his voice was a deep-throated purr. "It's time, Serry. Take me in your hand, darlin'. Guide me. Now. Please."

The feel of her warm fingers closing around him sent a bolt of white-hot lightning through Rafe. He sucked in his breath, willing everything in himself to hush, to hover, to hold tight as she touched him. Tenderly. Ah, wonderful.

And as she guided him, he felt guiltily glad that he wasn't her first, that he wouldn't give her pain but only pleasure. Glad, too, that she wasn't a delicate wisp of a woman, but sturdy and strong and able to take him, all of him, deep inside.

"Now, Serry. Take me," he groaned.

Her long legs slid around him, smooth as water, as she lifted her hips. Her hand slipped away and then he was sinking like a man drowning in a hot ocean, rising and falling on the crests of rough, relentless waves.

Serena was all liquid heat beneath him, singing his name like a flame-haired siren, then shuddering as she clenched him to her and drew him deeper still as the hot tide of his release ripped through him.

They lay for a long time then, coupled, drenched, silent except for their tattered breathing, seeking one another's eyes in the failing light, and smiling.

## Chapter Fifteen

Bacon! In her dream the fragrance was so powerful, so real it was nearly visible, scrolling from the kitchen in fancy curlicues and wavy ribbons that twined around her and tickled her nose and stomach. Aunt Pete had left the kitchen door open on purpose, Serena supposed, in order to tempt her awake. She snuggled deeper into the blanket, poised between sleep and wakefulness, between fanciful curls of bacon and the memory of deft hands, a delving tongue, a... Oh, Lord!

Her eyes flew open. It hadn't been a dream. None of it. Not the bacon, and definitely not the man who was squatting by the fireplace now muttering low little oaths as he attempted to turn the splattering, sizzling pieces of meat. His back was to her, allowing her a leisurely perusal of his wide shoulders, his narrow hips, and the angry stripes in between. There were probably a few more of those than there had been originally, she thought, thanks to her roving fingernails.

The mere thought of her actions the night before sent a rush of warm desire through her. Serena closed her eyes and hugged the blanket more closely, unwilling now to get up, to leave the warm nest where she'd spent the night in Rafe Sugarman's arms—although not sleeping much. She bit down on a yawn, then gingerly stretched her aching muscles. Her calves hurt, and her thighs. It seemed as if even the soles of her feet were protesting. For a minute she wasn't even sure if she would be able to walk, but the thought didn't bother her much. In fact, she decided she wouldn't mind one little bit if she were stuck right here in this dingy cabin with its hard floor and papered windows as long as Rafe was here.

She rolled onto her side now, one arm cocked under her head, watching the muscles shift beneath the scars on his back, loving the way the firelight wove through his dark, curly hair, aching for him all over again.

"Marry me, Sugarman." The husky tone of her voice surprised her as much as the words themselves. She'd meant to say good-morning, only it came out otherwise.

He shifted on his haunches, slanting her a warm grin. "I thought we'd already settled that, Serry."

Languidly now, in the sunshine of his smile, Serena stretched. "Did we?"

"If I'm not mistaken, I believe I asked you to marry me last night."

"Did you?" She took the stretch to its limits, then drew back her arms. "And did I answer?"

"Uh-huh."

"Did I say yes?"

Rafe chuckled. "Sort of. You said you'd accept as long as I kept doing what I was doing when I—"

"I remember," she said quickly, cutting off his description of one of the previous night's more ardent moments. "Shame on you, Rafe Sugarman. There are some things for telling and other things just for the doing." Her cheeks were flaming now as she finally met his impudent gaze and his infectious grin. Serena couldn't keep her own lips from tipping up in response.

"Lord, it's hot in here all of a sudden." She lifted an edge of the blanket to fan herself. "Well?"

Rafe arched an eyebrow. "Well what?"

"Did I ever give you an answer?"

He stood, lazily unbuttoning his trousers. "You know, Serry, I don't rightly recall," he drawled. "I guess I better ask you again."

She wanted to turn away. At the very least, decency dictated that she close her eyes. But, holy hellfire, watching that man shuck off one leg and then the other of his pants was pure magic. Serena felt like a kitten having its belly rubbed. And he wasn't even touching her. Yet.

Rafe slid beneath the blanket, gathering her into his arms and claiming her mouth all in the same smooth motion. When she purred, he lifted his head to kiss her nose and whisper, "This'll have to be quick, darlin', or my bacon's going to burn."

Serena offered him a smile she had never used before in her life, a smile that seemed to begin at the tips of her toes and gather warmth as it traveled upward to her lips. She fit her hips to his. "I certainly hope so, Sugarman."

Later—a good while later—after the cabin filled with acrid smoke, Rafe stabbed his legs into his pants, grabbed the red-hot skillet with his shirt, and rushed it outside where he dropped it onto the porch boards.

"God bless it!" He shook his hand, then clamped it under his arm as he glared at the scorched bacon.

Serena, in just her underclothes, sidled up behind him, slipping her arms around his waist and pressing her cheek to the sleek spot between his shoulder blades. "I don't care if I ever eat again," she said with a sigh.

She felt his rib cage expand as he drew in a beleaguered breath.

His sigh was more aggravated than winsome. "Hell, honey, if this keeps up, we'll both be skin and bones."

"I love your skin." Her fingers fanned open on his hard, corrugated abdomen. "And your bones." Her tongue gently teased his raw shoulder blade.

Another sigh escaped him, this one weaker than before. "Still," he murmured, "it'd be nice to keep a little muscle in between."

"Hmm." Serena smoothed her hands across the hard curve of his chest, pressing herself even closer against his back, wishing she could simply move into him, her own flesh melding totally with his. Never before in her life had she felt so complete, so fulfilled. Or so playful. The fact that the act of love was actually fun was a stunning revelation. "Flapjacks," she whispered sensuously.

"Oh, yeah," he groaned.

"Swimming in maple syrup."

Rafe's stomach rumbled beneath the spread of her hand.

"Big flaky biscuits covered with gravy."

He made a sound now strangely akin to a whimper.

"Steaming grits with—"

He turned, planting his mouth solidly over hers, stifling her speech. It was, after all, just what she craved. Then, in spite of the way her heart was pounding and her knees were liquefying, Serena's stomach growled loudly.

Rafe lifted his head. A smirk grazed his lips. "Pardon me?"

Exasperated, she pushed out of his embrace. "Well, all right. I'll admit it. I am just a little bit hungry."

He pulled her back against his chest, then rested his chin on her head. "We both have big appetites, Serry. For everything." Rafe chuckled softly now. "But, I'm telling you, darlin', if we don't get something to eat we're going to wind up as the skinniest couple in Quinn County."

"I wouldn't mind," she murmured.

"I would." He grasped her backside with both hands. "I'm growing kind of partial to these curves."

Serena wriggled against him. "We fit so well, Rafe. Like we were made for each other."

"I expect we were, Serry."

"I wish..." Her voice trailed off, just a breath against his skin.

"What, honey?"

Her arms tightened around him. "I wish it had been you seven years ago. I hope those damn Yankees are burning in hellfire now for stealing what should have been yours."

"Shh. It's me now, darlin'. The past doesn't count—for either one of us." He stroked her hair. "Let's just look forward, Serry. Let's not let all those hurts and sorrows get in the way of our blessings."

"Blessings," she echoed. It was true. She did feel blessed and so full of love she could barely breathe now. The present was absolute bliss, and the future promised more. The future that she had dreaded only a few scant weeks ago now stretched out before her like a glorious road. A road unfurling through Quinn County like a victorious banner.

Her father, she thought, would be nearly as happy as she was. It occurred to her then that he was probably already happy—licking his chops, no doubt—after getting the news yesterday from Little Joab that she would be spending the night out here. Well, fine. She didn't begrudge him. Now that she had found her man and her future, Serena thought she'd be only too happy to comply with her father's demands for grandchildren.

"I have an idea," she said, fingers straying into Rafe's dark, curly locks.

Rafe uttered a small groan. "Honey, I can't keep doing this without at least a little fuel in my belly."

"That's my idea. Food. Food and blessings. Not necessarily in that order."

"I'm all ears, darlin'. Especially about the food part."

She stepped back, raising her eyes to his. "Did you mean it, Rafe? About marriage? That wasn't just some kind of fancy love talk men use when they're..."

His big hands cradled her face. "I meant it. Every word of it. If you want, Serry, I'll go down on my knees right here, right this minute."

Rafe's expression was so earnest, Serena couldn't help but smile. "That isn't necessary." Then she laughed. "Anyway, as I recall, you were somewhat on your knees when you asked last night. Not to mention your elbows."

He grinned. "As good a stance as any for a proposal, I reckon. And it earned me a pretty resounding yes, if you'll recall."

"Well, I'm not the only one you have to ask, Rafe Sugarman. Just in case you've forgotten, I do have a daddy. It's customary and quite proper to seek a father's blessings and to ask for a young lady's hand." With a wicked grin, she added, "Along with whatever parts you might not want to mention."

Serena had expected him to laugh, but he didn't. His face, in fact, darkened perceptibly. Was he that nervous, she wondered, about confronting her father? Probably, she decided. For a moment she was tempted to put his worries to rest. After all, her father's blessings had been simmering for years, and they'd plain boil over with joy when the word *marriage* passed from Rafe's lips to Con Quinn's eager ears.

On second thought, though, she rather enjoyed the idea of his nervousness. It was good for a man, even a giant, to shake in his boots every now and then. And since she doubted she'd witness too much of that emotion in the future, Serena decided to just let him shake.

"Blessings," Rafe muttered to himself, planting one boot on the Quinn walk, the other boot still on the dusty road as he turned to look at Serena. Serena dawdling. Serena stopping every quarter mile to pick feverfew and chicory to add to her growing bouquet. Serena, red head over pretty heels in love with a lying, conniving Yankee, on her way to gather her father's blessings, which Rafe had already received—in spades.

He dragged in a deep breath. Nearly summer now, the noon air was warm and rich and tinged with the fragrance of every growing thing. Down the walkway, the big house was keeping cool in the mossy shadows of live oaks. Quinn County felt solid, like the entire earth under his boots. This was all he'd ever wanted, all he'd ever dreamed of possessing. And it was more than he ever believed he could lose.

But it was the thought of losing Serena that gnawed at his gut now. Ever since she'd mentioned asking her father for her hand, Rafe could hardly look her in the eye for fear she'd sense the deal he had made with

Con, for fear she'd read it on his face like the devil's own mark.

His concerns about his Yankee past had so overshadowed the agreement that he really hadn't given it a lot of thought. What difference did it make? he'd said to himself. He loved her, deal or no deal. And whether she came naked or wrapped in Quinn County acreage no longer mattered a damn.

But this morning, when he had seen the proud glitter in her eyes, the diamond light that fairly shouted, "Somebody loves *me*. This man wants *me* to be his wife," guilt had swept over him, black as a crow's wing. It had cast a shadow across his heart, and now it was pecking away at his soul.

God Almighty! How they were cheating her—her father and her future husband—of all that was sweet and sacred about love. Nothing was worth that. Not a thousand acres. Not every inch of Quinn County. Nothing on earth was worth the shine he'd witnessed in Serena's eyes.

The shine he was looking at now as she strode to his side, her arms full of flowers, her eyes replete with a joyous light that pierced his heart. Hadn't he loved her before? Rafe wondered suddenly. Had it been just some combination of old dreams and a startling new passion that had moved him until this very moment? What moved him now—with the force of an earthquake—was love.

His knees nearly buckled. That was all right, he thought, because he was about to go down on them anyway and beg her to share his life, to give him even a fraction of the love he felt for her right then. Most of all, to forgive him for raping her innocent heart just as the men in blue before him had raped her innocent body.

Serena hooked her arm through his just then, keeping him upright, as she pointed her chin in the direction of the big house where Con Quinn's bulky form had appeared on the veranda. Her voice was rich with amusement as she announced, "There's the man with the pocketful of blessings now."

Strolling down the brick walk, her arm linked through Rafe's, Serena took pure delight in her father's expression as they approached the veranda. The nearer they got, the higher Con Quinn's eyebrows crept up his forehead and the harder his teeth clamped on his cigar. By the time they reached him, she was surprised he hadn't bitten the fat stogie right in two.

He plucked it from his mouth now. "Good morning, Sister. Or maybe I should say good afternoon."

Serena swung her skirts up the steps and kissed him solidly on the cheek. "Good afternoon, Daddy." She cast a quick glance back at Rafe who had remained at the bottom of the steps. Big as he was, he reminded her now of a scared little boy the way he stood staring at the tips of his boots, working his lower lip with his teeth. Perhaps, she thought, she could ease the way for him just a bit.

"Daddy, Mr. Sugarman has come to ask for my hand in marriage."

"Well, now." Con Quinn's dark eyes rested on Serena a moment, then swung to Rafe. "Well, now. I suspect I should tell Uncle Peter to put that old shotgun of mine back in the rack." He settled his cigar in the corner of his mouth as he bellowed over his shoulder. "Uncle Peter."

The moment was uncomfortable, but Serena decided to hold her tongue. A father, after all, had a right to defend his daughter's reputation. Judging from his stony expression and his silence, Rafe, too, seemed to believe he deserved the patriarchal rebuke.

She was relieved, though, when Uncle Peter appeared to break the silence.

"Did you call me, Mr. Con?"

"I surely did, Uncle Peter. We got any champagne left over from the big shindig last month?"

The old man glanced up at the sun. His brow wrinkled. "Ain't much past noon," he murmured.

The remark earned him a scowl from his employer. "I don't do my drinking by the clock, Uncle Peter, much as you'd like me to." His fierce look softened as he gestured toward Serena. "I'm celebrating. My little girl is getting married. Now go on. You bring back a bottle and three glasses. No. Four glasses. Where's Esme?"

"She's not here, Mr. Con."

"Well, hell. You get Aunt Pete then and a whole tray of my fine crystal. We're going to toast these young people in style. Bring me a couple more of these, too." Con waved his cigar in the air.

While her father was giving the servant more and more elaborate instructions, Serena turned toward Rafe, who continued to study the tips of his boots.

"You're being awfully quiet," she said softly.

He raised his eyes to hers. There was just the slightest glint of humor in them, like matchlight reflected in bourbon. "Seems like your daddy's making enough noise for all of us."

"He does go on, doesn't he?" Serena laughed. But when Rafe persisted in looking downcast, she tried to reassure him. "He didn't mean that. About the shotgun."

His hard mouth offered up the ghost of a grin, but the whimsy was gone from his eyes. He appeared more sober than Serena had ever seen him. Sober and regretful. The look unsettled her. He wasn't already getting cold feet, was he? Maybe the prospect of having Con Quinn for a father-in-law was suddenly dawning on him.

Serena shot her father a harsh look, hoping to deflate his ebullience, but he ignored it as he draped his arm around her shoulders and tugged her to his side.

"This is a happy day, daughter. A fine day for me. For all of Quinn County." He hugged her even tighter, crushing both Serena and her bouquet. "I've got a future now."

"I'm glad you're happy, Daddy. You might want to consider somebody else's happiness, though." She nodded toward Rafe. "All I've heard you say so far to my intended is that you're glad you don't have to use your shotgun on him. Don't you think a few kind words of congratulations might be in order?"

Con snorted. He swung his gaze to Rafe. "I plan on giving your intended more than just a few kind words,

Serena. What do you say, Sugarman? After we've had our champagne, why don't you accompany me to the bank and we'll draw up that little agreement you and I discussed?"

Rafe started to speak, but Serena cut him off. "What little agreement?"

"Well, now, Sister, let's just call it your dowry. 'Course, your wedding is merely the preamble. It's those babies that'll make everybody happy." Con aimed a slow, knowing wink at Rafe before he crooned. "And rich."

Serena's face went chalk white. Even the blue of her eyes seemed to fade until the color matched the chicory blooms in her bouquet. Rafe watched her while he smothered the oath that rose in his throat.

He'd intended to take Con aside as soon as he could to make it clear that he wasn't interested in his proposition anymore, to let the old man know in no uncertain terms that it was Serena he wanted and nothing else. It had never occurred to Rafe that Con would mention the bargain, much less crow about it in Serena's presence. That announcement had stunned him as completely as if it had been a wooden club connecting with his skull. Except for the rough curse he'd stifled, he stood there—blank, stupefied and mute.

If he could have gotten a word out, he would have lied through his teeth and denied he'd ever even spoken with Con about the matter. If he could have, he would have tried to save his own skin. But it wasn't his own skin that was troubling him now; it was Serena's—so pale, her rosy flush of only moments ago now withered away. Sweet Lord, he could practically hear her pride cracking down the middle. He knew for sure he was hearing her heart break. He could feel it in his own.

The bouquet fell from her hand then, and that empty hand groped for the edge of a shawl that wasn't there. She stood there utterly defenseless. Undone. Drowning. Rafe had never wanted to protect her more, had never felt less qualified to do it, since he was the source of all that pain.

"Sorry." His voice was a rough whisper.

She met his gaze then with ice blue eyes. Just ice. The flame in their depths had disappeared. Even so, she managed to sear him.

She broke from her father's hold on her then, and advanced on Rafe, her fists balled and her lips tight and white. Thinking she was going to strike him, he stood fast, ready to take the deserved blow. When she struck, though, it wasn't with her fist but with her voice.

"Swine," she hissed, her breath hot, close to his ear where only Rafe could hear. "You're worse than a Yankee, damn you. At least they were honest when they used me."

He took that, as he had intended to take the flat of her hand across his cheek. And then he couldn't speak, couldn't find words to tell her she was wrong because the terrible truth was that she was right.

After she had fled into the house, Rafe still stood there.

Con Quinn took a long, thoughtful pull on his cigar, then exhaled a hard stream of smoke, aiming it directly at Rafe's downcast face. "Hell and damnation, boy," he muttered. "All I asked was for you to marry her. I never said you had to fall in love with her, did I?"

## Chapter Sixteen

Serena sank deeper into the porcelain tub. The water was tepid now, despite her boiling anger, and her fingertips were wrinkled as currants. Her toes would have been, too, but they'd spent the better part of the past two hours hanging over the end of the too-short tub.

"I hear you two whispering out there like a couple of thieves." She glared at the door. "Esme? Aunt Pete? I know you're there because I can hear you breathing."

Earlier it had been her father, breathing fire and blowing smoke through the keyhole, then banging on the door with both fists and at least one foot. Serena had nearly blistered the paint on her side of the door telling him exactly what she thought of his scheming and conniving. At last she heard the tromp of his footsteps going down the stairs and felt the reverberations of the front door as he slammed it on his way out.

Now it was her sister-in-law and Aunt Pete who were tormenting her while she was scrubbing once more in an attempt to wash away every last trace of that other conniver.

"Go away," Serena yelled.

"I most certainly will not, Serena Quinn," Esme called back. "If you won't come out to listen to reason, then I'd like to remind you that you're not the only one residing in this house. Other people need to bathe. Myself in particular after working all morning in the mercantile. I'm perspiring, Serena. Now you get yourself out of there right this minute and give me a chance to wash up. I'm promenading with Arlen Sears this evening and I intend to do it clean."

"Oh, all right," Serena growled. Lord, she'd never heard her delicate sister-in-law admit to breathing much less sweating.

"That's better," the little blonde said when a dripping, towel-wrapped Serena opened the door.

Leaning out to peer down the hallway, Serena asked suspiciously. "Where is everybody?" She had half expected to see her father standing there with a gun and a hank of rope, not to mention a preacher.

"Well, let's see," Esme said. "Daddy Quinn's down at the bank in a snit as big as Mississippi. And the last time I saw Mr. Sugarman he had a jug of liquor tucked under his arm and he was stomping out toward Chickapee Bend." Esme smiled sweetly. "How are you, Sister?"

"I gather you know what took place here earlier." Serena pushed past Esme, tugging her towel around her as she strode down the hall. "Daddy sold me like a damn brood mare," she shouted over her shoulder, then cursed as her feet tangled in the bath sheet and she stumbled into her room.

Esme stood in the doorway, smoothing out her skirts. "You're being too hard on Daddy Quinn. He only wants what's best for you."

"Best for me!" Serena howled, shaking her fists at the ceiling while the towel plopped around her bare feet.

In the doorway, Esme let out a little gasp and quickly averted her eyes. "Sister, really!"

"Oh, hush, Esme. I'm too damn mad to be modest." Naked, Serena stomped to the dresser where she pulled a pair of cotton pantalets from a drawer and snapped them smartly before stabbing her legs in. "Anyway, who cares if a brood mare walks around stark naked? As far as Daddy and Rafe Sugarman are concerned, I'm only good for one thing, and that one thing doesn't require clothes."

She dragged a camisole over her damp head. "There. I'm decent now. You don't have to keep blushing and staring at your damn feet." Turning toward the mirror then, Serena attacked her hair with a brush.

Esme stepped into the room and perched on a corner of Serena's bed. "You're acting like a hotheaded fool, Serena," she said quietly.

"Thank you very much, Esme." The brush snapped through Serena's tangled tresses. "I appreciate your concern. I'll be equally sympathetic when Daddy makes *you* the centerpiece of a business deal."

"He already did," Esme retorted.

The hairbrush held still. Serena sought her sister-in-law's green eyes in the mirror. Their characteristic sparkle was absent. Esme's hand flitted to her mouth as if trying to retrieve her words.

"What?" Serena demanded, her curiosity piqued now. "What did Daddy do? You can tell me. Nothing that man's ever done could possibly surprise me."

Esme clasped her fingers together now and let them fall onto her lap. "Life's full of surprises, Sister. Surely you've learned that by now."

"Well, go ahead," Serena challenged. "Surprise me."

"All right. Maybe a good shock would help to cool that hot head of yours. I swear I'm at a loss trying to talk any sense into you." Esme smoothed her skirt over her knees. "I *was* the centerpiece of one of Daddy Quinn's deals. To put it bluntly, he bought me. For Con, Jr."

Serena sniffed and went back to brushing her hair. "I think all that perspiring in the mercantile affected your brain, Esme." But her tone lacked conviction as she continued to stare at Esme's strange expression. "What are you saying?"

"I'm saying—and this is for your ears only, Sister, and only because it might make you see things differently—that your brother didn't marry a New Orleans belle like everybody was told."

"Ha! That bayou simper of yours didn't come from anywhere else," Serena retorted.

"Oh, I'm from New Orleans, all right, but Con, Jr., didn't fall head over heels in love with me at any cotillion. It was in a sporting house." Esme paused, narrowing her eyes as if to gauge Serena's reaction. She sighed then. "Lord, honey, I'm not even sure you know what a sporting house is."

"I know," Serena insisted, "but I don't for a minute believe—"

"Believe it." Esme's voice was harsher now, all traces of her simper gone. "Believe it, Serena."

The sharp tone, so unlike Esme, convinced her, and Serena turned to face her sister-in-law. "Esme," she breathed, unable to think of anything else to say, unable to get enough air even if she had known what to say.

"Have I surprised you?"

Still mute, Serena nodded.

"Good," Esme said with a twitch of her shoulders. "Now maybe you'll listen to me."

"Tell me about...about New Orleans," Serena said. "How did you...?"

"Become a soiled dove?" Esme finished for her. "I was a poor dove. A very hungry dove, too. It was either that or starve, Serena. My heart was never in it." She laughed softly. "Only my stomach. Anyway, Con, Jr., wanted to just run off with me, and I was too scared. I thought they'd kill us both. Not that I minded so much about myself. Con, Jr., telegraphed your father, and, bless his conniving heart, he came down to New Orleans the very next day. That man looked me over like a side of beef. Then he asked me one question. Just one simple question. Did I love his son?"

Esme smiled wistfully now, tears shimmering in her green eyes as she continued. "I drew myself up proud-like, all five feet and ninety pounds, and I replied, 'Yessir. I love your son so much that I'm begging you to take him back to that precious county of yours and keep him there until he forgets he ever met me.''

Serena, having recovered her breath now, asked, "And what did Daddy say?"

"He smiled that big old hammy smile of his." Esme tilted her head. "You know, the one where he's hatching a plan in the back of his head while he's conversing about something else altogether?"

Serena nodded. She knew it well. Only too well.

"He smiled that particular smile, and then he said, 'Miss Esme, I like your style.' And the next thing I knew he had bought out my contract at gunpoint and had whisked me back here."

Serena continued for her as she recalled that day when Esme had arrived, a blushing young blonde on the arm of Con, Jr. "And told everybody you were from the richest, most well-respected family in Louisiana."

"And told *me* I'd best behave as if I were," Esme added. Her moist eyes locked on Serena's then. "I did, too, didn't I, Sister? All these years."

"Yes, you did," she whispered as she sat beside Esme and put a gentle arm around her fragile shoulders. "I wish Con hadn't been killed, Esme. I know how much you loved him. I know that even better now."

Esme sniffed and blotted her eyes with the hem of her skirt. "I still love him. And I'm still here. You know, after all these years of acting like a virtuous lady, I almost believe I've earned the right to be one. Well, anyway..." She rose from the bed and stood looking down at Serena. "I suppose I've given you one of the biggest shocks of your young life. I hope you don't hate me, Serena. Or think too ill of me."

And now Serena surprised herself as she said and truly meant, "Actually, Esme, I like you better now that I know there's a little substance under all that pretty wrapping."

The little woman let out an audible sigh of relief. "Listen to me going on about myself when I meant to go on about you."

"There's nothing to say," Serena said adamantly, letting her simmering anger come to a boil once more.

"Well, let's just chat about that big, handsome man of yours."

She crossed her arms. "I won't discuss that lying, grasping, greedy son of a—"

Esme's bright laughter cut her off. "All right, Sister. Don't let's forget how virtuous my ears have become. Just tell me one thing. Do you love the son of a bitch?"

"I hate him," Serena flung back as her eyes filled with hot tears.

"And with a passion, that's for sure." Now it was Esme who was easing a comforting arm around Serena's shoulders. "It's all right, honey," she murmured as those shoulders began to shake.

"I thought he loved me, Esme. I believed it with all my heart. And now I know it wasn't me at all." She dragged in a wet gulp of air. "It wasn't me he wanted. It was just the money or the land or whatever Daddy went and promised him. Rafe was only using me."

Esme touched her forehead to Serena's, speaking softly. "Did he use you gently, Sister?"

"Yes," Serena sobbed.

"And do you still want him to touch you that way? To be with you that way?"

"No." The anguished denial tore from her throat. She leaned harder against Esme's shoulder.

"Listen to me, Serena Quinn. There's nothing wrong with loving a man that way. From what I've seen, Rafe Sugarman can hardly draw a decent breath when he's around you. If ever a man was in love, I'd say it's him."

"In love with Quinn County," Serena sobbed.

Esme took Serena's chin in her hand. "Look at me. And you listen. You've never been poor, Serena. You don't know what it is to want. I suspect Rafe's been wanting his whole life. Your daddy understands that, and it's one of the ways he controls people. One of the ways he bends them to his will. I'm not saying it's right or wrong. It's just a fact."

"It's an awful fact." Serena sniffed.

"Maybe so. But what would you have had Rafe do when your daddy smiled that snake-in-the-garden smile at him and made him all those promises? Should he have said, 'No, thank you, Con. You keep all that land and all that money. I'd just as soon take your daughter and share my hardscrabble existence with her.' Would that have made you believe he loved you, Serena?''

"Maybe."

"I doubt it very much," Esme snapped. "I sincerely do." She stood then. "You think on it awhile, Sister. Daddy Quinn's set on your marrying and giving him grandchildren." Her voice dropped ominously. "He'll have his way, one way or the other. You can count on that. And if it's not The Sugarman, Serena, it'll be some other man. Is that what you really want?"

"I don't know what I want anymore," Serena wailed. "I'm just all muddled and confused."

"Well, you best get unmuddled, honey, and quick." Esme walked to the door, then paused with her hand on the knob. "I'm going to take my bath now. I might just have a good cry myself after all this confessing and remembering. Then maybe I'll be all cried out by the time Arlen comes calling on me."

Esme's tone was so forlorn, it made Serena forget her own problems for a moment. "You don't really care for him, do you, Esme? For that awful..."

The blonde stiffened her shoulders. "My socializing pleases Daddy Quinn. I owe him, Sister. I owe him so much."

"But not Arlen Sears, Esme," Serena countered. "He's—"

"He's as good as anybody else for settling my debts. You worry about yourself, Serena. Lord knows you've got plenty to worry about. After last night, it might already be too late.''

Serena's wet eyes widened. "What do you mean?" she asked in a hushed voice, knowing all too well what Esme meant, but willing, even longing to deny it.

"I mean that Daddy Quinn's dearest wish might already have been granted." Her gaze lowered to Serena's belly. "You worry about that, Sister, if you haven't already."

There hadn't been time to worry. Between loving Rafe and hating him, between desire and fury, there hadn't been a minute to contemplate the consequences of anything. But after Esme's stern counsel, Serena spent the long afternoon lying on her back in the middle of her big four-poster bed—deathly still, her eyes closed, her hands fisted at her sides. If she resembled anything, it was an angry corpse.

After a while, however, she found it all but impossible to feel mad and dead at the same time.

Slowly, Serena opened her eyes. Even more slowly, she relaxed her clenched hands. Then, ever so gradually, tentatively, she moved those hands until they came to rest over the slight swell of her abdomen.

"Dear God," she whispered as her worry turned to wonderment. It was possible. A life taking hold inside her. A bloom. A future stretching far beyond hers. Suddenly, she not only understood her father's insatiable hunger for heirs, but she shared it.

"Rafe." Her trembling lips shaped his name.

Serena struggled with her pride then, weighing love against loss. To marry Rafe now would cost her a good chunk of that pride. But not to marry him. That would cost her heart and the better part of her soul.

What Esme had said had been right. *If it's not the Sugarman, it'll be some other man.* And she'd been right also that life was full of surprises, not the least of which was that, in spite of the fact that Rafe Sugarman loved Quinn County more than he loved her, Serena believed she could live with that. For a while, anyway.

There were worse things to covet than the green, rolling countryside of Quinn County. Let him marry her out of greed. She'd marry for love and let the future take care of itself. That future—she splayed her hand over her stomach—her future and Rafe's might already be here.

Serena sat up. If her future had already arrived, she wasn't doing much about it by lying like a corpse in her bed, was she?

Ten minutes later she was dressed and trotting down the stairs, her shawl billowing like a paisley sail.

"Whoa, Sister. Where are you off to like a hound in a lather?"

"You're just the man I was looking for," she said to her father as she strode into the parlor where he was ensconced in his reading chair, his dark eyes quizzing her over the rim of the afternoon paper.

"Well, you found me," he replied, folding his paper with deliberation.

Serena planted her hands on her hips. "Tell me about the deal you made with Mr. Sugarman, Daddy. I believe I have a right to know just what I'm worth."

"Oh, now, honey, don't go getting all—"

"Don't you 'honey' me, Con Quinn. You tell me. You tell me now. What did you promise him?"

He scowled, pressing his lips together.

"I'd rather hear it from you than him. And I *will* hear it," Serena threatened. "What did you promise him?"

Con let out a long, raspy sigh. "A certain amount of acreage per child."

"How much?"

"Now look here, Sister—"

"How much, Daddy?"

He sighed again. "One thousand acres."

Serena crossed her arms. "That's not nearly enough," she said, then watched her father's eyes snap to sudden attention. She smiled inwardly as she continued. "For starters, Daddy, you'll build us a house with a carriage house big enough for Hester and Big Joab and their children. They'll be working for us in the future." Serena glanced out the front window. "I want the house close enough so Little Joab and baby Flora can just skip over and visit Aunt Pete if they've a mind to. That pretty little oak grove up on Crescent Hill will probably do fine."

"I suppose I could do that," he said, eyeing her keenly.

"Also, I want you to give Rafe a thousand acres immediately. Whether or not there's a child. He ought to have something of his own."

"All right." Con crooked an eyebrow. "Anything else?"

Serena wrinkled her brow. Now that she had him, she thought, was there anything else she wanted to wring out of the old conniver? There wasn't a thing in the world she wanted for herself—except Rafe Sugarman.

"I'll think on it, Daddy," she said finally. "Of course, I'll expect you to honor your agreement with my husband by signing over acreage when our babies come along. I'll bid you good-afternoon now. I have some business out at Chickapee Bend." Serena turned and strode toward the front door, sensing that her father was smiling behind her back. Well, as much as any man could who'd just been picked clean in his very own front parlor.

Arlen Sears rose lazily from his chair when Serena walked out onto the veranda. Lazily enough, she thought, so that his rising implied a deliberate rudeness rather than courtesy.

"Afternoon, Miz Serena. It's a little late for you to be going back to the store, isn't it?"

"I'm not going back to the store, Arlen," she replied stiffly. "Not that it's any of your business. You're waiting on Esme, I gather."

A leer cut across his mouth. "Not that it's any of *your* business, Miz Serena."

His arrogant gaze made her want to pull her shawl tightly around herself. Surely, she thought, Esme could find somebody else to spend time with in order to settle whatever debts she felt she owed Con.

"Just see that you treat my sister-in-law like the lady she is, Arlen. There'll be the devil to pay if you don't."

He laughed. "The devil or your daddy?"

"Both of them," Serena snapped as she yanked at her shawl and stepped off the veranda. "And me, too," she called back over her shoulder.

## Chapter Seventeen

On the hill behind his cabin, Rafe hooked his thumb through the jug handle, then hefted it on his forearm to take another long pull. For all the good it did, he thought. He'd put away at least half the crock of corn liquor and he was still sober as a judge's old maid aunt.

What he wanted to do was get so falling-down drunk he wouldn't be able to stumble or even crawl back to town. To Serena.

"Leave her be," Con Quinn had said this afternoon when Rafe had gathered his wits enough to start after her into the house. "Leave her be. I know my daughter, Sugarman. She's going to spend the afternoon in a steaming tub, soaking her pride and softening up that rigid spine of hers and repairing the damage our gentlemen's agreement did to her dignity."

Rafe had pointed out with a few well-chosen words that neither one of them was a gentleman, and he had gone on to tell Con Quinn precisely where he could shove his agreement.

But the old man just smiled. "She'll come around by sunset, boy. You mark my words. A little frayed dignity never kept a Quinn from getting what he wanted. And my daughter wants you."

It wasn't much consolation, Rafe thought now, lifting the jug again. It didn't make him feel a whole lot better to know that Serena would be coming back for more—more secrets and more sorrow and maybe more hurt than her dignity could bear.

He should have come straight back to the cabin, yanked his suitcase out of the cupboard, and taken off. Should have gotten the hell out of Quinn County and Mississippi while he still had a few shreds of his soul left. Only here he was, tipping a jug, trying to knock his legs out from under him so he couldn't move at all.

The slant of the sun setting brought to mind a similar evening five years ago near Fredericksburg, Virginia. Seemed as if the sun had been hanging over the horizon forever, fighting to stay alive the way it was right now. He and General Grant had been sitting on a hilltop, just the two of them, sharing a bottle, staring at the day's losing battle against the night.

"It's winding down, Sugarman. Everybody's holding back now. Nobody wants to be the last soldier to die in this war. Everybody but you. You're about the only warrior I've got left. A goddamn hero." Grant had slapped him on the back and they both had coughed when the dust rose from Rafe's blue jacket.

"No, sir. Just dirty and tired. I only keep fighting hard so I can go home." Rafe had laughed then. "Right now all I am is drunk."

"And stupid," Grant had grumbled, "thinking you'll be doing anything but looking over your shoulder the rest of your life, answering for your whereabouts during the rebellion. Lying and hating yourself for it, or telling the truth and getting hanged for your honesty. That doesn't strike you as stupid?"

"Maybe so. This whole war is beginning to strike me as pretty stupid, General, if you want the unvarnished truth. I'll be glad to get back to Mississippi and whatever's waiting for me there."

"I'll tell you what's waiting. Damnation, that's what." Grant had passed the bottle and its dwindling contents to Rafe again. "Damnation and more damnation. Sheer Southern hellfire. You won't find a woman to love you or a man to shake your hand. You remember I said that, Sugarman. Then you come looking for me when you've had your fill. My offer stands, son."

Rafe raised the jug of corn liquor again as he watched the angry red sun surrender to the horizon. The breeze kicked up then and riffled the young leaves in his orchard. It wasn't as if he didn't have a choice, he reminded himself. He could light out tonight and be in Washington by day after tomorrow.

Hell, he could walk up to the front door of the confounded White House and get a hero's welcome from President Grant instead of skulking around Mississippi where they kept greeting him with hot tar and whips. Yet, here he sat on a hill with a couple dozen saplings, wishing he could be like one of his trees—just stand in one spot with roots pushing from the soles of his feet and the rest of him sprouting bark and leaves.

Choices, he thought dismally. He'd always had them, and it seemed now as if he'd always chosen, if not wrong, then badly. Fate would put him at a crossroads and he'd go left instead of right, down the hard road instead of the wide, easy path. He'd gone north rather than south. Then he'd come back home when he should have followed General Grant to the capital and glory. And he'd stayed in Mississippi when he should have packed up years ago and bid the whole damn state a fond, dry-eyed farewell.

Loving Serena wasn't a choice, exactly. It felt more like a destiny. But marrying her... now there he still had some say. And if his choices up till now had all been bad and hurtful ones, then maybe it was time to take that other road, to turn left when he wanted to turn right.

It only made sense, he thought, hefting the jug once more. He'd do the opposite of what his heart was telling him, then everything would turn out fine. For Serena, anyway.

Serena slid off the Morgan's back, then rushed up the porch steps and pulled the door open. The tin cans clattered and bumped against the wood. Inside the cabin, however, there was only silence. Silence and an emptiness that made her heart sink.

He couldn't be gone. She refused to believe it. But when she knelt by the fireplace and saw that the ashes were cold, a chill coursed through her. She hugged her shawl tighter. No. No. She wouldn't let him be gone.

Her panicky gaze roamed the dim interior of the cabin and came to rest on the closed cupboard. She sat there a moment, just staring at the pine doors, thinking a gypsy's crystal ball couldn't have held a clearer picture of her future. If Rafe's suitcase was inside, tucked up on the top shelf...

Weak-kneed, Serena stumbled on her hem as she rose. One hand shot out to the mantel for balance while the other clutched at her stomach to still the churning there. Her gaze stayed locked on the cupboard as a wave of nausea swept over her, threatening to drown her, to drag her down. Only that suitcase, like a life raft, could save her, could keep her afloat. But if it wasn't there... God help her, if it wasn't there....

The tin cans jangled on the door and a slice of dusky light widened on the floor until the cabin was all amethyst and amber, and Rafe's long, still shadow reached across the room. He filled the doorway as he filled her heart.

He'd barely had time to comprehend that it was Serena rather than an intruder before she ran into his arms, her own arms stretched out to him and her shawl falling from her shoulders as she moved, falling soundlessly and mindlessly away as she came to him.

Rafe buried his face in the hollow of her neck, breathing in the warm fragrance of her hair and the sweet, clean smell of soap...or spring...or woman. His woman, so solid, so perfect in his embrace, as if his arms had been hewn just to hold her.

"I thought you were gone," she whispered. "I—I think it would have killed me if..."

"Shh. Hush, now." He said it to her as much as to himself, knowing there was a time for words and a time when words were useless, no better than birds with broken wings. Like now. This moment. This perfect moment when every choice he'd ever made became glorious and absolutely right because it had brought him here. To her. Where he had no choice but to stay.

Rafe laid claim to her mouth then with a force he could barely contain, the sweep of his tongue communicating as words never could that he was hers as much as she was his.

Serena surrendered to the kiss, a rich, intoxicating blend of whiskey and wanting. He was here. He was hers. Her weak knees went weaker still but it didn't matter because Rafe's strong arms were around her, holding her.

She dragged her mouth from his, needing to speak the words her heart was pushing into her throat. "Don't ever leave me, Rafe. Don't ever let me go."

"Serry," he groaned, pressing her head to his chest. "Listen to my heart. All it can say anymore is *Serena, Serena.*" The cadence of his deep voice matched the hard surge of the heart beneath her ear. "*Serena, Serena,*" he murmured. "Listen to how much I love you. Feel it."

She could. And she could hear her own heart pounding out his name as if it were scrolled in her blood. "I hear it."

Rafe reached for her hand and pressed it to his chest. "It's yours, Serry. My heart. All of me. This whole sorry life of mine." He tipped her chin up then. His eyes were dark in the faltering daylight, darker still with desire. "There's so much I need to tell you."

But now it was Serena who silenced him with a finger to his lips and with husky whispers. "Just love me now. Teach me more about loving you. Show me how to touch you, where to touch you so you catch fire the way I do." She smiled bewitchingly, then touched her tongue to a corner of his mouth. "Don't talk at all, Rafe. Teach me. Touch me."

Whatever he meant to say, whatever words he'd intended to use, were incinerated the minute her sweet, seeking tongue touched his. She was mistress of the kiss, in command for a moment only—the moment during which his bloodstream ignited like a tangled trail of kerosene—and then the kiss was his. He deepened it, taking command of Serena's mouth, drinking in her moans and letting the taste of her and the subtle textures pervade all his senses.

He undressed her slowly, but only because his fingers trembled from his exertions at control and each sweet bit of skin he uncovered became a tantalizing distraction for his tongue or his fingertips. And finally, when she stood before him clothed only in the fiery shawl of her hair and the last glimmering of daylight, Rafe sank on his knees before her in the pool of cast-off cotton and silk.

"I love you, Serena Quinn." His hands slid up her thighs, splayed to the shape of her hips. "I want to pleasure you. Now. Always." Then his arms encircled her tightly and he whispered into the sweet warmth of her. "Promise, Serry. Promise me."

She threaded her fingers through his dark curls. "Promise you what, my sweet, sweet Sugarman?"

"Don't ever stop loving me. Please. No matter what, Serry. Love me. Please."

"Yes." The word tore from her throat, less answer than a guttural encouragement as his hot mouth moved over her and touched off spark after spark deep inside her.

"Say it," he breathed. "Promise me."

"Yes. Oh, yes. I promise. I love you, Rafe. I always will."

And then she had no breath left for promises or for any kind of speech as the shimmering inside her quickened to an all-consuming fire.


Later—how much later Serena wasn't even sure— they lay on the floor in a tangle of arms and legs, among pants and pantalets and petticoats. Her head was pillowed on Rafe's shoulder. Neither one of them had spoken since the last ragged endearments of their coming together.

"Lassitude," she said with a sigh now. "I'm drenched in lassitude. Is it always like this, Rafe?"

He drew her closer against his side, sliding one hand along her flank then resting it between her thighs. "That's me you're drenched in, darlin'. And, yes, I suspect for you and me it'll always be...well—" he chuckled deep in his throat "—strenuous. We're two big healthy people, Serry, with appetites to match."

"Hmm." Serena moved sinuously against his hand. "Imagine if we had a bed."

Rafe sighed. "Let's just lie here and let our hearts do a little catching up before we go imagining again."

She spread her hand over the hard curve of his chest. "I don't feel your heart pounding out my name anymore."

"That's because it's about as speechless as the rest of me."

"Rafe Sugarman," she chided with a warm thread of humor in her voice, "you're not saying I tired you out, are you? Or wore you down to a nub?" Now Serena's hand slid south, over the washboard ridges of his abdomen, into a thick patch of hair.

"Oh, my," she breathed as her questing fingers encountered his solid length.

"What's that you were saying about a nub?" Rafe levered up on his elbow and at the same time shifted Serena so she was lying beneath him. He whispered as he smoothed her tangled hair back from her face. "I'm going to take good care of you, Serena Quinn. This way. Every way."

"Let's have lots of babies, Rafe." Serena's arms curled around his neck.

"I expect we will," he said as he dropped kisses on her eyelids and cheeks, "considering all the, uh, *imagining* we're bound to be doing."

Serena moved sensuously beneath him. Her fingers combed through his hair. "In a bed," she said with a sigh. "A big, soft bed."

"That'd be nice," he murmured. "I think my knees are smiling with pure gratitude."

"We'll need at least four or five bedrooms to accommodate all those children, I should think." She felt his lips curve upward against her mouth. "What are you grinning at?"

"I'm thinking about all those beds."

Serena laughed. "Do you suppose we'll ever sleep?"

"Is that what you want, Serry?" His tongue traced the outline of her mouth, then dipped teasingly inside. "Do you want sleep?"

Her fingers twisted in his hair now. Her voice was low and husky as she arched against him. "Maybe in twenty or thirty years."

Rafe shifted the arm that was cushioning Serena's head, slowly flexing his hand to get the circulation going again, trying not to wake her as she lay curled against him like a kitten. Her breathing was deep and even, a sweet, soft riffle against his cheek while he lay staring into the darkness. Maybe in twenty or thirty years he'd be able to sleep, he thought. Maybe, once his conscience stopped clawing at his insides and his head stopped buzzing like a persistent swarm of gnats, he'd be able to get some rest. Lord knew he needed it.

He needed to tell Serena everything—not after they were married, but tonight, now. To take her body under false colors wasn't the most noble act of his life, but to take her vows of love, honor and obedience was unconscionable when she'd be swearing her allegiance to an enemy, a Yank.

Words and visions scrolled through his brain. Once more he saw the flayed skin of the field hand. Once more he envisioned the hellish leer on the face of Dr. Daniel Merriweather's overseer as the man laid the lash again and again on the slave's bleeding back.

*I did what I had to, Serry. I'd rather have died than put on gray and fight to preserve that unspeakable inhumanity. And if I have to pay the price forever, then so be it.*

But, God Almighty, Rafe thought as his eyes drifted closed, if it cost him Serry—her love and her trust— then he'd just as soon stop breathing.

He was poised on the edge of sleep, slipping into a dream of church bells, wildflower bouquets and pretty white dresses, when she stirred against his side.

"What's that?" Serena bolted upright.

Slowly, Rafe sat up, rubbing the circulation back into his arm. "I don't hear any—"

"Shh. Listen," she hissed.

And then he heard it, too. Church bells ringing wildly. Not the gentle clamor of his dream, but an urgent, almost desperate clanging.

She was up in an instant, tugging her underclothes out from under him. "There's trouble in town."

Now she was wrestling with her petticoats and her breath was coming in quick gasps and raspy, half-spoken oaths.

A sense of foreboding as dark as the night settled over Rafe. He couldn't move for the dread that flowed through him. His confession—the words he'd been so sure would have bound Serena to him for life—sank in his stomach now like cold rocks.

Gritting his teeth, he rose and dressed with grim deliberation, less like a groom headed for wedding bells than a man on his way to a funeral that might very well be his own.

## Chapter Eighteen

Rafe slid off the winded Morgan's back and walked briskly beside Serena up the hill to the big house. The church bells had stopped, replaced by the random crack of rifles and an occasional shotgun burst. Recognizing the sound of a gathering mob, Rafe was anxious to get Serena safely back under the protective wing of her father. There was no safer place in Quinn County.

All during the ride from his cabin, Serena had wondered aloud about the commotion. For his part, Rafe had remained silent, his arms locked around her, his chin seeking the warm hollow of her neck while his heart beat a funeral dirge against her shoulder blade. After five years of picking up and running in the dead of night, he had no need to speculate about angry men and mobs. They were gathering for him. And when there were enough of them, when their outrage was sufficiently fired up by rumors and their courage suitably boosted by whiskey, they would come.

Probably, he thought as he strode beside the lathered horse, he should have told her right then. But the words that had been so difficult during the quiet interludes of their loving were all but impossible now with gunfire and angry shouts punctuating the night. He wasn't sure yet just what he was going to do. He couldn't think beyond seeing Serena to safety. After he accomplished that, then perhaps he'd be able to contemplate his own.

It was just past midnight, but the big house glowed like noontime at the top of the hill. Serena leaned forward in the saddle. "Good Lord! What in the world is going on?"

She had expected to see the lamp lit in her father's room, and perhaps some faint illumination in the kitchen where Uncle Peter had risen to prepare a hot toddy for the wakeful master of the house. But this...

Her hand rose automatically to her tangled hair and despite the darkness she could plainly see the wrinkles and the utter dishevelment of her clothes. With her hopes of sneaking quietly up to her room now dashed, Serena sighed. Not that her carrying-on with Rafe was exactly a secret, but this was too close to being caught in the act for her taste.

"I might as well be stark, staring naked," she muttered as Rafe led the Morgan closer to the house.

The knowing grin he flicked her over his shoulder made her feel as if she were. And for a brief, blood-rushing moment it wasn't such an embarrassing state. Serena couldn't keep her mouth from flaring up at the corners.

"Guess you'll have to marry me now, Sugarman," she chided him warmly. "There'll be no escape for you, I'm afraid, now that you've brought me to wrinkles and ruination."

She laughed then, but when Rafe didn't join her, Serena added quickly, "Don't worry. My daddy will be too busy clapping his hands with joy to even consider propriety or the lack of it."

He stopped then so abruptly that the Morgan snorted and laid back his ears.

Serena reached out her hand to smooth the startled horse's neck just as Rafe turned toward her with an expression on his face she had never seen before. Nor did she ever want to see it again. His handsome face had lost every trace of humor, every glimmer of hope. His eyes burned, not with desire but with a kind of bright despair. His mouth—that greedy, glorious mouth—held hard and still as stone. Then it twitched, a small, nearly imperceptible movement as if that stone would speak.

"Rafe?" Serena's heart slammed against her ribs and her breath fled as if she had been dealt a stunning blow. She couldn't have said how she knew the meaning of that look. She didn't know it so much as feel it dragging through her chest, dulling every nerve. He was telling her goodbye. As surely and as completely as he had ever told her hello, he was bidding her farewell.

She didn't understand. Even more, she didn't want to understand. A rush of wild emotions swept through her. If she didn't listen, she decided in a panic, then it wouldn't be true.

Rafe's grim, implacable face seemed to blend with the surrounding dark then. He seemed to be fading away even as she watched. Serena swayed in the saddle, and the next thing she knew she was being guided down from the Morgan's back and Uncle Peter's voice was buzzing in her ears.

"Mr. Con says you got to get in the house right quick, Miz Serena," the servant insisted. "There's trouble. Terrible trouble's coming down on us all."

When her feet met with solid earth, all Serena could do was stand there for a moment, baffled that the ground was even beneath her when she felt as if she were five miles out to sea and about to slip beneath the surface.

"What trouble, Uncle Peter? What's going on?" Rafe's urgent tone cut through her bewilderment. It pulled her back to reality as surely as a rope and it grounded her at last.

Now she noticed the enormity of the elderly servant's eyes and recognized the panic in them. Her own eyes seemed to mirror his as she grabbed his sleeve.

"Is it Daddy? Has something happened to my father? Has he taken ill, Uncle Peter?"

The old man shook his head. "Oh, no, Miz Serena. Bless you, child. It ain't your daddy. He—"

"What, then?" Rafe cut in. "For God's sake, tell us."

"It's Miz Esme—" Uncle Peter began, only to be silenced by a shotgun blast that rolled toward them through the humid night like a great wave breaking on a shore. With a rush of breath then, the old man continued. "Miz Esme's been hurt real bad. The constable carried her home 'bout an hour ago. He says it was Big Joab, that he done raped Miz Esme."

The ground that had felt so solid under Serena's feet a moment before seemed to shift precariously now. Rafe's arm immediately steadied her.

"What does Esme say?" Rafe asked.

It was the question Serena would have asked if she had been able to move her lips just then.

Once more, Uncle Peter shook his head. "Miz Esme ain't saying. Seems like all she can do is stare."

Con Quinn, huge and rumpled in his robe and slippers, was pacing back and forth outside Esme's bedroom. The lamplit hallway was blue with cigar smoke when Serena and Rafe reached the top of the stairs. Ashes darkened the carpet beneath the big man's tread.

Considering her dishevelment and the late hour, Serena fully expected him to bristle like a boar when he greeted her. Instead her father wrapped his arms around her tightly and held her close.

"You're safe, daughter," he said thickly. "That's good. That's one less worry to prey upon my heart tonight. Did Uncle Peter tell you about Esme?"

"Where is she, Daddy? I want to see her." Serena stepped back and lifted her chin. "I want to find out exactly what happened."

"So do we all," her father muttered. He tilted his head toward the closed door. "Aunt Pete's seeing to her now."

"It wasn't Big Joab," Serena said forcefully.

Con Quinn's eyes narrowed and his voice was smooth and low. "Were you there, Sister? Were you a witness to this abomination?"

"Well, no, but I—"

"Then I'll thank you to keep your opinions and your heartfelt speculations to yourself." Con swung his dark gaze toward Rafe, who was leaning against the wall, arms crossed, eyes downcast. "I assume the two of you were together and that you don't know any more about this than my daughter does. Is that a correct assumption, Sugarman?"

Rafe met Con's steely gaze with one of his own. "Yes, sir."

"I'm not just speculating, Daddy," Serena broke in. "I know Big Joab. So do you. Don't you know in your heart that man would never do something like this?"

"I know what I was told by the man I employ to keep law and order in my county. A man who was there and who has the cuts and bruises to prove it. Arlen Sears informed me that—"

"Arlen Sears!" Serena huffed. "I wouldn't take his word if he had both hands spread on Bibles and another one balanced on his head." She turned her back on her father, twisted the doorknob and strode into Esme's room.

The lamp was turned low. Aunt Pete hovered like a massive shadow beside the bed where Esme lay, her tiny and delicate body barely displacing the covers that had been drawn over her.

"'Bout time you got back, missy," the black woman snapped as Serena approached the bed.

"How is she?" she whispered. On closer inspection, she could see the dark bruises on Esme's face and the split in her swollen upper lip. Anger rolled through her at the sight. "What monster did this to her? Did she say anything, Aunt Pete?"

The older woman shook her head. "Seems like Miz Esme been struck dumb. Couldn't even cry, poor baby."

Lowering herself to the edge of the bed, Serena reached for the damp cloth on the nightstand. She pressed it gently to Esme's forehead and cheeks, then used it to push back a few pale, tangled strands of hair. She spoke softly, almost to herself. "She's so fragile. So small. I wish it had been me."

"It was you—once," Aunt Pete said.

Serena's hand held still at Esme's temple. She blinked, amazed that she could have forgotten for even a moment the event that had branded her like no other. And yet she had. Right now it was as if her own rape had never happened. She was healed, she thought, and was suddenly and completely over-whelmed by the notion. Rafe had done that. In a matter of weeks, he had erased seven years of pain.

"Only Miz Esme don't have the steel in her back-bone that you got, child. She's not as strong as you," Aunt Pete continued. "I hope my Hester's got your mettle. They'll be coming for her soon. Coming to get her to lead them to that no-'count runaway."

"Big Joab didn't do this," Serena said fiercely. "I know that, Aunt Pete."

The big woman angled her head toward the window. "Those men out there don't know that."

"Well, we'll just have to tell them, won't we?" Serena grasped Esme's frail shoulders. "Sister Belle, you listen to me now. You've got to tell us who it was. Do you hear me?''

Esme's eyes remained closed and her swollen lips moved only to draw breath.

"Esme!" Serena shook her harder to no avail.

Aunt Pete walked to the window and nudged back the curtain. Her voice was dull with resignation as she announced, "Torches coming up the walk."

Her father stood on the veranda, straight and sturdy as the columns that flanked him. Rafe had taken up a similar stance a few feet away, and now Serena's shoulder brushed his as she moved beside him. He offered her a quick, sidelong glance before returning his gaze to the crowd that continued to gather on the lawn. Most of the men gripped torches in their raised fists, and their angry features twisted with wavering torchlight and shadows. The smell of burning pitch drifted up to the veranda, mingling with the fragrance of Con's cigar.

Arlen Sears shouldered his way through the mob, then stood with one hand resting on his holster, looking up at Con. There were scratches on the constable's face, Serena noticed, and on the backs of his hands.

"The men have offered to help me bring that runaway in, Mr. Quinn." Sears shot his chin over his shoulder toward the crowd. "What you see here before you is a duly sworn-in committee of anxious townfolk who don't want their wives or their daughters to be next."

Con crossed his arms and shifted his feet farther apart. "Looks mighty like a mob to me. I hired you to keep a lid on things around here, Arlen. Not to go stirring them up."

"After what happened to Miss Esme, it didn't take much stirring," the constable replied.

"We ain't going to stand for it, Con," one of the men yelled. "It's one thing when that black devil helps hisself to our chickens and pigs. But it's our women now."

"Now hold on—" Con began, only to be cut off by a shout.

"Big Joab's earned himself a rope this time for certain."

"My daughter-in-law hasn't said yet just who accosted her," Con called out.

Arlen Sears put a foot up on the veranda step. "She doesn't need to say. I was there. I got a real good look at him before the bastard knocked me out." He swiped his hat off and ran his fingers through his hair. "Take a feel of this lump on my skull. I'm damn lucky he didn't split it open."

Serena stepped closer to the edge of the veranda. "Judging from the scratches on your hands, Arlen, I'd say it's more than likely you were in the middle of a cat fight."

"That's enough, Sister," her father warned before addressing the crowd again. "If you all came up here for my blessings, you're not getting them. I don't hold with mob justice. You all know that."

"We came for Hester Inch," somebody called.

"We know she's here." Another voice rose from the crowd. "And she knows where to find Big Joab."

"Send her out, Con."

"Send her out."

The demand rippled through the crowd in a low and ominous chant. Serena felt the heat of Rafe's body as he moved closer to her. She sensed the tension in him and the readiness to yank her back into the safety of the house at any second. Her father, on the other hand, stood there calm as a preacher at a Sunday school picnic.

Con Quinn lifted a hand. The crowd grew quiet.

"I'm not going to waste my breath telling you what to do, men. I doubt if you'd listen, anyway. But Hester Inch is in my house and that's where she's going to stay. You all want Big Joab so bad, then you're just going to have to track him down yourselves." He pulled on his cigar and launched a thick stream of smoke over their heads. "I can't stop you, but I sure as hell won't join you."

Arlen Sears's eyes cut across Serena to Rafe. "What about you, Sugarman? Where do you stand?"

Rafe hooked his thumbs through his belt. "Right where you see me, Sears."

The lawman sneered. "Quinn property is what I see. Signed, sealed and delivered." He turned then and walked into the crowd, shouting, "Y'all spread out and keep those torches high."

"My God," Serena breathed. "They'll hang Big Joab for sure."

"Provided they catch him, Sister," her father drawled. He arched an eyebrow at Rafe. "What do you think, Sugarman? Can Big Joab outrun a fired-up mob?"

A grin flared at the edges of Rafe's mouth. "I expect he can," he said, "if he's got somebody giving him a big enough push."

After her father had gone back into the house—having given Rafe a somber, almost funereal handshake—Serena clasped her arms around herself and gazed out across the lawn. Moonlight glossed the leaves on the big magnolia and cut a silver swath across the grass. A good night for hunting.

Her lips barely moved when she whispered, "Don't go."

Rafe's arms encircled her then, holding her close, so close the buckle of his belt bit into her spine.

"Daddy should have stopped them" she said. "He would have, too, if it had been anybody but Big Joab. Anybody white. He makes a great to-do of sending table scraps to all the former slaves, but he's too much the politician, too much the dyed-in-the-wool Mississippian to stand by them openly." Sighing, she leaned her head back on Rafe's broad shoulder. "I'm ashamed of that. I'm ashamed he has no honor, no principles."

"Don't be. The man's doing his damnedest to hold this county together." He laughed softly. "For what it's worth, Serry, and in my own very humble opinion, honor can make a pretty big mess of things. Turn around now and let me kiss you before I go tearing off through the woods."

## Chapter Nineteen

It was dawn when Serena turned down the wick beside Esme's bed, then sat watching the eastern sky run through its repertoire of blues and pinks, finally settling for a pale, translucent shade the color of a robin's egg.

Esme hadn't stirred all night, although her eyes had opened frequently. Each time she would gaze around the floral-papered room in a kind of panic, then, as if finding comfort in the familiarity of her surroundings, she would let her lids flutter closed again. Serena had long since given up encouraging her sister-in-law to speak, having decided that the little blonde was probably better off adrift in her peaceful limbo than being wrenched back to reality.

For now, at least, the truth barely mattered while two men—one black and one white, one Hester's and one hers—were running for their lives.

She sagged back in her chair. Bird song drifted through the window, a choir of robins and meadowlarks greeting this day as if it were just like any other. The sun was well above the horizon now, shining away. How dare it shine? Serena thought. How dare the air feel clean and fresh when she could barely breathe for worrying? How dare life go on if she couldn't begin each day with Rafe?

In the distance, a rifle cracked. It was followed a moment later by another shot, then another, each one louder and closer. The stillness of the house was broken by the rush of footsteps up the stairs. Then the door of Esme's room flew open and crashed back against the wall.

"My mama said come quick, Miz Serena." Little Joab dragged in a breath. "They got 'em. They got my daddy and The Sugarman, too."

Blood trickled down the side of Big Joab's face, running faster when it mixed with the sweat that glistened on his dark skin. Already the rope around his neck was stained a rusty red. The runaway's eyes were closed and his lips twitched as he stammered, "Thy kingdom come. Thy will be done."

"That kingdom's not coming today," Rafe growled as he continued to loosen the rope around his wrists. "If you swing, it'll only be for a minute. You take in a deep breath, Big Joab, and tighten your neck muscles for all they're worth, you hear?"

Big Joab mumbled an "I hear" in the midst of his second invocation of the Lord's Prayer.

They might have made it. Hell, they would have made it if it hadn't been for the dogs. He and Big Joab had spent the dark hours crossing and recrossing the river, slipping beneath the water when anyone came near, but always moving. Until they'd brought out the damn dogs. The former slave's eyes had rounded with panic when he'd heard the yapping and baying. "Dogs," he had whispered. "It was dogs that ripped the innards out of my pa." And then Big Joab was just plain frozen, waist deep in the middle of the river, and stood there stone-deaf to Rafe's pleas that he keep moving.

By the time Rafe had decided that the only way to save him was to knock him out, it was too late. The dogs had lined up along the riverbank, snarling and baring their teeth, and the men with the guns and the ropes had quickly joined them.

Now he and Big Joab were standing in the bed of a hay wagon with ropes around their necks and the big, utilitarian limb of a sycamore directly over their heads. It was the prelude to a hanging. These things couldn't be done too quickly, Rafe noted morosely. The crowd had to work up the proper amount of righteous anger to legitimize their actions, and their victims were obliged to sweat and stammer prayers and, just to make it a real spectacle, maybe even blubber and beg for their worthless lives.

Only he wasn't going to die today. Rafe couldn't have said how he knew that, but he did. Even with a noose for a necktie, he knew he'd see the sun go down today and watch it rise tomorrow. A similar calm used to come over him prior to battle. A calm like an impenetrable shield.

Funny, he thought now. What General Grant had taken for courage was nothing more than a powerful vision of the future. It had been the men who had gone into battle knowing they were going to die who were the brave ones. All Rafe had been was certain.

As certain as he was right now. He wasn't going to die. It followed, then, with a grim sort of logic, that Big Joab wasn't going to die, either, since Rafe refused to let it happen as long as he was still drawing breath.

His hands were tied behind him and his wrists were raw from working the rope, but with each twist the hemp gave another fraction. It was only a matter of minutes before his hands would be free to reach for the knife that was stashed in his boot. Then, if he had to send half the men in Quinn County to meet their Maker, he'd do it—because he sure as hell wasn't ready to meet his own.

The first man he'd go for was the constable, who had been weaving back and forth through the crowd, flashing his badge while he shouted invective, keeping the crowd riled and making sure nobody's temper cooled. Sears was climbing up into the back of the wagon now and it was all Rafe could do not to lash out a boot that would shatter the lawman's kneecap. He would have, too, if he'd thought for a minute he was going to hang. If that were the case, then it was only fair that the man primarily responsible for his death should be crippled for life.

The lawman grinned like a jackal as he rearranged the rope around Big Joab's neck, then he scowled when the blood-and-sweat soaked hemp left its grisly traces on his fingertips.

"Blood on your hands, Sears?" Rafe growled. "Hard to believe that bothers you."

Wiping his hands down the sides of his pants, Arlen Sears stepped closer to Rafe. His mouth twisted. "You bother me, Sugarman. You've stuck in my craw ever since you walked into this town like you were set on owning it. From the outset, I just plain didn't like you."

"You don't hang a man 'cause you don't like him, Sears."

"Lucky for me you picked the wrong man to throw in with, isn't it? You're gonna hang for aiding and abetting a rapist. At least, that's how it'll go down on the books."

Arlen Sears turned toward the crowd then. "What do you say we get on with Quinn County justice, men?" he called. His cry was met with cheers and dozens of raised fists. "Now, who wants to haul these ropes over the tree?"

A few fists lowered, but enough remained in the air to make Rafe sweat. Even a man who knew he was going to see the sunset couldn't help but squirm a little when he saw just how many men were eager to see his eyes closed permanently.

The supreme irony was that they were planning to stretch his neck for all the wrong reasons. His Yankee past—the past that in so many opinions had indeed earned him a rope—was still unknown. Though it might not be much longer, he realized as he turned his head in the direction of a group of hooting, hollering boys who were tossing his suitcase back and forth between them.

At almost the same, sickening instant Rafe saw Serena rushing toward him across the town square.

His chest seized up and for a minute he couldn't even breathe as he watched his past and his future about to collide. For a man who had been certain he'd live to see the sun go down, right then he wasn't so sure he wanted to.

Halfway across the square, Serena stopped. Her throat was raw from gasping for breath, and the stitch in her side felt like a hot knife lodged between her ribs. But it wasn't the pain that brought her to a sudden halt. It wasn't even the sight of the man she loved standing in the back of a wagon with a rope around his neck. It was the look in his eye as his gaze held hers all the way across the courthouse square. Hopelessness. A sorrow deep as a bottomless well. Rafe was saying goodbye—again—forever.

It was the same look he had given her the night before, and, as then, it tore at her soul. Serena wondered now if he hadn't had some sort of premonition of this terrible moment, some inkling of his fate.

But, as before, everything in her rose up in denial. And despite the evidence before her this very moment, Serena refused to accept it. This was not the way it was going to be. If Rafe had envisioned this, then his vision was wrong. Just plain wrong. Perhaps it had focused on him alone and had failed to encompass one very important element. Her.

Little Joab caught up with her now and snatched at her hand, crying frantically, "Come on, Miz Serena. You got to stop them. You got to."

Only then did she shift her gaze to the other man on the wagon. Big Joab's face, bloody and twisted with fear, was nearly unrecognizable. However this turned out, she thought, she didn't want Little Joab to remember his father this way. She sank to her knees and grasped the boy's fragile shoulders. "I want you to run back to the house, Little Joab. You tell Mr. Con what's coming to pass down here in the square, you hear? You tell him Miz Serena said to come quick."

The child's eyes sought his father again. "But . . ."

"No buts." Serena gave him a solid push in the direction of the house. "Just run. And don't you come back here, Little Joab. I'm speaking for your daddy now. He doesn't want you anywhere near these infernal carryings-on. Now go."

Serena watched his bare feet kicking up the dust in the dry street as Little Joab raced back toward the house. For a moment she wanted to run, too, away from the horrible event taking place in the square. She wanted to pretend it was just a bad dream and that she would wake in Rafe's arms to have his solid warmth surround her once more like a shield. Nothing could hurt her then. Not even a regiment of Yankees.

He watched her wheel and march across the square, her eyes glittering fiercely and her shoulders stiff with purpose. In her fury, she was the most beautiful creature he had ever seen. With her hair on fire in the morning sun and her skirts whipping at her legs with each long stride, she reminded him of a goddess coming down with a vengeance on a gathering of mortals. And he was the most mortal of them all, he thought bleakly, with his heart aching for what was to come and his throat tightening with dread.

She latched onto the constable's upper arm with a tight, white grip.

"Stop this, Arlen." She spat the words at him. "A single word from you will put an end to this horror right now."

Arlen Sears's cold gaze slid over her and his thin mouth snaked sideways. "Now why would I want to stop it, Miz Serena? It's my duty to see that justice is carried out."

"This isn't justice," she snarled. "It's cold-blooded murder and you know it. These men are innocent."

"Why'd they run, then?" His question, shouted at the top of his lungs, was directed more toward the seething crowd than to Serena. "Tell me that. If they're so damn innocent, why'd they run?"

"That's why." Serena gestured toward the knotted ropes. "They ran for their lives because they knew this was what they could expect from Quinn County justice. If they're guilty, then go ahead and prove it, Arlen." Now Serena lifted her voice in a tremulous appeal to the crowd. "But you can't hang them just because they ran. You can't hang Big Joab for something he didn't do. And, by God, you can't hang Rafe Sugarman for trying to help an innocent man."

"Then let's hang him for a traitor."

The sharp cry came from somewhere near the front of the hay wagon. A hush fell upon the crowd then as everybody turned toward the boy with the broken nose.

Everybody but Rafe, whose dull gaze had been fastened on the boy for a while now, following his every movement—from the smashing of the metal clasp to the moment his fingers had touched the embossed gold buttons and his hands had tightened on the dark blue sleeves. The boy had shouted out then—*Traitor!*—before standing to wave the incriminating uniform over his head as if it were Old Glory itself.

A stunned murmur rolled through the crowd, increasing in volume and heat and fervor as each man grasped the meaning of the color of the cloth in the boy's upraised hands. But Rafe's eyes were locked on Serena now. Serena. She was all he could see. And what he saw was the color draining from her face and her mouth slackening as if she had just seen a ghost. As if she had just seen several ghosts, all of them in Yankee blue.

Her eyes sought his then. Desperate and wide, they begged him to tell her it wasn't true. Deny it, they implored from behind a shimmering of tears. Please.

As he stood there mute and guilty, unable to draw a breath now and the noose burning into his neck like a brand, Rafe watched his most hellish dreams come true and saw his every hope evaporate just like the tears in Serena's eyes the instant she understood the truth.

Her pale cheeks went paler still, and she took a faltering step backward as if she couldn't bear being even that close to him now, as if she wanted to run but her legs wouldn't carry her. She swayed then like a tree in a great gust of wind. Arlen Sears's arm snagged around her waist to keep her upright.

It was the sight of that arm—winding around her like a snake, touching her—that hauled Rafe out of his guilt-ridden daze, that snapped every nerve in his body into action and set all of him ablaze. His vision blurred for a moment and all he could see was Serena's lush, generous body, so perfectly hewn for his. His, by God. She was his. No matter that she despised him now. No matter that his own life had just become as worthless as his dreams. As long as he lived, even if it was only a matter of minutes now, Serena was his. As long as he was breathing, no other man would touch her.

Howling like a wounded animal, and with a strength born of agonized fury, he wrenched his hands from the ropes, wrested the noose from around his neck, then leapt down from the wagon bed. But before his feet even touched the ground, a fist slammed into the side of his head, an elbow caught his jaw and the butt of a rifle smashed into his ribs.

Down on his hands and knees then, he sucked in a painful breath, spread his fingers on the ground, trying to hold on. To hold on to what was his. To Serena. To his dream, if not his life. To Mississippi—sifting like dust through his fingers now and mixing with his blood.

# Chapter Twenty

Once Rafe was down, the men closed in a tight circle around him. Shoulders and jostling elbows formed a wall that shut Serena out, but her ears weren't shut to the sound of boots, one after another, thudding into flesh and bone, or to the sound of a chuffing groan each time a kick connected. Her eyes weren't shut, either. They were fastened on the uniform that had been dropped and trampled in the dust.

Her first instinct was to step on the dark blue frock coat, to grind the symbol of all her pain and loss so deep into the soil she'd never have to see it again, to bury it just as she had buried her mother's silk handkerchief that horrible night.

Memories churned through her. She felt as if she were caught up in the dark tangle and twist of a nightmare even though she knew she was wide awake. Yankee blue pressed down on her again. She could smell the hay and the stinking blue wool and hear the newborn Morgan snuffling in the nearby stall. As if it had happened only yesterday, as if it were happening right now, she heard the first Yank laugh as he rolled

off her and crowed to his comrades that he'd probably just had the only virgin in the whole goddamn
Confederacy.

She lurched forward, intent on crushing the despi-
cable garment beneath her feet, stamping it into the
ground until it disappeared. And then, as in a nightmare, the vision in her head shifted and the strag-
gler's face altered even though the uniform remained
the same. Rafe! His whiskey-warm eyes were even
warmer in the reflected blue of the coat. The same hue
shaded his firm jaw and threaded through his dark
curls.

Then, instead of planting her foot on the uniform,
Serena sank beside it and gathered it to her bosom.
The size and substantial heft of the wool cloth immediately convinced her that it was his. Her fingers
drifted the length of a sleeve, then brought the frayed
cuff to her lips before she buried her face in its dark
folds. If she had hoped to find his warm scent there,
she was immediately disappointed. The jacket smelled
musty, like old, forgotten clothes folded for years in a
trunk.

It wasn't Rafe, and she let it fall onto her lap in a
heavy heap as a sudden longing for his scent and his
warmth and his touch overwhelmed her. "A Yankee!" The word she'd always spat as a curse came out
now as a little cry of amazement. Who'd ever believe
in a million years that Serena Quinn could love a
Yankee? Yet she did. And it wouldn't have mattered
then if his suitcase had opened to reveal a devil's
pitchfork. She could just as easily have given her heart

and soul to a lieutenant of Lucifer—as long as he came in the guise of The Sugarman.

They had hauled him back up into the wagon and wrenched the rope around his neck again. Rafe had to lock his knees to remain upright. From his sorry vantage point on the makeshift gallows, he could see Serena where she sat on the ground, stroking his coat like a big blue cat on her lap. She was too dazed to hate him. Yet. Too much wind had been knocked out of her to curse him. Yet.

Beside him, Big Joab was praying again. Dully, Rafe realized he couldn't even do that. He couldn't ask for a forgiveness he didn't deserve. What he'd done to Serena was unforgivable. He'd gladly swing for that. Only let it be now, this minute, so he didn't have to witness her hate.

"Do it," he snarled at the lawman, who stood nearby.

Arlen Sears's mouth snagged sideways. "You're in a big hurry all of a sudden, aren't you, Sugarman?" He crossed his arms and took up a leisurely stance. "I don't know why it didn't come to me that first day you walked into town. A man like you doesn't drift unless he keeps getting the ground yanked out from under him. I should have figured it out from the first."

"Well, face it, Arlen. You're just not all that smart." Rafe started to grin but winced instead when the constable's fist shot into his ribs.

"I'm smart enough to know when somebody's pretending to be what they're not," he snarled. "Man or woman. A Mississippi Yank or a damn New Orleans whore.''

Rafe twisted his head to look at him, but just then Con Quinn's buggy clattered to a halt in the courthouse square and the clamor of the crowd changed abruptly, subsiding to a hush as The Man waded through their midst.

"Seems like things have gotten a little bit out of hand here, Arlen," he called up to the lawman. "Last time I looked there was a jail in my courthouse. Wasn't it you who had me send all the way to New York City for that newfangled lock?" The big man shrugged slightly as he took a cigar from the breast pocket of his coat, then bit off the tip and spat it on the ground. While he patted his pockets for a match, he squinted back up into the wagon bed and stated calmly. "I'd like to get my money's worth out of that lock, Constable."

Rafe could almost hear Arlen Sears sweat. The son of a bitch was caught now between the devil Quinn and the deep blue sea of the mob. Hell, he thought he'd almost like to stick around for a few minutes just to have the pleasure of watching him squirm, not to mention taking one more lesson from that master politician, Con Quinn.

Despite his offhand manner, Rafe knew the man was intensely aware of the crowd and its mood. He was testing it, sniffing it the way a housewife sniffs a melon, weighing it on his personal scale that balanced Quinn—the man and the county—against everything and everyone else. How that scale would tip was a mystery to Rafe right then, and he wasn't sure

if he liked Con Quinn or despised him, but he knew
for a fact that he respected him and he figured he was
leaving Serena in the most capable hands around.

Serena. He swung his gaze in her direction in time
to see her rise unsteadily. His blue coat slid off her lap
as she drew herself up and took a first tentative step
toward her father. The expression on her face was
fierce. And beautiful. Dear God, how glorious was her
hate! It sliced through his heart like a saber and forced
him to close his eyes in pain.

"You took your sweet time getting here, Daddy,"
she snapped, covering the last few yards with long,
sure strides.

"I'm here now," he flung back.

Serena crossed her arms. "Just what do you intend
to do about this?" Her chin lifted toward the wagon
bed.

Con Quinn jammed his cigar into the corner of his
mouth, squinting against the rising smoke. "Right
now, missy, I'm pondering the situation."

Her eyes raised heavenward in frustration. Damn
him to hell and back for his political sensibilities, Serena raged inwardly. Just once in his life couldn't he
do what was right rather than deliberate endlessly on
the consequences for himself and his precious county?
Like Rafe. He hadn't speculated long into the night
about the dangers or drawbacks of helping Big Joab.
He hadn't wrung his hands and agonized. By God,
he'd just gone and done it. Because it was right.

It occurred to her then that that was probably how
he'd crossed over the rebel lines to join up with the
Yanks. She knew plenty of men who'd signed up to

wear the gray only because they feared the consequences if they didn't. Whatever had impelled him to aid Big Joab had also pushed him across that line. He must have believed it was right. And maybe she could believe it, too. If given the chance.

And she'd do anything for that chance. Anything. Beginning with a lie. "Well, while you're pondering, Daddy," she said with as much calm as she could muster, "you might want to consider that I'm carrying Rafe Sugarman's child. Your grandchild. The one you'll never see if anything happens to that man."

Up on the wagon, Rafe's eyes shot open in time to see the cigar twitch in Con Quinn's hard-set mouth. His own mouth went slack with surprise. It wasn't true, was it? he wondered wildly. Their loving had been passionate enough to create life a thousand times over, but—as far as he knew about these things—it was too soon for Serena to know. And if it wasn't true, what the hell was she thinking? In her fury, didn't she believe hanging was good enough for a damn Yankee?

But if she was lying, nothing in her face or her rigid stance betrayed her. Her father's hard eyes were testing her now and she didn't flinch. Rafe practically heard the calculations clicking in Con's head. When did The Sugarman come to Quinn County? Weeks ago? Months? Had there been a certain look in his daughter's eyes, a glitter his crafty old eyes had failed to notice? Did she lie with the Yankee long before he suspected, or was she lying now?

A child! Rafe had to redouble his efforts to stay upright. A child he himself would never see. A big, strapping son or a healthy, flame-haired daughter—a child to put down the roots he never could. He wanted that suddenly with every ounce of his being. Wanted it as he'd never wanted anything before. Enough to pray. *Dear God, let it be true. Let me live—in her and through her.*

Her father's eyes narrowed to slits as he studied her face. "Is this high drama, Sister? Or some convenient fabulation? Because if it is..."

She shook her head vehemently. "It's true, Daddy. I swear." It would be true as soon as she could make it happen, she swore to herself.

Taking the cigar from his mouth, Con contemplated its fat ash a moment before he flicked it away. The gray remnant was immediately crushed beneath the constable's boot as he jumped from the wagon.

"She's lying, Con." Arlen Sears pushed his way between father and daughter, turning his back on Serena. "She's trying to save his Yankee neck."

"And you're doing your damnedest to stretch it, aren't you, Arlen? Now why is that?"

"He's a traitor." He jerked his thumb toward the uniform lying on the ground. "Take a look at what he's been carrying around in that suitcase of his."

Con glanced at the dusty jacket. "The war's over," he growled.

"Not around here."

One dark eyebrow arched and Con's mouth quirked in a rueful smile. "I wouldn't go bragging on it, if I were you, boy. Kinda stretches out our loss and makes us all look like damn fools." He raised his voice to the crowd. "We got better things to do in Quinn County than beat dead horses and stir up sleeping dogs, don't we?''

A kind of shuffling quiet moved through the mob.

"Well, don't we?" Con bellowed.

Murmurs of agreement rippled from man to man then. Serena could almost feel the tension seeping out of the mob as shoulders lifted and fell, fists uncurled, and dozens of heads tilted attentively toward her father. Directly in front of her, however, she could feel the heat blazing from the constable's rangy body.

He planted his feet wide and stabbed a finger at her father's massive chest. "Horses and dogs, my ass! What we've got up there is a rapist and a nigger-loving bluebelly. You hired me to keep law and order around here, Con. Now, do you want me to do my job or not?"

"My law!" the big man shouted. "My order!" With one huge hand, he grabbed the front of the lawman's shirt and pulled him closer. "Do you understand, boy?"

Sears drew back as if Con's hot breath had scorched him. His reply was a tight-lipped "Yes, sir."

"All right, then. Somebody get on up there and cut those ropes off my prospective son-in-law," Con ordered.

"Big Joab, too," Serena added quickly. She was rucking up her skirts, preparing to climb up on the wagon herself, when her father latched onto her wrist.

"Not so fast, Sister," he warned under his breath. "These men aren't done yet. You just be satisfied your child's going to have a father and leave the other one be."

She stared at him—at the firm set of her father's jaw and the resolute fix of his gaze. Suddenly, with bone-chilling comprehension, Serena knew what her father was doing. Somewhere in that wily tangle of his brain, he had determined that a runaway accused of rape was a fair trade for a Yankee. It wasn't even a question of guilt or innocence anymore. The master of Quinn County was going to allow the mob to drink Big Joab's blood in order to ensure the perpetuation of his own.

Dear Lord, he was going to purchase Rafe's life with Big Joab's. And, to her everlasting shame, she yearned to stand aside and let her father do it. Despite right or wrong—despite honor—Serena longed for that. So great was her temptation that she couldn't even look at Rafe now for fear of giving in. It would be too easy to find heaven in that glance, too easy to seize that heaven now and let the devil take her later.

So when, out of the corner of her eye, she saw him easing down from the wagon, standing there, his eyes burning into her, begging her to turn to him, to come to him, she turned to her father instead.

"You do what's right, Daddy. Or else."

Her father eyed her keenly. His dark brows drew together and his head tilted quizzically. "Or else what, daughter?"

"Or else you can leave Quinn County to the buzzards and the wolves. I'll have no part of this, and no child of mine will ever draw breath in a place where innocent blood is served up like whiskey punch."

"Whiskey punch, huh?" he growled as his lips worked his cigar toward a corner of his mouth. "Is

that what you think I've been doing for thirty years?
Just serving up whiskey punch to keep everybody in
my county happy and drunk?''

"You haven't exactly been serving up justice," she
replied.

Con Quinn snorted. "Justice! That's some skinny
lady wearing a blindfold who doesn't care which way
things turn out. I care, daughter." Tears glistened in
his dark eyes and he shook his head as if to dispel
them. "Maybe I care too much."

His sudden tears touched her heart, and Serena
reached out to touch his cheek, but her hand was
brushed aside by Arlen Sears.

"These men are still worried about their wives and
daughters, Con. Maybe you can make them choke
down a Yank, but they're not going to stand for letting Big Joab go. They don't want what happened to
Miz Esme to happen to any of their womenfolk."

As if to emphasize the constable's words, the men
edged closer. Her father had read them right, Serena
thought. They still wanted blood.

Arlen Sears leaned closer to her father now to
whisper seductively, "If you've lost the stomach and
the will for this, Con, why don't you just go on home
and let me take care of it."

For a single, heart-stopping moment, Serena
thought her father was going to do just that when he
failed to reply. Then slowly, silently, he withdrew his
watch from his pocket and perused it as calmly as if he
were waiting for a train.

In all her twenty-four years she had never seen him
consult a timepiece unless he was expecting someone

or something. Time, like everything else in Quinn County, waited on him. He clicked the watch closed just as a carriage came to a clattering halt in the square.

"That'll be my daughter-in-law," he announced coolly. "I figured it was only right to let the injured party taste her fair share of this blood you're all so damned eager to spill."

# Chapter Twenty-One

Rafe's belongings had been scattered from here to kingdom come and he stalked from one dusty garment to another, cursing as he bent to pick each one up, snapping the dirt out of them before shoving them into the battered suitcase. The crowd ignored him now, thanks to Con Quinn and his dramatics. Hell, if the old man knew who was guilty from the start, why'd he let it get this far? Rafe grumbled to himself as he snatched another garment from the dust.

Dramatics! The man had a flair for drama to rival John Wilkes Booth, and he was probably just as dangerous. Rafe paused to watch little Miss Esme making her painful progress from the buggy to the outstretched arm of her father-in-law. The men stepped back to let her pass, whisking their hats from their heads and averting their eyes. But Miss Esme's eyes were hot as green fire and they were trained not on Big Joab but on Arlen Sears with all the force of a double-barreled shotgun.

All Rafe wanted to do was get the hell away from here—from her, from Mississippi and all its sorrows—before his bruised muscles stiffened up and left him no choice but to crawl out of town.

He should have been grateful just to be alive. But gratitude would have to come later when he wasn't feeling so damn desolate and sick. He was probably the first man in history who had jumped down from the gallows, then immediately longed to climb back up.

One searing look from Serena might have helped. Like white-hot metal, it might have cauterized his wounds. But she had turned her back, unable even to look at him. Yankee. Liar. It didn't make any difference. He no longer existed as far as she was concerned.

Fine. A man who didn't exist didn't have to worry about anything. He was free. As free as a damn bird. As free as a dead man—as if the rope had done the trick and his soul were soaring heavenward now, or fluttering like a dry leaf on a hot breeze headed straight for hell.

He snatched up the last of his belongings—the Yankee blue coat—and stood there looking at it. His pride and his perdition, he thought. It was what was best in him, and what Serena hated most. Somehow, somewhere, he was going to have to fit those two ragged pieces of his soul together again.

Rafe dropped the jacket in the dust. He was about to walk over it on his way out of town when a startled cry rose up from the crowd.

"Come on, Con," Arlen Sears snarled as he aimed his revolver directly at the big man's heart. "Let's hear

some more about the law according to Quinn. We've
all seen just how you can turn a Yankee traitor into a
respectable reb. Why don't you tell these good people
how you've been pulling the wool over their eyes all
these years by passing a New Orleans whore off as a
lady."

"Stop it, Arlen," Serena hissed. "Haven't you done
enough damage already?"

Esme was sagging like a wilted flower against Con
Quinn's side, the strength she'd mustered to confront
her attacker having failed her as soon as she'd uttered
his name. Serena's father had demanded the lawman's badge, but instead Arlen Sears had drawn his
gun.

At first Serena had expected her father to laugh in
the lawman's face and then reach out one big competent hand and simply take the gun away from him. If
not that, then she fully expected his silver tongue to
bamboozle the weapon right out of Arlen Sears's
grasp. What she didn't expect, however, was the dull,
nearly leaden emotion she saw in her father's dark
eyes.

Doubt where there had never been doubt before.
She could see it so plainly. As plainly as she could read
their dull glaze. *Mistake,* they seemed to say. *The first;
the last.*

The constable was poking him with the pistol now,
taunting him. The crowd was holding its collective
breath, staring wide-eyed and slack jawed, just as
Serena herself was. And all the while her father
seemed to be aging before her very eyes, his body
shrinking beneath the ample swatch of his vest and the

huge folds of his coat, standing there mute and submissive, buckling under that vile tongue and that prodding gun.

In comparison, Arlen Sears appeared to expand. Like a hound whose hackles were raised. And like a hound homing in on his quarry, his lips pulled back now in a vicious snarl. "Beg me, old man. Get down on your knees and beg me not to kill you."

Surely that was too much, she thought. Surely that would snap him out of his terrible trance. But it didn't. Oh, God, he was sinking, slowly, taking Esme with him.... Well, by God, if her father could no longer master the situation and if everybody was going to just stand around and allow this to happen, then she'd just have to take matters into her own hands.

Her whole body stiffened with resolution and her eyes flicked toward the wagon, desperate to light on something, anything that might serve her as a weapon. But what she saw then was a weapon of a different sort. Huge and lethal. Silent as smoke. Moving slowly as a smoke-colored cat. Those whiskey eyes fastened on the gun in the constable's hand.

Serena held her breath. How could she not have guessed? she wondered. They were so much alike— Con Quinn and The Sugarman—and working in concert now as an arrow and its bow. Her father's apparent weakness was drawing Arlen Sears to him like a buzzard on dead meat, sucking him in like so much quicksand, and distracting the crowd sufficiently to allow Rafe to come on undetected and undeterred....

And, finally, fast, as in the blink of an eye, his hand came down like an ax on the lawman's arm.

* * *

The Man got his dignity back, Rafe noted, the way he had gotten just about everything else in his life. He grabbed it. By the time the old conniver was on his feet and swatting at the dirt on his knees, there wasn't a man within earshot who didn't believe Con Quinn had been in control all along.

A brush with death hadn't changed him. Nor had it changed Serena, who was tending to Miss Esme now. Right after he had brought the constable down, Rafe thought he had seen a certain warmth in her eyes, but she had directed it all toward the sobbing little Esme then, ignoring him.

Hell, that was probably preferable to clawing his eyes out. And hurt just about as much.

"Uncle Peter," Con Quinn bellowed, despite the fact that his servant was only a few feet away. "You take Miss Esme home now. And put Big Joab in the buggy with you, too. See he gets a decent meal and some of my good brandy, you hear?"

Uncle Peter nodded. "Thank you, Mr. Con. My Hester will thank you, too. Her man may be a no-'count runaway, but he surely didn't deserve to hang."

"Only one man around here deserves hanging," Con snorted as he looked toward Arlen Sears. The constable sat on the ground, rocking, cradling his broken arm as if it were a newborn. "But I believe I'll just try out that fancy new lock of mine. Who wants to escort our former constable to the jail?"

Suddenly, the men who had hung on Arlen Sears's every word only a short time before were now only too happy to yank him to his feet and shove him unceremoniously toward the courthouse door. A few of them murmured thanks and gave Rafe an awkward pat on the back in passing.

Those gestures barely registered on him, however, as he watched Serena help Esme into the buggy. She'd get in then and never even glance back. But that was all right, Rafe told himself. She hated as hard as she loved. He wouldn't have had her any other way.

Con Quinn's big arm nudged him. "Now that we're all alone, son, I want to express my gratitude." He paused to clear his throat. "I haven't had to thank many men in my day. Ordinarily it's others who are thanking me."

Rafe grinned. "Well, it didn't choke you, did it, Con?"

"Not quite," he grunted, "but I don't like the taste of it, and I don't like owing favors. I want to give you something, Sugarman. Acreage? Cash? What do you want? You just name it and it's yours."

He could name it—name her—he thought, but she'd never be his. "Just take care of her," he said, leaning down to grip the handle of his suitcase. "And if there is a baby..." His voice thickened and he fell silent for a moment before shaking his head. "Hell, I can't tell you anything you don't already know, you old coot."

"Then maybe you can tell me."

How she came up behind him so quietly Rafe didn't know. All he knew that moment was that he was more afraid than he'd been all day. Standing with a rope around his neck, even charging into the thick smoke of a battle was nothing compared to turning and looking into Serena's unforgiving eyes.

She watched the slow rise and fall of his big shoulders, and watched his broad back grow broader still as he took in a breath. Her heart was fluttering in her throat like a half-swallowed butterfly, and by the time he turned, Serena thought she'd just plain pass out from anticipation.

But her throat closed and her heart held still when she saw that he was wearing his goodbye look once more.

"Come on, children," Con Quinn boomed, draping an arm around each of their shoulders. "Let's go on up to the house and make us some wedding plans."

Serena found her voice then, but it sounded distant and cool. If she hadn't shut all emotion out of it, her words would have tumbled out in a painful howl. "I think not, Daddy. There's not going to be any wedding."

"If there's going to be a child, then, yes, by God, there is going to be a wedding, daughter. And soon. The sooner the better."

"There's no child," Serena whispered.

Her father's arms fell to his sides. His dark eyebrows lowered as they drew together like storm clouds. Lightning threatened in his eyes. "You *were* lying."

"To save Big Joab," Serena protested.

"Or she's lying now." Rafe dropped his suitcase, then strode toward her. Serena stood immobile, unable to move and nearly unable to breathe in the hot wash of his whiskey eyes. He grasped her upper arms then and sank his fingers into her flesh.

"Hate me all you want, Serry. Go ahead. Wish me in hell or worse. But, for Christ's sake, don't send me away believing there's no baby if there is." He dragged in a rough breath, then finished with a tortured whisper. "You're breaking my heart, Serry. Isn't that enough? Don't rip my soul to pieces, too."

He gave her one last shake, hard enough to rattle her teeth, then, afraid of his own desperate strength, he dropped his hands helplessly to his sides.

"Well? Which is it, Sister?" her father bellowed. He glared at her, along with Rafe, both of them waiting for her reply.

The reply that was bubbling up in her now, a wild combination of champagne and vitriol.

"You've got your nerve, the two of you, to talk to me about lying." She shook her hands in the air. "Neither one of you would know the truth if it flew right at you and flapped its wings in your face. You, Daddy. Truth is something you like to twist until it takes on a whole different shape. And you, Sugarman. What is it to you? Just something you conveniently forget to tell as long as you're getting what you want?"

Serena jerked her thumb toward the blue coat lying on the ground. "Did you know about that, Daddy?"

Con flinched. "Well, er, after a fashion."

"After a fashion, I assume, means yes," Serena snapped, stomping toward the garment. She snatched it off the ground, raising a small cloud of dust that she promptly waved away with one hand. Then she locked her fiery eyes on Rafe.

"And you, I suppose, were going to tell me?" she yelled.

Rafe shifted uncomfortably. "I was working up to it."

"Working up to it," she echoed scornfully.

"Now, look here, Serena," her father sputtered. "That's just a damn blue jacket. It doesn't mean anything anymore."

"Oh, yes, it does, Daddy." She strode back and shook the garment in Con's face. "It means everything."

She whirled on Rafe then, the blue wool clenched in her fists and her blue eyes shining with tears. "It means somebody did what he thought was right, no matter the cost. It means somebody did what was fine and decent and honorable, knowing he'd never be thanked for it but only reviled." She blinked in an effort to keep back the tears and her lips trembled. "How could you have thought for a moment I'd see it any other way? How?"

Rafe shook his head as much in confusion as surprise. In retrospect, he wondered, too, how he could have doubted the generosity of her heart or the strength of her love. Still, he'd been running so long, he couldn't quite believe his feet were on sure and steady ground. "I was afraid, Serry. I didn't want to lose you."

"Lose me!" Her voice rose, arced on an aching laugh as she clutched the jacket to her chest. "Rafe Sugarman, you're the only man who's ever found me.

You couldn't lose me if you buried yourself under a regiment of blue coats. Don't you know that?"

He did know it—suddenly and with a force nearly as powerful as a hurricane that ripped through him and threatened to take him to his knees. But Serena rushed into his arms and her warm, sturdy body kept him upright. While she was kissing him and whispering words of love, Rafe kept thinking how he'd wanted to be a tree, how he'd ached to stand still and to put down roots. He would now, he thought, but in the meantime there was Serena like a sure and steadfast oak. His sustenance. His shade and shelter. His love.

Nearby, Con Quinn cleared his throat. "That's all well and good, Sister, but you haven't answered the question yet. Now, are you or aren't you?"

Serena dragged her lips away from Rafe's with great reluctance. "Am I what, Daddy?" The sly smile that stole across her mouth was a good indication that her question was meant simply to nettle him.

And nettle him it did. He clamped down on his cigar and narrowed his eyes into slits. "You know perfectly well what I'm talking about, Serena Quinn. Are you or are you not in a family way?"

"Well, Daddy, if I'm not," she said as she linked her arm through Rafe's, "I will be just as soon as I can manage it."

Her father grunted. "I'd appreciate your managing it while I'm still drawing breath. I'm going back up to the house now. It's been a long morning." He took a few steps across the courthouse square, then called over his shoulder. "Didn't I tell you to burn that damn blue coat?"

Rafe grinned and called back, "Didn't I tell you no?"

"Did you?" Even though Con Quinn bit down hard on his cigar, he couldn't quite stifle his own grin. "I probably misunderstood. That's not a word I hear too often around here."

# *Epilogue*

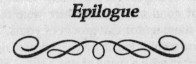

Serena held back the lace curtain and gazed down on the well-dressed, well-behaved crowd on the front lawn. A far different sight from a month ago, she thought, when the same men had stood there with guns in their hands and torches waving over their heads. The men of Quinn County, wives and children in tow this afternoon, formed a greeting party now rather than a hunting party.

Behind her, a watch clicked open and closed for the hundredth time.

Serena sighed. "Daddy, you're going to wear out your pocket the way you keep fussing with that timepiece. I swear, anybody'd think you were getting married today instead of me."

A characteristic grunt issued from Con Quinn's throat as he thumbed the watch back into his vest pocket.

"Growl all you want," Serena said. "It doesn't bother me. This fancy wedding was your idea, not mine. If I had had my way, Rafe and I would be three weeks married now." And sharing a big, soft bed, she added to herself, instead of sneaking off to his cabin as often as possible and practically ruining themselves on that hard, unforgiving floor.

"Well, it wasn't my idea to telegraph all the way to Washington to import the best man," Con grumbled. "Plenty of good men around here were more than willing to stand up for that groom of yours."

There was a quick knock on the bedroom door, then Esme swept in with a rustle of green silk. "He's coming," she said breathlessly. "His carriage is just coming up the hill. I must have a whole flock of butterflies inside me." She paused before Serena's dressing table, frowning in the mirror. "Oh, Lord. These bruises make me look yellow as a Chinaman."

"You look lovely, Esme. Just like a flower," Serena said reassuringly.

"A yellow flower," the little blonde moaned, stroking a powder puff over her face and neck. In the four weeks since her vicious beating and Arlen Sears's very public accusations about her past, Esme had refused to leave the house. Serena had had to practically twist her arm to get her to be her matron of honor.

"You look like the lady you are, Sister Belle," Con said now, eyeing her in the mirror. "And if anybody even breathes otherwise today or any other day, they'll have me to deal with." His scowl gave way to a smile then as he crooked both arms in invitation. "Are you ready, daughters? Now that our *late* guest of honor has arrived, I suppose we can finally get this show on the road."

"You be respectful now, Daddy Quinn," Esme warned as she slipped her arm through his. "After all, he is president of the United States."

Serena laughed brightly as she latched onto her father's other arm. "Esme, you might be better off directing those admonitions at Ulysses S. Grant." She leaned forward, winking at her sister-in-law across Con Quinn's bulk. "After all, he's not exactly in the United States anymore, is he? He's in Quinn County."

"Miz Serena said you was to wait in here, Sugarman, and not to come out till the piano starts playing 'Oh, Promise Me.'" Little Joab opened the door to the small library off the front parlor and gestured with a thin arm. "You, too, Mr. President, sir. The Shawl Lady'll skin me alive if I don't do this right."

President Grant patted Little Joab's head. "We wouldn't want that to happen, would we, son?" He looked around the room, his eyes lighting on a cut glass decanter. "I wonder if Miss Serena has any strong feelings about imbibing prior to sacred occasions."

"I don't know about Miz Serena, sir, but Mr. Con was down here not too long ago and he was tipping that bottle a time or two." The boy's eyes appealed to Rafe. "You want me to go and ask her?"

Rafe, decanter already in hand, smiled and shook his head. "That's all right, Little Joab. You just run along now and tell whoever's in charge of this shindig that the groom and the best man are as ready as they'll ever be."

When the boy was gone, Rafe handed Grant a glass of brandy. "Thank you again for coming, sir." The two men had already warmly embraced outside, and now, in private, the stocky, bearded Grant's eyes shone as he clamped a hand on Rafe's arm.

"Well, it doesn't look as if they've whittled you down any," he said.

Rafe laughed. "Not for lack of trying."

The president took a healthy swallow of brandy, closed his eyes a moment, then opened them to study Rafe's neatly pressed uniform. "Still fits you, I see. I'd have thought that jacket would have been ripped to shreds years ago. Or you."

"I had a couple of close calls."

"I can well imagine." The president laughed now as he lifted the glass to his lips again, then his bearded mouth crooked downward at the corners. "This is a hell of a job I've got now. I often think I made a better soldier than a politician. I could use you in Washington, Sugarman."

"Thank you, General, but I'm home now."

Grant sighed. "That's what I figured you'd say. And in light of that..." He reached into the breast pocket of his frock coat and withdrew a small velvet box. "I brought the mountain to Mohammed, so to speak." He opened the box to reveal a medal on a wide, sky-blue ribbon. He cleared his throat and lowered his voice to a somber, ceremonious tone. "This is the Congressional Medal of Honor, son. It's only a token of what these United States and I personally owe to the Mississippi Yank."

President Grant lifted the ribbon to place it around Rafe's neck, then his hands held still in midair and he tilted his head toward the window where several curious townsfolk were peering in. "You're sure you want to wear this? I mean, here? In Mississippi?"

"Hell, yes, General." Rafe's mouth twitched in a grin. "Anyway, this isn't Mississippi. It's Quinn County, and that's a whole other place."

He crooked his knees slightly and bowed his head to receive the honor, thinking in only a matter of moments now he would be repeating the same pose to claim the even greater honor of his wife's first kiss.

\* \* \* \* \*

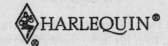

# THE VENGEFUL GROOM
## Sara Wood

Legend has it that those married in Eternity's chapel are destined for a lifetime of happiness. But happiness isn't what Giovanni wants from marriage—it's revenge!

*Ten years ago,* Tina's testimony sent Gio to prison—for a crime he didn't commit. *Now* he's back in Eternity and looking for a bride. *Now* Tina is about to learn just how ruthless and disturbingly sensual Gio's brand of vengeance can be.

**THE VENGEFUL GROOM,** available in October from Harlequin Presents, is the fifth book in Harlequin's new cross-line series, **WEDDINGS, INC.** Be sure to look for the sixth book, **EDGE OF ETERNITY,** by Jasmine Cresswell (Harlequin Intrigue #298), coming in November.

WED5

# HARLEQUIN®

**Georgina Devon**

brings the past alive with

# Untamed Heart

One of the most sensual Regencies ever published by Harlequin.

Lord Alaistair St. Simon has inadvertently caused the death of the young Baron Stone. Seeking to make amends, he offers his protection to the baron's sister, Liza. Unfortunately, Liza is not the grateful bride he was expecting.

St. Simon's good intentions set off a story of revenge, betrayal and consuming desire.

Don't miss it!

Coming in October 1994,
wherever Harlequin books are sold.

# ᴅᴇꜱᴛɪɴʏ'ꜱ ᴡᴏᴍᴇɴ
# Trilogy

The DESTINY'S WOMEN TRILOGY by Merline Lovelace is sexy
historical romance at its best! The plots thicken and the
temperatures rise with each page of her books. A fresh new voice in
historical romance, Merline has already begun to lure readers with
her exciting, bold storytelling. In ALENA, #220, May 1994, Roman
Britain exploded with passion. In SWEET SONG OF LOVE, #230,
July 1994, love blossomed amid the rich pageantry of the
Middle Ages.

Now, in September, look for SIREN'S CALL, #236, the final book in
the DESTINY'S WOMEN TRILOGY. Set in Ancient Greece, passion and
betrayal collide when a dashing Athenian sea captain finds his life
turned upside down by the stubborn Spartan woman he carries off.

**Available wherever Harlequin books are sold.**

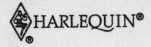